ROBIN FORSYTHE
MISSING OR MURDERED

Robin Forsythe was born Robert Forsythe in 1879. His place of birth was Sialkot, in modern day Pakistan. His mother died when a younger brother was born two years later, and 'Robin' was brought up by an ayah until he was six, when he returned to the United Kingdom, and went to school in Glasgow and Northern Ireland. In his teens he had short stories and poetry published and went to London wanting to be a writer.

He married in 1909 and had a son the following year, later working as a clerk at Somerset House in London when he was arrested for theft and fraud in 1928. Sentenced to fifteen months, he began to write his first detective novel in prison.

On his release in 1929 Robin Forsythe published his debut, *Missing or Murdered*. It introduced Anthony 'Algernon' Vereker, an eccentric artist with an extraordinary flair for detective work. It was followed by four more detective novels in the Vereker series, ending with *The Spirit Murder Mystery* in 1936. All the novels are characterized by the sharp plotting and witty dialogue which epitomize the more effervescent side of golden age crime fiction.

Robin Forsythe died in 1937.

Also by Robin Forsythe

ROBIN FORSYTHE

MISSING OR MURDERED

With an introduction
by Curtis Evans

DEAN STREET PRESS

Published by Dean Street Press 2016

Introduction copyright © 2016 Curtis Evans

All Rights Reserved

Cover by DSP

Cover illustration shows detail from a
1935 wood engraving by Eric Ravilious

First published in 1929 by The Bodley Head

ISBN 978 1 911095 09 5

www.deanstreetpress.co.uk

To

ELIZABETH

Robin Forsythe (1879-1937)
Crime in Fact and Fiction

Ingenious criminal schemes were the stock in trade of those ever-so-bright men and women who devised the baffling puzzles found in between-the-wars detective fiction. Yet although scores of Golden Age mystery writers strove mightily to commit brilliant crimes on paper, presumably few of them ever attempted to commit them in fact. One author of classic crime fiction who actually carried out a crafty real-life crime was Robin Forsythe. Before commencing in 1929 his successful series of Algernon Vereker detective novels, now reprinted in attractive new editions by the enterprising Dean Street Press, Forsythe served in the 1920s as the mastermind behind England's Somerset House stamp trafficking scandal.

Robin Forsythe was born Robert Forsythe—he later found it prudent to slightly alter his Christian name—in Sialkot, Punjab (then part of British India, today part of Pakistan) on 10 May 1879, the eldest son of distinguished British cavalryman John "Jock" Forsythe and his wife Caroline. Born in 1838 to modestly circumstanced parents in the Scottish village of Carmunnock, outside Glasgow, John Forsythe in 1858 enlisted as a private in the Ninth Queen's Royal Lancers and was sent to India, then in the final throes of a bloody rebellion. Like the fictional Dr. John H. Watson of Sherlock Holmes fame, Forsythe saw major martial action in Afghanistan two decades later during the Second Anglo-Afghan War (1878-1880), in his case at the December 1879 siege of the Sherpur Cantonment, just outside Kabul, and the Battle of Kandahar on 1 September 1880, for which service he received the War Medal with two Clasps and the Bronze England and Ireland until his retirement from the British army in 1893, four years after having been made an Honorary Captain. The old solider was later warmly commended, in a 1904 history of the Ninth Lancers, for his "unbroken record of faithful, unfailing and devoted service."

His son Robin's departure from government service a quarter-century later would be rather less harmonious.

A year after John Forsythe's return to India from Afghanistan in 1880, his wife Caroline died in Ambala after having given birth to Robin's younger brother, Gilbert ("Gill"), and the two little boys were raised by an Indian ayah, or nanny. The family returned to England in 1885, when Robin was six years old, crossing over to Ireland five years later, when the Ninth Lancers were stationed at the Curragh Army Camp. On Captain Forsythe's retirement from the Lancers in 1893, he and his two sons settled in Scotland at his old home village, Carmunnock. Originally intended for the legal profession, Robin instead entered the civil service, although like E.R. Punshon, another clerk turned classic mystery writer recently reprinted by Dean Street Press, he dreamt of earning his bread through his pen by another, more imaginative, means: creative writing. As a young man Robin published poetry and short stories in newspapers and periodicals, yet not until after his release from prison in 1929 at the age of fifty would he finally realize his youthful hope of making his living as a fiction writer.

For the next several years Robin worked in Glasgow as an Inland Revenue Assistant of Excise. In 1909 he married Kate Margaret Havord, daughter of a guide roller in a Glasgow iron and steel mill, and by 1911 the couple resided, along with their one-year-old son John, in Godstone, Surrey, twenty miles from London, where Robin was employed as a Third Class Clerk in the Principal Probate Registry at Somerset House. Young John remained the Robin and Kate's only child when the couple separated a decade later. What problems led to the irretrievable breakdown of the marriage is not known, but Kate's daughter-in-law later characterized Kate as "very greedy" and speculated that her exactions upon her husband might have made "life difficult for Robin and given him a reason for his illegal acts."

Six years after his separation from Kate, Robin conceived and carried out, with the help of three additional Somerset

House clerks, a fraudulent enterprise resembling something out
of the imaginative crime fiction of Arthur Conan Doyle, Golden
Age thriller writer Edgar Wallace and post Golden Age lawyer-
turned-author Michael Gilbert. Over a year-and-a-half period,
the Somerset House conspirators removed high value judicature
stamps from documents deposited with the Board of Inland
Revenue, using acids to obliterate cancellation marks, and sold the
stamps at half-cost to three solicitor's clerks, the latter of whom
pocketed the difference in prices. Robin and his co-conspirators
at Somerset House divided among themselves the proceeds from
the illicit sales of the stamps, which totaled over 50,000 pounds
(or roughly $75,000 US dollars) in modern value. Unhappily
for the seven schemers, however, a government auditor became
suspicious of nefarious activity at Somerset House, resulting in a
1927 undercover Scotland Yard investigation that, coupled with
an intensive police laboratory examination of hundreds of suspect
documents, fully exposed both the crime and its culprits.

Robin Forsythe and his co-conspirators were promptly
arrested and at London's Old Bailey on 7 February 1928, the
Common Serjeant--elderly Sir Henry Dickens, K.C., last surviving
child of the great Victorian author Charles Dickens--passed
sentence on the seven men, all of whom had plead guilty and
thrown themselves on the mercy of the court. Sir Henry sentenced
Robin to a term of fifteen months imprisonment, castigating
him as a calculating rogue, according to the Glasgow Herald, the
newspaper in which Robin had published his poetry as a young
man, back when the world had seemed full of promise:

It is an astounding position to find in an office like
that of Somerset House that the Canker of dishonesty
had bitten deep....You are the prime mover of this,
and obviously you started it. For a year and a half you
have continued it, and you have undoubtedly raised an
atmosphere and influenced other people in that office.

Likely one of the "astounding" aspects of this case in the eyes of eminent pillars of society like Dickens was that Robin Forsythe and his criminal cohort to a man had appeared to be, before the fraud was exposed, quite upright individuals. With one exception Robin's co-conspirators were a generation younger than their ringleader and had done their duty, as the saying goes, in the Great War. One man had been a decorated lance corporal in the late affray, while another had served as a gunner in the Royal Field Artillery and a third had piloted biplanes as a 2nd lieutenant in the Royal Flying Corps. The affair disturbingly demonstrated to all and sundry that, just like in Golden Age crime fiction, people who seemed above suspicion could fall surprisingly hard for the glittering lure of ill-gotten gain.

Crime fiction offered the imaginative Robin Forsythe not only a means of livelihood after he was released in from prison in 1929, unemployed and seemingly unemployable, but also, one might surmise, a source of emotional solace and escape. Dorothy L. Sayers once explained that from the character of her privileged aristocratic amateur detective, Lord Peter Wimsey, she had devised and derived, at difficult times in her life, considerable vicarious satisfaction:

> When I was dissatisfied with my single unfurnished room, I tool a luxurious flat for him in Piccadilly. When my cheap rug got a hole in it, I ordered an Aubusson carpet. When I had no money to pay my bus fare, I presented him with a Daimler double-six, upholstered in a style of sober magnificence, and when I felt dull I let him drive it.

Between 1929 and 1937 Robin published eight successful crime novels, five of which were part of the Algernon Vereker mystery series for which the author was best known: *Missing or Murdered* (1929), *The Polo Ground Mystery* (1932), *The Pleasure Cruise Mystery* (1933), *The Ginger Cat Mystery* (1935) and *The Spirit Murder Mystery* (1936). The three remaining novels—*The Hounds of Justice* (1930), *The Poison Duel* (1934, under the pseudonym Peter Dingwall) and *Murder on Paradise Island* (1937)—were non-series works.

Like the other Robin Forsythe detective novels detailing the criminal investigations of Algernon Vereker, gentleman artist and amateur sleuth, *Missing or Murdered* was issued in England by The Bodley Head, publisher in the Twenties of mysteries by Agatha Christie and Annie Haynes, the latter another able writer revived by Dean Street Press. Christie had left The Bodley Head in 1926 and Annie Haynes had passed away early in 1929, leaving the publisher in need of promising new authors. Additionally, the American company Appleton-Century published two of the Algernon Vereker novels, *The Pleasure Cruise Mystery* and *The Ginger Cat Mystery*, in the United States (the latter book under the title *Murder at Marston Manor*) as part of its short-lived but memorably titled Tired Business Man's Library of adventure, detective and mystery novels, which were designed "to afford relaxation and entertainment" to industrious American escape fiction addicts during their off hours. Forsythe's fiction also enjoyed some success in France, where his first three detective novels were published, under the titles *La Disparition de Lord Bygrave* (The Disappearance of Lord Bygrave), *La Passion de Sadie Maberley* (The Passion of Sadie Maberley) and *Coups de feu a l'aube* (Gunshots at Dawn).

The Robin Forsythe mystery fiction drew favorable comment for their vivacity and ingenuity from such luminaries as Dorothy L. Sayers, Charles Williams and J.B. Priestley, the latter acutely observing that "Mr. Forsythe belongs to the new school of detective story writers which might be called the brilliant flippant school." Sayers pronounced of Forsythe's *The Ginger Cat Mystery* that "[t]he story is lively and the plot interesting," while Charles Williams, author and editor of Oxford University Press, heaped praise upon *The Polo Ground Mystery* as "a good story of one bullet, two wounds, two shots, and one dead man and three pistols before the end....It is really a maze, and the characters are not merely automata."

This second act in the career of Robin Forsythe proved sadly short-lived, however, for in 1937 the author passed away from kidney disease, still estranged from his wife and son, at the age of 57. In his later years he resided--along with his Irish Setter Terry, the "dear pal" to whom he dedicated *The Ginger Cat Mystery*--at a cottage in the village of Hartest, near Bury St. Edmunds, Suffolk. In addition to writing, Robin enjoyed gardening and dabbling in art, having become an able chalk sketch artist and water colorist. He also toured on ocean liners (under the name "Robin Forsythe"), thereby gaining experience that would serve him well in his novel *The Pleasure Cruise Mystery*. This book Robin dedicated to "Beatrice," while *Missing or Murdered* was dedicated to "Elizabeth" and *The Spirit Murder Mystery* to "Jean." Did Robin find solace as well in human companionship during his later years? Currently we can only speculate, but classic British crime fans who peruse the mysteries of Robin Forsythe should derive pleasure from spending time in the clever company of Algernon Vereker as he hunts down fictional malefactors—thus proving that, while crime may not pay, it most definitely can entertain.

Curtis Evans

Chapter One

Mr. Gregory Grierson, Chief Clerk, sat at his desk at the Ministry of X— near an open window overlooking the Thames with his gaze fixed on the swiftly outflowing tide, all sparkling and flashing in the bright October sun. The wide stretch of water below him was pulsating with golden light, but, though his vision was intent on this splendour, his thoughts were elsewhere. They were evidently occupied with some unpleasant subject, for every now and then he frowned and the lids of his eyes narrowed until the pupils were almost hidden.

At length he rose impatiently from his chair, as if summarily wrenching himself free from the domination of that distasteful train of speculation, and walked leisurely over to the tall vase of sweet-peas standing on the mantelpiece. He gazed with genuine admiration at the delicate blossoms and tenderly re-arranged them with a sensitive and rather finely shaped hand. Then he stood back a pace and regarded them critically. Yes, they were undoubtedly superb blooms; they had more than repaid the incessant care he had bestowed on their culture. A look of satisfaction, even of pride, gathered on his features—the pride and satisfaction of the successful horticulturist. From that vase of sweet-peas he wandered over to gaze lovingly at an etching by Forain, and another by Zorn, hanging on the wall opposite the fire-place. These two etchings constituted the sole personal note struck by Gregory Grierson in the furnishing of Room 83, which in all other respects conformed to the taste of the mysterious genius responsible for the embellishment of Government interiors.

Mr. Grierson was a man of considerable refinement, and he had often felt grateful to that mysterious genius for the amazing skill with which he had eliminated every vestige of himself—of a human being with predilections—from his work. The unobtrusive greens of the walls, the silent, non-committal carpets, the mute and passionless reserve of the hearth-rugs (worked with the Royal monogram to obviate theft rather than add ornament) could never impinge on the consciousness or offend the susceptibilities of the most sensitive soul that might have to pass the greater part of his earthly existence among them. Mr. Grierson glanced round the room and for a moment entertained the seductive vision of Room 83 furnished to the standard of his fastidious taste. But to indulge the vision was only a pleasant folly after all...

He returned to his desk, sat down and commenced the day's work. He had not been seated long when Bliss, one of his staff, entered with a précis of some correspondence and laid it on his chief's desk. Bliss was about to return to his own room when Mr. Grierson swung round in his chair and spoke to him.

"Any telephone message for me this morning, Bliss?" he asked.

"No, sir. Have you had any further news of Lord Bygrave?"

"None whatever. Scotland Yard rang me up last night and told me that one of their representatives would call here to-day. Show him in to me at once on his arrival."

"Yes, sir."

"Altogether it's a most extraordinary business—I can't understand it. However, now that the police are on the track there's just a possibility that they'll shed some light on the mystery. The Press have already raised the hue and cry, and this morning one Daily published a photograph of Lord Bygrave with the offer of £100 reward for information that will lead to his discovery, dead or alive. What a topic of conversation for the town!"

"I can't imagine what can have happened to him!" exclaimed Bliss with a perplexed air.

"There's no knowing in these days of unrest and anarchy what may suddenly happen to any public man," replied Mr. Grierson gravely. "However, perhaps I'm looking on the matter with undue pessimism. Let's hope there'll be a happy solution to the mystery after all."

Mr. Grierson turned again to his desk to signify that the conversation might be considered at an end, and Bliss passed through the door leading into the juniors' room (as it was always called), where his colleague Murray was eagerly awaiting him.

"Any news of Bygrave?" asked Murray, unable to allow Bliss a protracted enjoyment of an air of importance which the possession of secret information had already bestowed on him.

"None at all," said Bliss curtly and sat down at his desk.

"I hope they've rung up Bygrave Hall," remarked Murray. "Bygrave may simply have gone home slightly indisposed."

"True, Murray, true! You seem to wish to be helpful," replied Bliss mockingly, "but you must fling off these luminous remarks to the Scotland Yard official when he arrives this morning."

"Good Lord, are we going to have a visit from Scotland Yard?" asked Murray excitedly.

"Yes," replied Bliss, noticing with some satisfaction the electrical effect of his communication.

"My hat!" exclaimed Murray. "The shadow of romance has actually fallen across the prosaic threshold of the Ministry."

"I think we may consider that it's our day," said Bliss with a faint smile. "By the way, Murray, have you decided how you're going to pose for the Press photographer?"

"Bless my soul, no, not yet. Things are moving so swiftly. I'm glad you've called my attention to the point—it's important. What do you think of, say, a three-quarter view, seated at my desk, telephone receiver in one hand and quill pen in the other? Have we any quills left? I feel a quill is essential. But have you got your story ready for the interviewer? 'Mr. Bliss's Story' they'll call it."

"I shall work that up at lunch over my sausages and mash and one veg., as the waitress calls it," replied Bliss quietly. "What is intriguing me at present is whether I shall be photographed with my morning coat open or buttoned. It's most difficult to decide."

At this moment the door opened and a uniformed messenger ushered in a heavy-jawed, forceful-looking man in a blue serge suit, holding in his hand a bowler hat which gave Murray the swift impression that it was much too small for the owner's massive head.

"Detective-Inspector Heather of Scotland Yard," said the messenger to Bliss. "Is Mr. Grierson in, sir?"

"Yes," replied Bliss; "he's at present in his room and is expecting Inspector Heather. Please show the inspector in, Johnson."

The messenger opened the door leading into Mr. Grierson's room, and Detective-Inspector Heather passed out of Murray's devouring vision. The door closed and Johnson vanished with a topic of conversation that would vie in interest with the "probable winners" among the other occupants of the messengers' room for the remainder of the day.

Mr. Grierson rose at once from his desk on Detective-Inspector Heather's entry and offered him a chair close to his own.

"No news of Lord Bygrave yet, inspector?" he asked anxiously as he passed the officer a box of cigarettes.

"None so far, sir, but I feel somehow or other that it won't be long before we hear something definite," replied the inspector in a quiet conversational tone. His eye, apparently occupied with the general aspect and arrangement of the room, was actually weighing up Mr. Grierson as far as that gentleman's outward appearance gave food for conjecture as to his nature and habits.

Though ever on the alert and suspicious of every one, Inspector Heather was not long in forming his opinion of Mr. Grierson. His opinion of Mr. Grierson was that he was simply a Government official—a man who is very highly paid for doing very little work. It was unusual of Inspector Heather to make hasty assumptions of this type, but then his mind was working under the compelling influence of a great British tradition—the legend that no work has been or is ever done by a civil servant. In justice to the inspector's fairness, it must be admitted that he coupled Mr. Grierson's facile evasion of work and capture of salary with an unquestionable probity, an unimpeachable respectability. He was moderately safe in this, for an official of the Mint has never yet been caught making spurious coin, nor a Treasury official yet run away with a million of the Treasury funds.

He also thought Mr. Grierson a gentleman: there was an air of culture and refinement about his bearing, and just the requisite amount of superiority which Inspector Heather found in most of the people he called gentlemen.

"Can I do anything for you, inspector?" asked Mr. Grierson urbanely.

"Well, I should like to ask a few questions which may be possibly of some assistance in my investigation, if you can spare the time just now," replied the inspector, producing notebook and pencil.

"I'm at your service," replied Mr. Grierson, lighting a cigarette and settling himself comfortably in his chair.

"As far as I have been able to gather up to the present, Lord Bygrave left London for the village of Hartwood on Friday, the 1st of the month, intending to spend a fortnight or so in the country. He arrived at the White Bear Inn rather late that night, left early next morning and seems to have vanished completely. Before going down there for more detailed information I should like to know, Mr. Grierson, when he left this office."

"He usually leaves at four, but on that night—so Murray, one of my clerks, tells me—he left at five. I myself had an appointment at four, and left at 3.30, so that I was not here. You can, however, take Murray's statement as accurate, because he would probably be eagerly awaiting Lord Bygrave's departure before he himself felt free to go."

"He would be blessing Lord Bygrave for staying late, if I am any judge of these young gentlemen," remarked the inspector.

"We were all young once," replied Mr. Grierson, with fatherly tolerance.

"Have you yourself made any Inquiries in likely quarters since you heard of Lord Bygrave's disappearance?" asked the inspector, looking sharply at Mr. Grierson.

"Oh, yes," replied the latter at once. "I immediately rang up Bygrave Hall and asked Farnish, his butler, if he had any information of his lordship. Farnish knew nothing of Lord Bygrave's whereabouts and had received no instructions from him since the morning of the 1st."

"I believe Lord Bygrave is a bachelor?" asked Inspector Heather.

"A confirmed bachelor, like myself," replied Mr. Grierson.

"Has he any residence in town?"

"None; and if he is obliged through his duties to stay in town—a contingency he detests—he always puts up at Jauvrin's Hotel, in Jermyn Street. I have inquired there also, but found that Lord Bygrave had not stayed there since April last."

Detective-Inspector Heather was lost in thought for some moments.

"I suppose a gentleman in Lord Bygrave's position can come and go pretty much as he chooses," he remarked. "Now, Mr. Grierson, from your knowledge of him do you attach any importance to his disappearance?"

"I'm inclined to think something serious has happened to him, inspector, though naturally I hope that my fears are groundless. The whole occurrence is most unusual and quite incompatible with my knowledge of him; yet, for the life of me, I cannot suggest anything to elucidate the mystery," replied Mr. Grierson, thoroughly mystified.

"That's bad, that's bad!" exclaimed the inspector. "Know a man and you can make a fair guess at what he'll do, and indirectly what may be likely to happen to him. What sort of a man is his lordship?"

"Though he is a Minister and always to a certain extent in the public eye, he is by nature a shy, reserved and retiring man. Public life is really a martyrdom for him. He has only suffered that martyrdom because of a profound conviction that it is his bounden duty to serve his country, regardless of his own personal preference for the peaceful oblivion of the life of a country gentleman. His tastes are those of a naturalist, and he has often said that, when he is too old for the service of the State, he will retire and commence his own life in earnest. There is nothing he likes better than to bury himself in some out-of-the-way English village and forget that the world of politics and business exists."

"H'm," replied the inspector. "You feel sure that there's nothing more than the desire for a peaceful life that takes Lord Bygrave on these quiet excursions. No lady in the background—eh?"

"No, inspector," said Mr. Grierson, unable to suppress a smile at the suggestion. "You can take it from me that it's not a case of *cherchez la femme*. Nor is Lord Bygrave a man of mysteries. On his return from these holidays he is full of his experiences, which he never fails to relate to me."

Inspector Heather was silent for a few moments.

"Has he any personal enemies that you know of?" he asked.

"It would be difficult, I think, to find anyone of whom it could be more truly said that he hasn't an enemy in the world," replied Mr. Grierson impressively, and then added: "I use the word enemy in the sense of a harbourer of personal hatred that might lead to physical violence. Political hatred is merely the rancour that arises from bad sportsmanship in a Party game; in England I suppose it may be considered negligible from a criminal point of view."

"Nothing is negligible from a criminal point of view," remarked Inspector Heather, as if it were a line from a Criminal Investigation Department credo. His eyes roamed slowly over the pattern of the carpet. "Has Lord Bygrave been to Hartwood before?" he asked.

"I believe he spent a few days at the White Bear Inn at Hartwood some years ago—but I may be wrong, my memory is not one of the best. He had a mania for staying in what he called good, old-fashioned, country inns."

"They're all right if the beer's good," commented the inspector seriously. "Did he travel on these occasions as Lord Bygrave?" he asked.

"I believe he often reverted to the family name of Darnell—Henry Darnell—to avoid attracting unnecessary attention. He used to say he didn't mind being considered a man of the people if it meant being charged popular prices."

At this point in the conversation Johnson entered and informed Mr. Grierson that a Mr. Algernon Vereker would like to see him.

"Mr. Algernon Vereker!" exclaimed Mr. Grierson, with a faint show of surprise. "A friend of Lord Bygrave's! I have often heard Lord Bygrave speak of him. He may be of some use to us, inspector. Show Mr. Vereker in, Johnson."

Johnson disappeared and Mr. Algernon Vereker slowly entered the room. Having watched the door close behind him by means of a pneumatic arrangement fitted for that purpose, much as a child would gaze upon some new wonder stumbled upon for the first time in experience, he turned and glanced rapidly at Mr. Grierson, and then at Detective-Inspector Heather.

"Quaint device," he remarked, pointing with his whangee cane at the door. "Closing mechanism. I could play with it for hours. Mr. Grierson, I believe," he continued, his eyes returning to that gentleman.

Mr. Grierson nodded assent.

"I have come to see if you know anything of Lord Bygrave. Is there any truth in the Press statements that he has mysteriously disappeared? I see one alert Daily has already made a prize competition out of him. I at once phoned Bygrave Hall, but found that Farnish, the butler, knew nothing of his lordship's whereabouts."

"I have just been discussing Lord Bygrave's extraordinary disappearance with Detective-Inspector Heather of Scotland Yard," replied Mr. Grierson, and he proceeded to give Vereker a summary of the conversation and the facts of the case as known to himself.

During this interval Inspector Heather's attention was riveted on Mr. Algernon Vereker, and he soon came to the conclusion, to put it in his own words, that he was a rum-looking specimen. There was something about the man's appearance that suggested the possession of a vein of eccentricity and a whimsical outlook on life. With such people Inspector Heather was inclined to be impatient. They're crazy; I have no use for them, he would say, and lightly flick them off the face of the particular earth that he himself inhabited.

When Mr. Grierson had concluded his statement, Vereker rolled his soft felt hat into a cone with his long nervous fingers.

"It's very strange altogether," he drawled; "so out of harmony with anything that one associates with old Bygrave. He hasn't disappeared of his own account—that's a certainty! No one could possibly imagine Bygrave vanishing with another man's wife or making a run for it with trust funds. The only thing I can think of is that he has gone to heaven."

"You really think that something serious has happened to him, Mr. Vereker?" asked the inspector, disregarding the levity of that individual's last remark.

"I am going to work on that assumption straightway," replied Vereker. "If anything untoward has happened to him—which God forbid—my hands will be pretty full, for I'm executor and trustee under his will."

"You know the contents of the will, Mr. Vereker?" promptly asked the inspector.

"Oh, yes. Translating it from legalese into the intelligible, David Winslade, his nephew, comes into all his property, save for five hundred pounds left to Farnish, the butler, and a thousand to me for acting as executor."

Inspector Heather made an entry in his notebook of these facts.

"I may as well tell you at this point, inspector, that I haven't got rid of my friend Bygrave for that thousand pounds," continued Vereker. "If you can accept this information as true it may save you some time, should further investigations be necessary. In the latter case I shall promptly suspect both Farnish and Winslade—it's only logical to do so, even though I am fairly certain that neither of them is a criminal. They at least supply a motive—a sordid one in all conscience, but a motive."

"Murders have been committed for less," remarked the inspector in a matter-of-fact tone.

"Yes," sighed Vereker wearily, "I suppose so. Keeping the fact in mind, it is difficult to cherish ideals as to the future of mankind. It would be quite as rational to entertain hopes of domesticating Bengal tigers. My faith grows weak, but I console myself that I'm only moderately imbecile when I think of the unbridled optimism of the Socialist."

Detective-Inspector Heather glanced uneasily at Vereker, whose eyes gazed dreamily across the sunlit river to the smoky haze that hung over the south, his thoughts lost in a vague, wistful conjecture about humanity's future, a subject which troubled Inspector Heather no more than, say, Einstein's theory of relativity.

Vereker rose abruptly from his chair.

"Well, I must be going," he said. "I shall probably see you down at Hartwood, inspector, for I shall get to work at once. Good day, gentlemen." The door opened quietly and Mr. Algernon Vereker disappeared.

"So that's Mr. Algernon Vereker, the artist!" exclaimed Mr. Grierson.

"Somewhat eccentric young gentleman," remarked the inspector.

"It's the first time I've met him," said Mr. Grierson. "Lord Bygrave, however, always speaks of him in terms of sincere affection. 'That lovable lunatic, Vereker,' he always calls him. He has a very high opinion of Mr. Vereker's character and must consider him, shorn of his eccentricities, a man of sterling worth. Otherwise he would hardly have appointed him a trustee and executor in his will—Lord Bygrave has an almost uncanny power of judging a man's character."

"Mr. Vereker seems a bit of a buffoon to me," commented the inspector quietly. "You say he's an artist?"

"According to modern standards, yes," replied Mr. Grierson cautiously. "He's making quite a name for himself among the newer school of painters. Whether his reputation or theirs will live is another matter."

"It's a subject I don't profess to understand, and I wouldn't give a pipe of good tobacco for the best picture in the world," boomed the inspector weightily and, with a sardonic smile spreading over his features, asked, "Does he earn a living at it?"

"I should say, confidently, that his work's a dead financial loss to him. Mr. Vereker, however, is a fairly wealthy man, though to judge from his appearance no one would believe it. He always professes a complete disregard for money—again, that may be, in a great measure, a pose. Suffers from a kink," remarked the inspector bluntly; "that's how I'd put it—a kink. Bless my soul if I don't think a University education gives every man a kink—some more, some less."

"Most up-to-date people would agree with you," said Mr. Grierson, raising his brows and looking over his glasses at the inspector. "However, in Mr. Vereker's case it's a harmless sort of kink—paint and canvas suffer more than humanity. Lord Bygrave tells me he's one of the most generous of men and is always helping some lame dog over a stile."

"He probably does a lot of good, but in a foolish, unsystematic way," concluded Inspector Heather, rising from his chair.

At this moment the door again opened and Mr. Algernon Vereker returned.

"I thought I'd just let you know my address, Inspector Heather, in case you want any personal information about Lord Bygrave.

But I shall be down at Hartwood from this evening—I start on the trail from the White Bear Inn. If I can be of any assistance—"

"Thanks, Mr. Vereker," replied the inspector.

"I like to do good even in a foolish and unsystematic way," added Vereker.

Inspector Heather looked up sharply. There was a trace of annoyance on his alert features. He deduced the fact that Mr. Vereker's ears were preternaturally acute.

"Ah, you overheard my remark," he laughed diplomatically. "I was speaking of you, Mr. Vereker."

"I wondered," replied Mr. Vereker, smiling broadly;" but I didn't think I'd extract a confirmation so easily from one of your profession. An unsystematic way of doing good is all that the complexity of life allows an individual; a wise and systematic method is reserved for some future blissful state. What do you think?"

"I'm unable to discuss the matter just now, Mr. Vereker," replied the inspector dryly.

"Then on some future occasion; say over a bottle of port, for I love to reconstruct the universe over good port. A man with your experience of the evil men do ought to be well worth listening to on the good they might do. By the way, inspector, I don't like the name of the innkeeper at the White Bear Inn."

"I don't see what a man's name has got to do with it," replied the inspector curtly.

"I'm rather influenced by names. Now George Lawless is an unpleasant name. Give a dog a bad name, you know! There's a lot in these old sayings—mother wit I think they call it. Well, once more good day, gentlemen," and Mr. Vereker took his departure.

"He's what is usually called a 'balm-pot'!" exclaimed Inspector Heather when he had made sure that Mr. Vereker had passed well beyond ear-shot. "By the way, is Mr. Vereker an amateur detective as well as an artist?"

"Oh, I wouldn't take much notice of Mr. Vereker's activities," replied Mr. Grierson, with a shrug of his shoulders. "He has been, so I have heard, actor, politician, amateur tramp, athlete, vegetarian and gentleman rider in turns. He will take Scotland Yard in his stride so to speak. Only the other day, so Lord Bygrave told me, he was going to equip an expedition to discover King Solomon's mines. He had dreamt they were in Borneo, and not in Africa, and he was convinced that their discovery would pay off the National Debt and give France a decent leg up. At the same time don't altogether class him as a fool. You will find, as far as I can gather, that he wears buffoonery as a kind of cloak—probably because he is in reality a very shy and self-depreciatory man."

Inspector Heather laughed as he let himself out of Mr. Grierson's room, and before he had reached the street he had come to a vague conclusion, the reason for which he would have been unable to express, that Mr. Algernon Vereker was probably not a bad sort even though he was undoubtedly a "balm-pot" to all outward appearances.

Chapter Two

The White Bear Inn lies at the western end of the village of Hartwood, and is a rambling edifice with a spacious courtyard in which the Hartwood Hunt often meets. The proprietor, George Lawless, was not an ideal innkeeper; but it requires a great genius to be an ideal innkeeper, and genius is rare in all professions. He was a man of little education and less refinement; of reserved manner, no conversation, an irritable temper and a heavy, almost repellent face. He was certainly not in keeping with the old inn. Its romance left him cold; its age—it was built in the reign of Richard III—never once lit in his imagination a thought of all those who had slept and eaten and drunk and fought and loved and danced and died beneath its heavy oak-beamed ceilings. He used daily to curse the place for not being on the main road for motor traffic to the south.

"White Bear, indeed," he would often mutter; "it has been nothing but a white elephant to me!"

On this October morning George Lawless was in a particularly irritable temper. He had cursed Terry, the barman, about the untidy appearance of the bar; Mary Standish, who was parlourmaid, housemaid, scullery-maid and barmaid all rolled into one, had come in for a share of his ill-humour, though he was always gentler in his speech with Mary than with any of his servants. Dick, who tended the garden, drove the buggy to the station for visitors and visitors back in the buggy to the station, groomed the pony and made himself useful and attentive in the garage, had actually sworn back at the "Guv'nor" and come to the verge of giving notice. It may be mentioned, however, that Dick had been on the brink of giving notice every day for the past ten years. George Lawless had, fortunately for his peace of mind, been unaware of this Damoclean sword.

All this unpleasantness was due to the sudden and inexplicable disappearance of Henry Darnell, Lord Bygrave. On Friday night he had arrived; on Saturday morning he had gone out and never returned. On Monday Lawless had met the village constable and casually mentioned the matter; on Tuesday the sergeant had been informed; on Wednesday the affair had been bruited abroad, Scotland Yard called in and every one in England who read a daily paper knew that Lord Bygrave had mysteriously disappeared. Had Henry Darnell been a shopkeeper, or a postman, the affair would have been important news to a modern daily paper. That he was a well-known peer almost raised the mystery to the level of "Beautiful London Girl of Eighteen Missing" in terms of headline and public interest.

George Lawless couldn't for the life of him understand why Lord Bygrave should disappear, and he lost his temper thoroughly over the whole business. It was unsatisfactory and altogether

unintelligible. People who stayed at the White Bear Inn, even
though they were titled folk, were expected to behave like ordinary
human beings in a common-sense, reasonable manner. Lawless
was not annoyed that Lord Bygrave had gone without paying his
bill; for in his room was a portmanteau with boots and clothes,
and on the wash-hand-stand he had carelessly left a heavy, gold
signet-ring with a crest cut in intaglio. On this property Lawless
felt that he had a lien—it was quite sufficient security for a bed and
breakfast. What had angered George Lawless was the behaviour
of Police Sergeant Bailey. It had been inquisitorial. He had asked
endless and seemingly irrelevant questions, and conducted
himself with an air of importance and secrecy that were noxious to
a degree—especially in an ordinary village police sergeant. When
he had been about to depart he had informed the proprietor of the
White Bear Inn that Detective-Inspector Heather of Scotland Yard
would be down in the afternoon to make further investigations.

"What the dooce does he expect to find?" George Lawless had
asked irritably. "Does he suspect I've done the gent in?"

Sergeant Bailey felt that this question was merely a verbal
diffusion of pent-up irritability, and did not condescend to
reply. When he had gone Lawless let himself go in a full-blooded
effectual way that was comforting to himself but withering to
the police force in general and to Sergeant Bailey in particular.
Remembering the cause of the trouble, his mind reverted once
more to Lord Bygrave.

"These London folk—more trouble than they're d—d well
worth! Never satisfied with a decent bed and plain food, but
always asking for something you ain't got and wot's not good for
'em in any case. Not that his lordship asked for much—in fact
he went to the opposite extreme and asked for *nothing*, which
is worse still. Then he's one of them blokes who goes chasing
butterflies like a kid of ten. Nice occupation for a grown man!
S'elp me if I don't think he wasn't quite right in the head. And now

he goes missing. 'Pon my soul, I don't know what the country's coming to!"

In the afternoon Detective-Inspector Heather arrived, and at once sought out the landlord of the White Bear. George Lawless had by this time resigned himself to the inevitable. He showed the officer into his own little parlour, from which he used to emerge into the bar at stated times and on specific occasions. It was a small room, comfortably furnished, according to the indeterminate ideas of Lawless about furnishing, with a small window looking on to the garden behind the inn. Inspector Heather settled himself comfortably in an arm-chair and lit a pipe.

"At what time on Friday night did Mr. Darnell, or rather Lord Bygrave, arrive here, Mr. Lawless?"

"About half-past nine. He came by the train arriving here at 9.15."

"Did he fill in the usual forms?"

"No. After he'd had his supper I thought it was too late to trouble him with the forms that night, and he'd left the inn before I saw him next morning."

"When did he leave next morning?"

"About half-past eight: he had breakfast at eight, and told Mary Standish that he'd be back for lunch."

"Ah, that's important. He intended to return. Did you notice anything peculiar in his manner overnight?"

"No. He seemed tired and after his supper drank a double whisky and soda and went to bed."

"You didn't see him next morning?"

"No. I was busy in the cellar. Mary waited on him and saw he had all he wanted for breakfast."

"Good. I'll interrogate her later. I'd like to see his room. I believe you said he'd left his luggage?"

"Yes, his bag is there just as he left it. No one has touched it."

"Anyone occupying that particular room now?"

"No. No one has occupied it since he left. Mary Standish found this signet-ring on the wash-hand-stand the same morning. She told me about it and we left it there until next day. When Lord Bygrave didn't come back I took charge of it."

"I'll take possession of it for the present," said the inspector, examining the ring closely. "I believe that's the crest of the Bygraves."

George Lawless picked up a key from a table, and together the two men went upstairs to a room on the first floor. In a corner of the apartment stood a capacious leather kit-bag.

"There's his luggage—just as he left it. I tried it, to see if it was locked, but found that it was open. Nothing inside has been touched."

The inspector lifted the kit-bag and brought it into the centre of the room. Unfastening the straps he opened it and carefully turned out the contents on the floor. Shirts, collars, socks, underclothes, a safety razor and strop, tooth-brush, hair-brushes, soap, etc., a suit of light-coloured Harris tweeds, a pair of walking shoes, a pair of morocco slippers, pyjamas, a bunch of keys attached to a key chain and a pound tin of tobacco which had been broken formed the main contents. Inspector Heather had just arranged these articles on the floor when the door of the bedroom opposite opened and there emerged into the corridor Mr. Algernon Vereker, wiping his hands with a towel.

"You lose no time, inspector," he remarked. "I didn't expect you down here to-day."

Inspector Heather smiled. "Can't allow you too long a start, Mr. Vereker," he remarked jocularly.

"Oh, I haven't left the mark yet. But I may as well jump off now. I see you are having a look through Bygrave's kit. I'll take an inventory too—as his executor I suppose I ought to, in case of eventualities."

Vereker, having dried his hands, threw his towel through the open door of his bedroom and came and watched the inspector making a detailed list of Lord Bygrave's personal belongings.

"Have you emptied the canvas pocket?" he asked.

"Is there one?" asked the inspector in turn.

"Oh, yes; rather neatly concealed. I've often borrowed that bag."

The inspector promptly examined the interior more carefully and, thrusting in his hand, produced a slim, well-worn notebook.

"By Jove, a diary—I hope it's modernly indiscreet!" exclaimed Vereker. "But it's a foolish hope, I'm afraid—Bygrave was a gentleman."

The notebook, however, merely contained a mass of lead-pencil jottings, the rough unpolished notes of an ardent and patient naturalist, of bird life, etc. They were all dated and referred to observations taken in the Western Islands of Scotland during a holiday the previous year. The officer tossed it over to Vereker with a disappointed shrug of his shoulders.

"An ordinary diary might have been of great use," he said quickly.

"Now, let's start making brilliant deductions, inspector," said Vereker.

"Fire away, Mr. Vereker," replied Heather, his eyes moving from one article to another on the floor as he jotted the items down in his notebook.

"Then I must withdraw the 'brilliant'; I was leaning on you for all the sparkle, inspector. But to business! I deduce Lord Bygrave was in a hurry on the morning of his departure."

"Good, Mr. Vereker. You came to that conclusion because he'd neither shaved nor washed his teeth. His razor and tooth-brush have not been unpacked."

"That's brilliant but problematical," remarked Vereker quietly, "because I know Lord Bygrave's habits, and he always put his toilet articles back in his bag after using them when staying at an hotel."

"Then how did you infer that Lord Bygrave was in a hurry?" asked the inspector, glancing with interest at Mr. Algernon Vereker, who seemed lost in profound thought.

"Mary Standish told me," replied the amateur dryly, "though I should have discovered it in any case from the fact that he forgot to put his ring on again after his ablutions. A man who habitually wears a ring must be in a hurry to omit so accustomed an action as resuming it after washing.

"Ah, you've heard all about the ring?"

"Yes, I've seen the ring all right. It was one of the first things Lawless spoke about when I arrived, and he knew I was on the trail."

"Anything else you can see?" asked the inspector.

"M'yes—I estimate that Lord Bygrave smoked about an ounce of tobacco a day. That pound tin had to last him the fortnight. However, this is art for art's sake—it won't help us much. I also feel sure I shall finish the tin for him, unless he turns up and takes possession. I'm rather fond of this brand; it's the only tobacco old Henry could enjoy." Vereker produced an outsize in briars and began to plug it.

Inspector Heather had now completed his notes and, rising from the floor on which he had been kneeling, made a keen survey of the room. Vereker also flung a searching glance in every direction.

"Another beautiful but useless discovery," he remarked. "Bygrave smoked a pipe of tobacco before going to bed or just before breakfast. He has knocked his pipe out in the fender, and there's the dottle."

Picking up the dottle between finger and thumb, Vereker showed it to the inspector and then flung it back into the fire-place.

The police officer walked over to a small writing-table and examined the blotting-pad lying on it. It had never been used, for not a mark was on its white surface save the price lead-pencilled in the corner.

"Not much to be learned here," he said. "I'll now see Miss Standish and learn what she can tell me."

"Lunch with me, inspector. I have ordered for both of us. Standish waits on us, and you can then cross-question her. The beer here is most excellent—I'm afraid it has biased me in Lawless's favour. I've almost ceased to suspect him of complicity in this business. Yet there's the cellar to be searched. I ought to have gone down and made a thorough investigation—before tasting the beer. By the way, do you want to examine the contents of that kit-bag again?"

"No, I think I've done with that," replied the inspector.

"Then I'll lock it," said Vereker, and taking out the bunch of keys, which had been thrust back into the bag, he locked it and slipped the bunch into his own pocket. "And now for lunch and beakers with beaded bubbles winking at the brim."

The two men descended to the dining-room, where George Lawless had done his best to have an appetizing lunch laid for his guests.

Chapter Three

Inspector Heather and Algernon Vereker sat down to a plain but substantial meal as devised by a man (with a healthy hunger) for hungry men. There was an excellent sirloin of beef, and Mary Standish had built up a salad with a sound foundation of beetroot, lettuces, onions and hard-boiled eggs, with an admixture of good Hartwood cream, and a crowning note of refinement in a nasturtium blossom or two.

"This is altogether delightful," remarked Vereker enthusiastically. "It's an age since I ate nasturtium flowers— they're a delicious adjunct to a salad, apart from pleasing the eye."

"That's a nice bit of Stilton," added Inspector Heather on a more solid note.

At this juncture Mary Standish brought in a dish of steaming potatoes and two pint tankards of ale and set them down on the table.

"If you want anything else, gentlemen, will you kindly strike the gong? The electric bells are not working to-day."

"Right you are," replied Inspector Heather, settling down with a business-like air to the meal.

Algernon Vereker, however, remained standing until Mary Standish had left the dining-room, for if anything in the world could disturb his equanimity it was the sudden birth of an inspiration to paint.

"A portrait, inspector, a portrait!" he exclaimed. "Now, I've been looking for such a face for years—an uncommonly beautiful face. How often the words are used, and how seldom charged with meaning save to an artist."

"How about her young man?" asked Inspector Heather with a heavy wink.

"There's something in what you say, inspector," continued Vereker, "but, as an artist, I want to paint her face, and he doubtless wants to kiss it. She's radiant!"

"You're already losing interest in the Bygrave case, Mr. Vereker," remarked the inspector. "I'm afraid you're a painter and not a detective. This salad's uncommonly beautiful too." He laughed as he helped himself to a liberal portion.

"No, I'm working steadily away on the case, inspector. It has not been out of my mind for a moment. You know that modern psychology has knocked the bottom out of the old theory that you can't think of two things at once—ay, and do them." Algernon Vereker's face was temporarily eclipsed by an upturned tankard.

"She's got the nicest nose I've ever seen on a woman," he continued on reappearance. "That's saying something; for my sister Marjorie's took some beating."

Inspector Heather smiled; noses, to him, always bordered on the ludicrous. They suggested colds and comedians and Ally

Sloper, and something to punch. They were as much a portion of stock British humour as kippers, landladies and mothers-in-law—but that anyone should have, so to speak, a taste in noses verged on sheer lunacy.

Vereker could see that his enthusiasm was unintelligible to his companion and, rising from his chair, walked over to the gong and struck it lightly.

"Can't see too much of a beautiful thing," he remarked, and when Mary Standish appeared he turned to Heather. "I think coffee and cigars would assist us over the mental strain of further brilliant deductions."

"Not a bad idea, but I prefer my pipe," replied Inspector Heather.

"Well then we'll cut out cigars, because I, too, prefer my briar, and now, while you seek any information you require from Miss Standish, I'll go and get that tin of Bygrave's tobacco."

Algernon Vereker left the room and went upstairs to Lord Bygrave's room. He pulled the bunch of keys from his pocket, looked at all the keys carefully and examined the leather buttonholed tab at the other end of the chain. Then, opening the kit-bag once more, he extracted the tin of tobacco, filled his pouch, relocked the bag and returned to the dining-room, where Inspector Heather was still interrogating Mary Standish.

"You say Lord Bygrave hadn't shaved before breakfast?" he asked.

"I'm sure he didn't, sir, because he hadn't that fresh look which distinguishes a cleanly-shaved man. The can of hot water which I left at his door had not been used, and I don't remember seeing his shaving requisites on his dressing-table."

"You bear me out," replied Inspector Heather, glancing at Vereker.

"That's something you've extracted," remarked Vereker quietly. "I don't see that it's vital, but it at once confirms the fact that Lord Bygrave was extremely agitated or in a most unusual hurry. He was the most leisurely of men in his actions as a rule; for an eight o'clock breakfast he would rise at six. Still I repeat that he always returned his toilet articles to his dressing-case every time after using them when he stayed in an hotel. It was merely an idiosyncrasy: I don't even remember whether he had a reason for it. However, in this instance it doesn't matter, for I think we can take it for granted that he hadn't shaved if Standish is so positive about it."

"Now, Miss Standish, did you see him with a pipe in his mouth on the morning of his disappearance?" asked the inspector.

"Good, Heather, good. You've forestalled me in the question," interrupted Vereker.

"No. He asked for a cigar after breakfast, but after looking at the various brands we stock he decided not to smoke at all. He used the words: 'I think I'll give it a miss this morning.' Whether he changed his mind before he left and lit a pipe I can't very well say, because I was too busy with my work to take any further notice of his lordship."

Inspector Heather looked at Vereker. "Well, that almost confirms the point that Lord Bygrave smoked a pipe before retiring on the previous night."

"And it fits in with what one would surmise," added Vereker. "We have come to the conclusion that Lord Bygrave was in the morning either in a desperate hurry or mentally agitated. Knowing him, I am inclined to think the latter. On the previous night he had events in perspective, so to speak, at some distance. He could smoke and ponder over them with comparative calmness even though they were swiftly approaching. There was nothing else to do."

"Just so," nodded the inspector.

"What kind of clothes was Lord Bygrave wearing? Can you remember whether they were light or dark?" asked Vereker suddenly.

"A dark tweed suit, sir."

"Good, that's something; but it makes matters more mysterious."

"I can't follow you," smiled the inspector. "The colour of a man's clothes matters little before a catastrophe," and he courteously signified to Mary Standish that his cross-examination of her was at an end.

She at once left the room. A slight colour had mounted to her cheeks under the questions of the officer from Scotland Yard, and she seemed relieved to find that her cross-examination had for the time being come to an end.

"There's something in her manner that instinctively tells me that she is not quite at her ease under the probe," remarked Vereker after the girl's departure. "I am very sensitive to these extremely delicate nuances, so to speak, in a woman's behaviour. Did you notice it, inspector?"

"No, I noticed nothing of the sort, Mr. Vereker. Most women are nervous under a fire of questions from a police officer."

"Doubtless you're right, inspector. I'm glad, however, she remembered that Bygrave was wearing a dark suit on arrival at the inn on the Friday night. Yet the business puzzles me—it seems to be so meaningless."

"I don't grip your line of thought. How does the fact that Lord Bygrave was wearing a dark suit puzzle you?"

"It proves that he didn't change his clothes while he was at the inn, for the only other suit he had brought was a light-coloured one. Now, when I found that he had detached this bunch of keys from his trousers and flung them into his kit-bag, I came to the conclusion that he had changed, for otherwise I saw no reason for his detaching them. That he detached them is an incontrovertible fact; and, as it is an unusual action to detach a key chain from one's trousers unless preparatory to changing one's suit, it gives us a little problem to solve. Why did he detach them? It may be a minor problem, but these little things often act as pointers to larger issues."

"Well, I can tell you that a bunch of keys is a nuisance on a long walk. If Lord Bygrave thought so too, your little problem is at once solved," replied the inspector, sipping his coffee.

"But, as he was going to return for lunch at noon, it would seem that he had no intention of taking a walk of inordinate length—not long enough to render keys anything in the nature of cumbersome impedimenta."

"I don't see much in it looking at it from any point of view," replied the inspector with a wave of his short, firm fist. The important task ahead is to ascertain if anyone saw Lord Bygrave after he left this inn on Saturday morning, and where."

"It's more important," replied Vereker, with eyes assuming a look of almost childish simplicity, "to ascertain if there's anyone who knows where he is now."

Inspector Heather glanced up at Vereker to discover whether that individual was serious, but his face gave no indication of the nature of the thoughts within.

"Now I'm going to consolidate my conclusions as far as I have gone, inspector," said Vereker, refilling his pipe.

"We know Lord Bygrave left town on Friday night and arrived at Hartwood 9.15. As far as we are aware, no message awaited him here, so that the subsequent events that led to his disappearance must, unless they were purely accidental, have been food for his anticipation on his arrival. That is, he must have had some appointment which he intended to keep on the following day. This, I think, we can almost take for granted. From the fact that he smoked a pipe in his room before he went to bed to soothe himself it is clear that he was worried about the matter, for it is a thing I've never known Lord Bygrave do, and I have known him very intimately for fifteen years. He was evidently more worried next morning, for, according to Mary Standish, he did not shave and left the inn to keep that appointment unshaven. I can imagine the degree of his perturbation from this rather startling information alone. He breakfasts, intimates that he will return for lunch at midday and incontinently vanishes. Now assume that Lord Bygrave went to keep an appointment, and an unpleasant appointment at that—why should he not return? It was his expressed intention. He must have been forcibly deterred, or events occurred which made his return either highly undesirable or altogether impossible. Now of these alternatives I'm inclined to assume that something happened which rendered his return impossible."

The inspector glanced up quickly.

"You infer that he has been killed?" he asked gravely.

"If my knowledge of Lord Bygrave's manner of life is correct—that is, presuming he is not another Dr. Jekyll and Mr. Hyde—I'm inclined to put a very grave construction on events. A well-known Minister of blameless repute doesn't vanish for the purpose of setting the country by the ears. An actress or an author seeking advertisement might be tempted to do so, but a responsible Minister—never."

"What about political enemies? Have you thought about that side of the question yet, Mr. Vereker?"

"Well, no; not more than admitting the possibility of an unwarranted attack on Bygrave by a political lunatic. You see, his position is not one to bring him into conflict with the people. You might as well try and work up a bloodthirsty hostility against the head of the Board of Fisheries as hate Lord Bygrave politically."

"H'm," replied the inspector, "you put your view plausibly. But my experience of public life to-day prevents my sweeping aside the idea of a political enemy as lightly as you do. In fact, after removing the beneficiaries under his will from the number of possible murderers—and in this case they do not at present impress me as of much importance—it seems to me one of the most reasonable lines to take. You never know what secret political organizations even the mildest public men may fall foul of. Well, there's nothing more to be learned here just now. I think I'll get about the village and see if I can glean any information from the inhabitants." And with these words Inspector Heather rose, thanked Vereker for the lunch and left the inn.

For some moments Algernon Vereker sat in silence, thinking over all the facts of the case as they presented themselves to him in their present amorphous state.

"The bally stuff lacks cohesion!" he exclaimed at length. "There's an absence of affinity among the atoms." He thereupon stood up and looked out of the coffee-room window into the rambling sunlit garden behind the inn.

It was a warm afternoon in early October, and that glance into the garden brought another and quite different trend of thought into Vereker's mind. He strolled leisurely into the sunshine and, picking up a wicker-chair, took it into a very sheltered nook screened from the rest of the garden by a thick evergreen hedge. He sat lazily down in the chair and thrust out his long, active legs in front of him.

"The essence of detective work," he soliloquized, "seems to be the power to concatenate." And after unburdening his mind of this wisdom the material influence of good food and sound ale eclipsed the spiritual side of Algernon Vereker, and he fell fast asleep.

An hour or two later he awoke, rubbed his eyes, stretched his arms lazily and sat up in a more erect posture. His thoughts involuntarily swung round to the subject of tea. He glanced at his watch. It was four o'clock, and the hour forced on him the conclusion that there were few things on earth comparable with good tea. Vereker was about to rise and order it when a ripple of laughter issuing from another corner of the garden fell on his ear. The voice was unmistakable; it was that of Mary Standish. Vereker rose and glanced over the evergreen hedge. In a summer-house on the other side of the lawn sat a youth with the fair hair, blue eyes and profile of the Greek god so acceptable to the consumers of everyday fiction. He purported to be drinking tea. The paraphernalia for the ceremony lay in front of him on a small wicker-table. As a matter of fact he was holding Mary Standish's hand between his own and gazing with unconcealed rapture into a pair of unmistakably responsive eyes. Vereker at once resumed his seat. There occur in life little tableaux which may be entrancing to the imagination; they appeal to the mind's eye of every lover and poet; they can be viewed with equanimity in an illustration if the illustration be good, or with sympathy on the stage, but they cannot be looked upon in actuality. So thought Vereker as he once more reclined at ease and out of sight. He began to probe further into the psychology of this little problem of human delicacy. It flung out a thousand elusive questions. He pulled out his notebook and roughly jotted down some of his musings. Meanwhile he was conscious that the idyll was still being enacted behind his back.

"And I want my tea!" he exclaimed petulantly to himself. Shortly afterwards he made convulsive efforts to stifle a sneeze. In vain. It burst and metaphorically dissipated a rainbow, Vereker heard the two voices grow distant as the pair left the garden, and when they were gone he suddenly brought his hand with a resounding slap on his thigh.

"Well, I'm damned!" he exclaimed. "It has taken me some time to place this tea-garden Apollo. Fancy my not recollecting his face at once: the association with Mary Standish evidently jammed the working of the subconscious mind. David Winslade—Lord Bygrave's heir!"

Chapter Four

For a long while Algernon Vereker sat lost in thought. His memory had flitted back some years to a glorious day during the May eights at Oxford—the day on which Lord Bygrave had introduced him to David Winslade. It was the last occasion on which he had seen him. Subsequently he had heard a great deal of him from his uncle, Lord Bygrave: how he had done moderately well at the University, been a very fair athlete and gone through the War with credit. Bygrave would have liked to see him called to the Bar; but, to a legal career,

Winslade had objected strongly. He had told his uncle definitely that his life was to be spent if possible in the open air, and shortly after demobilization he had bought Brookwater Farm, near Hartwood. So far he had found it an arduous and lean living, but he liked it and was determined to stick to it, and his pluck had won his uncle's unexpected admiration. Lord Bygrave, however, was a man of deeds rather than words, and he had made David Winslade heir to his considerable fortune as a result of that admiration.

"Mary Standish may prove rather a disruptive factor in the problem," thought Vereker. "I wonder what Bygrave would think of it?" He rubbed his chin and smiled thoughtfully. "Perhaps a piece of youthful philandering on young Winslade's part. But, if there wasn't a wedding-bell appeal in his glance, I'm no thought-reader! A domestic servant at a country inn! Not the usual type, I admit. Very pretty—I should like to paint her portrait—speaks perfectly correctly, has a nice taste in hosiery, might be anybody. She might even be an aristocrat already hiding from the wrath to come or that has come—who knows! In any case a jolly nice girl. I give up the problem. Tea, tea, that's the first consideration!"

He walked across to the little summer-house and rang the bell on the wicker-table within. The shrill note seemed to summon Hebe with some of the celerity of a genie of the magic lamp, and Hebe was Mary Standish, rosily flushed and undeniably exalted. Vereker made a mental note and gave his order. When she returned and was arranging what Vereker loved to term facetiously the "tea equipage," he metaphorically leaped from his ambush by asking:

"Does a Mr. David Winslade ever visit the White Bear?"

A penetrating glance, a deeper flush were followed by a swift self-control and the reply:

"Yes, sir, he often lunches here. He had tea here this afternoon. Do you know him?"

"I met him once many years ago. I was aware that he lived in the parish. He is Lord Bygrave's heir, and I was wondering whether he was here on the day of Lord Bygrave's arrival or on the day of his sudden and inexplicable disappearance."

"No, sir. I think I can say definitely that he wasn't."

"You would have remembered?"

"I think so."

"Can you remember when he was here last?"

There was a momentary hesitation. Miss Standish appeared as if trying to recollect; her lip quivered nervously—or rather Vereker thought it did.

"Tuesday following Lord Bygrave's departure, I think," she replied slowly.

"He never mentioned the subject of Lord Bygrave to anybody in the inn, I suppose?"

"I cannot say, sir. He never mentioned it to me. I was unaware that he was Lord Bygrave's heir."

"Don't think my persistent questioning of you rude, but a village inn is the centre of all village news and gossip. Perhaps you heard of Mr. Winslade's movements, say, during the period of Lord Bygrave's stay here?"

"I don't know the village well enough to be interested in its news or gossip, sir."

The reply had a forbiddingly cold tone, and a deeper flush had suddenly mounted to Mary Standish's cheek.

"By Jove, this is glorious toast!" came the swift and tactfully irrelevant exclamation.

There was a pause, a moment's hesitation and Mary Standish turned to go.

"If you want anything further will you kindly ring, sir?"

"Thanks. I'm quite all right. I shan't trouble you," replied Vereker, helping himself to a slice of cake.

Mary Standish had gone.

"My lady knows something more than she is willing to confess, I should say. Of course she would naturally be reticent about her admirer's affairs. Strange that she should know nothing of

Bygrave's relationship to Winslade. It looks as if it were nothing more serious than philandering—on his part; that's a fairly sound deduction from a worldly point of view. Young scamp!"

After tea Vereker put a sketch-book into his pocket and wandered out of Hartwood. Half an hour later saw him seated in a lane. Temporarily, the Bygrave case was completely forgotten; a certain massing of dark and light and the sky pattern through the foliage groups had seized him. His crayon was scribbling furiously; eye and hand were in glorious accord and driven by a fine emotion. It could be altered to the terms of design later; this was the first burning impression.

He walked back to the inn with a feeling of exultation—just the exultation of the sportsman who has made a good bag, or the poet who has created a beautiful line. The appearance of Inspector Heather brought him to earth. That officer was just returning from his round of inquiry. Vereker strove to read some message in his face, but it was entirely impassive.

"Picked up the key to the problem, Heather?" asked Vereker cheerfully.

"No. Have you?" from the police officer, with a quick glance at Vereker's beaming visage.

"Got the skeleton of the whole thing!" exclaimed Vereker, with undisguised delight.

"How did you manage that?" asked Inspector Heather dubiously.

"Quite by accident. Took a stroll keeping my eyes open— and there, in a lane in a certain play of sunlight, the germ, the skeleton!"

"Of the Bygrave case?" asked the inspector in a mocking tone.

"No, no. Bygrave case, no! I mean my next picture. I'm forgetting that I'm a detective; for an hour or two I'm an artist. I'll meet you at dinner. I shall possibly have returned to the fold by then."

Vereker was in his bath when a smile of bewilderment crossed his features and he uttered the exclamation: "Prize ass that I am! I had completely forgotten the existence of Sidney Smale, Bygrave's private secretary!"

He hurriedly finished his toilet and, feeling refreshed and ready for dinner, returned to the dining-room, where Inspector Heather awaited him.

"Heather, we've completely overlooked one person who may be able to shed a light on events prior to Lord Bygrave's disappearance."

"Do you think so?" asked Heather, looking up slowly from an evening paper that had just arrived.

"Lord Bygrave's private secretary, a man called Sidney Smale," said Vereker excitedly.

"He's out of the country at the present moment," remarked the inspector quietly.

"Where has he gone?"

"To Paris, for a holiday. We've cut it short by cabling for him to return to Bygrave Hall the day after to-morrow."

"Resourceful fellow, Heather! I hope your summons will be obeyed. I trust you cabled in a thoroughly peremptory tone. All my suspicions have suddenly veered round to Smale. I've reluctantly had to discard Lawless and have discharged him without a stain on his character."

"What makes you suddenly suspect Smale?" asked the inspector.

"Primarily because his Christian name's Sidney!" replied Vereker gravely.

The inspector tossed his head wearily as if to signify that conversation in that jocular key was distasteful. "What about dinner?" he asked.

"Do you think Smale will return in response to a cable? It might start him off like a pistol-shot on a race to the uttermost parts of the earth," queried Vereker.

"Not likely—Paris police!" replied the inspector laconically.

"It's not fair," sighed Vereker. "You don't give the hare a chance with your web of wireless and cables and police bureaux at the gates of the wilderness. For the only place that's paradise now for the criminal is the wilderness. You're not sportsmen at the C.I.D. I refuse to compete with you any longer."

Inspector Heather smiled.

"I'm going over to-morrow morning to Bygrave Hall. I hope you'll accompany me, Mr. Vereker. The servants know you pretty well; it would be diplomatic if you arrived with me."

"Very good. I'm sorry you've discovered nothing at Hartwood, inspector."

"It's extraordinary. Not a vestige of anything that's useful. Only one villager admits to having seen a gentleman that might have been Lord Bygrave, and that was as he emerged from the inn on Saturday morning. He couldn't even say in what direction the gentleman went."

"Yet I can't help thinking we might discover something here, inspector. I have no very definite grounds for thinking so, but there are all sorts of vague things in my mind. They're only ghosts of suspicions; I can't definitely lay hold of one definite surmise. But they're like spirits brooding. I feel certain they'll suddenly materialize and give me a clear, tangible something. It's sure to happen when I'm miles away from the place. It's always the way with me. Ah, here's the dinner at last!"

During dinner the conversation flagged. Inspector Heather seemed buried in his own thoughts and little disposed to discuss matters with his companion. Vereker, on his part, was absorbed in the quality of a bottle of Madeira that he had bought and was sampling with undisguised zest.

"You ought to try this wine, inspector," he urged at length.

"I seldom want anything better than good, honest ale," replied the inspector, and suddenly diving into his waistcoat pocket he produced Lord Bygrave's signet-ring.

"Did you look at that ring carefully?" he asked.

"Not very carefully," replied Vereker. "Why, what's wrong with it?"

"Nothing wrong; there's nothing mysterious about it. That is Lord Bygrave's crest, I suppose?"

"Certainly," said Vereker. "By the way, that ring is mine should anything have happened to Bygrave. He wants me to keep it as a little remembrancer."

"You had better take charge of it, then," said the inspector. "But should I require it again you can let me have it back."

"Most assuredly. I think I'd better wear it or I'll leave it lying about somewhere. You don't think it would be unlucky to wear it, do you, Heather?"

The inspector vouchsafed no reply, so Vereker put the ring on the third finger of his left hand and the meal ended in silence.

After dinner Vereker retired to his room. He drew an arm-chair to the empty fire-place and filled his pipe. Now that he was alone his usual look of irrepressible gaiety had vanished and his brow was furrowed with thought.

"The gloom seems to be luminous," he soliloquized, "but not a definite shaft of light!"

He then stretched out his hand to the mantelpiece for Lord Bygrave's tin of tobacco, and carefully read the label.

"Good Lord!" he exclaimed. "Why, he buys it at the Civil Service Stores! The plot thickens!" For half an hour Vereker sat gazing into the chill darkness of the empty grate, his right thumb and forefinger ceaselessly twirling the signet-ring on his left hand. Then he jumped up from his chair, hurriedly undressed and got to bed. He lay awake for more than an hour, arranging and re-arranging in his mind the salient facts of the case as he understood them.

"I won't rest, Darnell, till I discover the whole truth about this mysterious affair. I think I've already left Heather with all his myrmidons a lap or so behind."

Shortly afterwards Algernon Vereker was sound asleep—even Inspector Heather's loud snore, audible from the next room through the lath-and-plaster wall, failed to disturb his tranquil repose.

Chapter Five

When Vereker came down to breakfast next morning Inspector Heather was already there, and apparently busy. Seated at a small table in the breakfast-room, he was writing up all his memoranda in a notebook. On Vereker's appearance he looked sharply round; then, closing his book, carefully thrust it into his breast pocket.

"I've got a car down from town," he said, "and when you're ready, Mr. Vereker, we'll start. They tell me (from headquarters) that Mr. Sidney Smale has cabled that he is on the way back to Bygrave Hall."

"Famous, inspector, famous! There's something awe-inspiring about your methods. There's no getting away from you. Smale, instead of making giant strides for the Sahara, promptly walks back right into the jaws of death. Of course it's bluff, we know; he's going to pretend he's entirely innocent and all that sort of thing. What a fool he must be!"

"We'll soon take any bluff out of him," remarked the inspector stoutly.

"Prick the bladder of his audacity, so to speak," remarked Vereker, cracking another egg. "I shall enjoy the stern drama. I never did care much for Smale. He doesn't like me either, because I used to call him Mr. Snail—quite inadvertently, you know. I'm frightfully inexact about names."

Inspector Heather lit his pipe and continued to smoke thoughtfully until Vereker had finished his meal.

An hour or so later their car swung round the drive and pulled up before the stately porch of Bygrave Hall. As Vereker stepped out of the car he turned to Inspector Heather.

"What do you think of the place, Heather?"

"Bit of a ruin in parts, Mr. Vereker, but it looks a nice, old place for an English gentleman to live in."

"Very neatly expressed. I'm glad you like it. I wish the place were mine. It's a fine example of the late fortified manor of the Middle Ages. It radiates the spirit of medievalism, and that's why I love it. Do you know, Heather, just one glance at Bygrave Hall reveals to you one of the most remarkable defects of our own age."

"What's the defect, Mr. Vereker?"

"Lack of dignity. Our modern attempts at dignified architecture are so ineffectual because we are no longer dignified. The character of an age is expressed in its Art and, when we try to express the characteristic called dignity in these days, we are generally merely pompous. If you were to live any length of time in Bygrave Hall it would change you from a detective inspector into a knight, and you would forget all about the Bygrave case. It would ruin a modern politician in a fortnight—but I'm wasting time; let's get in and make our inquiries."

On their entry they were met by Farnish, who since Lord Bygrave's departure for Hartwood had had complete control of the household management. He was the typical trusted servant of the old type, a type that under the swiftly changing order of things is passing away. He knew Mr. Algernon Vereker as one of his master's most intimate friends, and that fact alone was sufficient to win, for Vereker, Farnish's loyalty and esteem. An English gentleman was to him one of the finest of God's handiworks, and he had very definite opinions as to who did and who did not come in that category. He had long since placed Algernon Vereker among those who could do no wrong. Whether he understood Vereker's whimsical attitude to life and everything under the sun it would be difficult to say. He may possibly have thought him a trifle insane, but his deportment before his social superiors was that of the trained gentleman's servant—the perfection of correctness; it was a tacit implication that he was a servant of the gods.

To Vereker, Farnish had always been a mystery. Whoever else took servants for granted as necessary adjuncts to life, and differentiated by only two characteristics—good and bad—Vereker did not do so. His inquisitive mind was interested in their mentality; he was always trying to discover the human being hidden so discreetly behind the servant. Their psychology intrigued him, and nothing would have pleased him more than to know Farnish's real opinion about the men and affairs that constituted a portion of the texture of his life and experience. But Vereker had never been able really to penetrate that deferential armour which Farnish wore when his inferior clay came in contact with what was socially supposed to be a superior earth. He had only managed once or twice to glimpse the soul sheltering within this decorous automaton, and the difficulty of the task had always interested him.

"He's a winkle—a bally mollusc!" he had often exclaimed.

Farnish was to-day looking more dignified than ever. The disappearance of Lord Bygrave was to him the most serious matter on earth, and he evidently considered that it required a corresponding gravity of countenance on his part. Vereker, however, thought that there was just a trace of anxiety in his manner, an extra sharpness in the lines of his thin face, a shade more pallor.

"No further news of his lordship, Farnish?" he remarked.

"None whatever, sir."

"This is Detective-Inspector Heather of Scotland Yard. He has come to look round the place and make inquiries. Put everything at his disposal and give him all the assistance you can. As you may know, Farnish, I am a trustee under Lord Bygrave's will, and in his absence you will take your orders from me and come to me for anything you want."

"Very good, sir," replied Farnish, and his eyes glanced up at Vereker with a strangely furtive, inquisitive look.

Vereker was astonished. Never before in his life had he seen the slightest trace of inquisitiveness in Farnish's manner, and here all at once the miracle had happened. Vereker, however, strove to hide any sign of the surprise that he experienced at this unusual occurrence, though it shook him to the extent of causing him to conceal his face and expression with his handkerchief, under cover of violently blowing his nose. When he had sufficiently recovered his equanimity and looked again at Farnish, the miracle had passed, but in Vereker's mind it had left a shadow, the first, almost imperceptible shadow of doubt and suspicion.

Inspector Heather at this juncture signified that he would at once have a look over the entire house, and would be glad of Farnish's guidance. He would also like to question Farnish about all Lord Bygrave's recent movements.

"Then I will go out and study the case in the Japanese garden," said Vereker, "and, Farnish, you might see that lunch is ready for one o'clock."

Vereker slowly made his way to his favourite spot in the Japanese garden, and sat down on a large boulder forming a bridge over a tiny rivulet of clear water. He sat there until lunch-time, deep in thought, his eyes glancing now and then at various aspects in the garden with swift and keen appreciation, but his whole mind bent on the problem of his friend's inexplicable disappearance. And, as he sat pondering, certain points in his experiences since he assumed the rôle of amateur detective began to assume significance and form the skeleton on which his supple imagination commenced to build.

"But I can't understand Farnish!" he soliloquized. "What did that note of interrogation in his eye mean? I wonder—I wonder if he knows anything. I must keep a sharp look-out." Vereker paused, and then a smile spread over his features. "Of course he may suspect that I have had some hand in Henry's disappearance and was trying to read me. The incident is most important and looks as if it is going to fit into a mysterious scheme of things."

*

After lunch Inspector Heather unburdened himself.

"Well, Mr. Vereker," he began, "I've thoroughly cross-examined Farnish. He's a rum specimen, is Farnish. I don't quite know what to make of him."

"His best manner is rather devastating," replied Vereker. "Do you know, Heather, in Farnish's presence I always begin to shrink. My clothes seem too big for me and I have a strange sensation that I am being firmly assured that my ancestors did not come over with the Conqueror. What effect did he have on you?"

"Nothing of that sort, Mr. Vereker. But he's so confoundedly discreet. He never answers in a hurry, and then weighs every word he utters. You feel that he is fencing all the time, that he is determined you shall know no more than he wishes to let you know. Anyone would think he was hiding something."

"Oh, he's a past-master at that sort of thing. You must remember that the life of a man like Farnish is apparently one long discretion. Have you any suspicion with regard to him?"

"I'm going to keep a watchful eye on him. As to my cross-examination of him, it uncovered nothing of any importance with regard to Lord Bygrave. His information was exactly what I expected it to be and revealed not a jot more than we both already know. Lord Bygrave left him in charge of the place until his return from Hartwood. There was nothing unusual in his lordship's behaviour prior to his departure. He said nothing out of the ordinary to Farnish before leaving, and Farnish entertains no ideas of any kind as to where his lordship has gone or when he may choose to return."

"Farnish is a blank slate, inspector, as far as you are concerned?"

"Absolutely."

"What is your next move?"

"I'm going to search the place thoroughly and look through all Lord Bygrave's papers."

"Good; but let me warn you to be careful when exploring the undercroft. There's a well down there in which you may inadvertently find yourself unless you are careful. I should take Farnish with you and observe him closely but furtively while you are searching. You remember Carlton's explanation of his method of discovering an object hidden in a town simply by watching the feet of the man who had hidden it, and who was accompanying him. No? Well, never mind. But it was a brainy idea. I should not hesitate to make use of it."

"You suspect Farnish?" asked the inspector quickly.

"I am not quite satisfied that he is innocent of everything connected with this affair. Merely an idea of mine, with very scanty foundations for it. Perhaps I'm entirely wrong—it's a duel between reason and the vague promptings of that shadowy faculty called intuition."

"Not much use for intuition in these matters, Mr. Vereker," sighed the inspector heavily and, rising from his seat, added, "Well, I think I'll have a good look round and examine Lord Bygrave's papers—at least those to which I can get access here. What are you going to do?"

"Oh, I'm going to read the most up-to-date novel of the day. I always carry it with me. It is so true to modern life—'The Satyricon.'"

"May I ask who's the author?" queried the inspector listlessly.

"A Mr. Titus Petronius."

"Perhaps he's a friend of yours, Mr. Vereker."

"One of my best friends—but I've not met him. Perhaps I shall in the distant future. I hope so."

The inspector made no further remark and left Vereker smiling, as he filled his pipe.

Vereker sat in an easy chair engrossed in his book for some time; then he suddenly closed the volume and rang.

Farnish appeared in response.

"Tell Walter I should like to speak to him, Farnish," said Vereker, eyeing the butler closely.

Farnish's physiognomy was now, however, as unreadable as that of the Sphinx, and his manner the old unperturbed manner of the Farnish known to Vereker for so many years.

Walter was one of Lord Bygrave's footmen; a tall, slimly built man with raven black hair, carefully brushed and sleek. His head was a handsome head, shapely in the skull; his nose aquiline; his eyes dark brown and frank in their expression. Vereker had always liked Walter.

"There's nothing much wrong with a man who has a symmetrical skull," was one of Vereker's favourite sayings. "Your brilliant men and scoundrels have all got asymmetrical heads."

Lord Bygrave also had a sincere affection for his servant, and at times, when he felt in an expansive mood, extracted much private amusement from Walter's opinions and unconsciously humorous outlook on life generally.

When Walter appeared Vereker at once saw that the man had something to divulge, and had only been waiting to divulge it in what he felt was the right quarter.

"I can see he's simply bursting to impart information," thought Vereker. "Heather has already cross-questioned him and probably learned nothing. I must handle him as gently as an egg—a very valuable egg."

"Oh, Walter," he began, addressing the footman, "I want to speak to you on a matter the nature of which you have doubtless already guessed."

"Well, sir, I have an idea it's about his lordship's disappearance."

"You say 'disappearance,' Walter. Don't you think his absence may be easily explained? For instance, if his lordship extended his holiday you'd hardly call it disappearing?"

"If he extended his holiday without letting us know, sir, I'd certainly call it disappearing. His lordship never did such a thing in his life before."

"Perhaps not, Walter, but there's no knowing what he might do under the force of circumstances never before encountered?"

"That's just what I think, sir; and some strange circumstances must have been the cause of his not returning on the date he said he would."

"You noticed nothing peculiar about his lordship's manner of late?"

"Not of late, sir, but six months ago a very strange thing happened."

"Oh! What was that?"

"Well, sir, I wouldn't tell you, only I know you were his lordship's greatest friend. I didn't say a word to Inspector Heather when he was questioning me, because, thinks I, if there's going to be a scandal about his lordship, I won't be the one to publish it. It's not my way, sir. Besides, his lordship has always been very good to me—a better master no man could wish for."

"Scandal, did you say?" asked Vereker, raising his eyebrows in surprise.

"Yes, sir. Where there's womenfolk there's nearly always a scandal. As his lordship once remarked—'Walter,' says he, 'I don't know whether the pleasure they give outweighs the trouble they create.' True words those are, sir. I never have anything to do with them—"

"Ah, so you're a misogynist, Walter, a confirmed misogynist?" interrupted Vereker.

"If that means keeping clear of trouble, sir, I'm one."

"And what about a woman and his lordship. You don't mean to say—"

"Pardon me interrupting, sir, but this is exactly what happened, and I'm certain sure it has something to do with his lordship's disappearance. I said no good would come of it at the time. Six months ago a lady came to see his lordship. Very few people ever call on his lordship, but I know them, sir, by name and sight. His lordship rarely made new friends. This lady was a stranger to me, and what's more she was one of those handsome, bold as brass sort as you see on the halls. She walked up the drive and handed me a note for his lordship. I took the note to him myself, and on opening it his lordship started violently and turned very pale. He told me to show the lady into the drawing-room, and he followed her in a few minutes later. It would be a good half-hour before she left, and his lordship seemed very agitated, more agitated than ever I've seen him before. That's all, sir."

"You've never seen the lady since?"

"No, sir."

"Does anybody else know about this lady's visit? Mr. Farnish, for instance?"

"I think not, sir. I believe Mr. Farnish was away from the Hall that afternoon, and even if Mr. Farnish knew—" Walter hesitated and said no more.

"Go on, Walter, tell me everything you know. Tell me even your suspicions. I feel sure there's something wrong about all this business and I'm going to get to the bottom of it. You may rest assured that I shall employ the utmost discretion in making use of anything you may care to divulge."

"Well, sir, Mr. Farnish always was a deep 'un. Not that I dislike him. We've always got on well together. But he was never what you call free in his conversation with any of us. Mighty big notion of his position, sir, he has. And of late—well, he's been more silent than ever, and sometimes downright queer. On one occasion since his lordship's disappearance he was a long while in the study by himself. Next morning he went off early to London without telling any of us his business. He left me in charge and just said, 'I have to go up to London, Walter; I shall be back as soon as possible.' After he'd gone, sir, I took the notion into my head to have a look in his lordship's study. Naturally, I was curious as to what Mr. Farnish had been doing so long in his lordship's study—it was a room, sir, into which none of us servants was ever allowed to go. His lordship used to say, 'Dust might be troublesome, but dusting was a damned noosance.' But when I tried the door I found it locked, and the key gone. Now the key was always in the door when his lordship was here or away, for I'm sure he had nothing to hide. He simply wouldn't have his books and papers put where he couldn't at once lay hands on them, and that was the only reason we were forbidden to enter his study."

"Nothing more has happened since?"

"Nothing unusual, sir. This thing has been on my mind and worried me considerable, so I had made up my mind to tell you, sir."

"Thanks, Walter; that's all I want to know."

"Very good, sir," replied Walter, and left the room.

He had not gone many minutes before Inspector Heather entered. He found Vereker engrossed in that up-to-date novel by Mr. Titus Petronius.

"Well, Heather, I can see by your face you've made a discovery," said Vereker, looking up.

"A small discovery and a few more facts."

"You've been in the study," remarked Vereker at random.

"H'm, yes—I've been all over the place. How did you know I'd been in the study?"

"You've got a document in your hand with the words Last Will and Testament engrossed almost life-size on the back, and easily legible from here. The rest was pure deduction."

"You're improving, Mr. Vereker. As for the discovery—I found one of the drawers of Lord Bygrave's bureau had been forced with an ordinary screw-driver. I asked Farnish if he could furnish me with a screw-driver, and he did."

"It was the identical one?"

"It was."

"By Jove, Heather!" exclaimed Vereker, but with little show of excitement.

"There doesn't seem much in it, though," continued Heather thoughtfully, "because hardly had Farnish handed the tool over to me than he volunteered the information that his lordship had lost a key to one of his bureau drawers and had broken it open some days before he left—'with the same screw-driver.'"

"You didn't believe him, of course."

"I won't say that, but I noticed that of the several bundles of papers in the drawer all were tied with a proper reef-knot, and only one with a granny-knot."

"And you deduced—?"

"Nothing as yet, Mr. Vereker, but I've taken the usual note. You know the contents of the will?"

"Yes—and I know you've taken a note that Farnish is left £500 under its terms."

"Quite so. But from my interrogation of all the servants I find that Farnish neither drinks, smokes nor intends to get married. He's a careful, honest, punctilious man and devoted to his lordship."

"Now, now, Heather, you're not going to tell me you're impressed by that stuff. I can already see you getting the handcuffs ready for dear old Farnish."

Inspector Heather laughed and continued:

"They've just rung me up from headquarters and told me that about six months ago Lord Bygrave got his bankers to dispose of about £10,000 worth of registered securities, and had them transferred into bearer bonds."

"Six months ago?" queried Vereker listlessly.

"Yes; but why?"

"Well, that was last May. Anything could have happened to them since then. Now, if this transaction had taken place just before Lord Bygrave's departure for Hartwood there might be some significance in it."

"I can find no trace of them, anyhow. They're not at his bankers and they're not in his private safe here, and it is unlikely that he would carry £10,000 about with him on a holiday," argued the inspector.

"Then I make another brilliant deduction, Heather—Lord Bygrave simply blewed them!" said Vereker.

"I've more news for you, Mr. Vereker," continued the inspector. "Mr. Grierson rang up to say that he would like to see you. He is coming down from town and ought to be here in a few minutes. Meanwhile I think I'll go and send off some telegrams."

Chapter Six

After Inspector Heather's departure Vereker sank back in a comfortable arm-chair, lit his pipe and gave himself up to a lengthy reverie. There was a look of uneasiness on his face; it could hardly be termed annoyance, for it took a great deal really to annoy Mr. Algernon Vereker. This uneasy look was the signal that he had been suddenly confronted with the unexpected, and it was all due to Walter's story of the heavily-veiled lady's visit to Bygrave Hall. This sudden irruption of a female figure into the chaotic tangle of events which constituted the mystery of Lord Bygrave's disappearance was undeniably disconcerting.

"A woman in the case—the last damned thing I would have expected!" he exclaimed. "What earthly right has a woman to figure in this case at all? It discloses a facet of Bygrave's life the existence of which I had never suspected. It's enough to make me forswear the rôle of amateur detective for ever and to give up the quest here and now."

He pondered over the incident, looking at it in many lights. There might be a romance, some romance of Bygrave's early life, of which he knew nothing. It might be one of the most prosaic of occurrences. But why had Lord Bygrave been agitated? There was no explanation forthcoming at the moment. It might disclose itself later. In any case it was not to be disregarded without some explanation. Again there was Farnish's strange behaviour—

according to Walter's account. Walter, perhaps an imaginative man in his own way, might be unduly suspicious. His kind, when they became suspicious, were nearly always recklessly so. They put the most damning constructions on the most innocent of occurrences. Then again, Heather's discovery of the drawer of Bygrave's bureau having been forced seemed to lend some vestige of importance to Walter's story of Farnish's visit to the study. Vereker felt that there was no reason to suspect the existence of a feud between the two men. Walter had spoken without any show of rancour or sense of injury at the hands of the butler.

He smoked quietly for the space of a few moments and then rose and went up to Lord Bygrave's study.

It was a sparsely but beautifully furnished room. The thick, luxurious carpet deadened the sound of his footsteps; the dark oak wainscoting and one or two old portraits of the Bygraves, sombre with age, lent a gravity and severity to the general aspect of the study, which seemed remarkably in keeping with its owner's serious and gentle turn of mind. The whole colouring of the furnishing was rich and low, for Lord Bygrave had often remarked to Vereker that nothing distracted him more roguishly from his studies than the sight of forceful or cheerful colour.

"Just sit down in a rose-and-white drawing-room and try to understand some of the problems that Bergson or Einstein has offered for our mental digestion," he had once said to his friend. "It's impossible—you'd dismiss philosophy and mathematics and wind up by whistling airs from light opera."

"You're wrong, Henry," Vereker had replied. "I should commence right away with the light opera. Bergson and Co. I should reserve for a scarlet room, where I could indulge in really loud laughter. I still think his essay on Laughter one of the humorous masterpieces of literature. Professor Sully's was dull in comparison."

Vereker's entrance into his friend's study had vividly recalled the moment of that conversation. Little had he dreamed that it would ever be recalled under the shadow of a tragedy or even a mystery. He glanced round the room; its sombre tones seemed suddenly to affect him—every aspect was an expression of the temperament and individuality of his friend. A disconcerting sense of helplessness all at once overcame him. So far, in his investigations, all sorts of diverse facts had thrust themselves forward in a wildly unintelligible sequence. At times, one feature of the case had seemed most important. No sooner had he decided this, and determined to follow up a line of inquiry based on that salient feature, than something new thrust itself irrepressibly forward and disjointed all his carefully-pieced construction. Facts and clues had the disturbing mobility of fragments of glass in a kaleidoscope. Up till now he had felt some confidence in himself, but Walter's story of the woman and the possibility that Farnish might have broken open Lord Bygrave's bureau came as devastating shocks to all his confirmed estimates of Lord Bygrave and of Farnish. He had always prided himself on his perspicacity with regard to human nature: the numbing thought assailed him now that human nature after all was too complex and elastic for such confidence in his own powers of vision and appraisement. Circumstances were very often more potent than principle, even though principle had armoured the soul through long habit. A human being never could be a fixed quantity. Chance might have at one stroke completely shattered that soul-stuff which went to the making of the individualities, Bygrave and Farnish, as he had known them up till now, and constructed and moulded it into two quite unrecognizable shapes.

Vereker crossed over to the bureau and opened the various drawers one after the other. A glance revealed the contents of each. He saw nothing of importance in any until he came to the drawer that had been broken open with the aid of a screwdriver. Here were various bundles of letters and papers all tied with white cord. He carefully examined the knots that bound the bundles. Heather was right—they were all reef-knots except the last, which was a granny. What could be deduced from this fact? Either that Lord Bygrave, who, Vereker knew, had once been a very keen yachtsman, had been in a great hurry when retying that particular bundle with the granny, or that the drawer had been broken open and that bundle opened and retied by some one else. Vereker took out all the bundles from the drawer, placed them on the writing-table and untied them all. He would glance through their contents rapidly and see if anything could be gleaned from the perusal. The task proved fruitless. He could find nothing in their contents that bore in any way upon the Bygrave case.

He rose and examined the marks made by the screw-driver in breaking open the drawer; it had been a thoroughly inexpert job—the clumsiest piece of work imaginable.

At this moment he was conscious of the presence of somebody behind him—a light footfall on the thick carpet had been detected by his extraordinarily quick ear. He glanced swiftly at a dark steel engraving above the bureau and in its glass saw Farnish standing near the door. Without turning round, or exhibiting any surprise in his voice, Vereker calmly said:

"I've been looking through his lordship's papers, Farnish; but I've drawn blank. I shall be glad if you will tie up all these bundles for me again and leave them here on the table. I may have another run through them before turning in tonight."

"Yes, sir. I've just come up to tell you that Mr. Grierson has arrived and would like to see you."

"Show him into the library—I'll be with him as soon as I have washed my hands."

Farnish departed as silently as he had arrived, and as Vereker was washing his hands, some moments later, he thought to himself:

"I'm afraid I was too quick for you, Farnish, that time. Even then, I failed to surprise >*you*—your face was simply petrified unconcern. You're a marvel, Farnish, a marvel!"

In the library, Mr. Grierson was awaiting Vereker's arrival with unmistakable anxiety.

"Have you heard or found out anything about my Chief?" he asked as Vereker shook hands with him.

"About Lord Bygrave we've heard not a word, Mr. Grierson. A number of suspicious facts have gradually disclosed themselves, but none of them gives direction to a fruitful line of inquiry. We can only go on in the hope that when we have secured more information certain parts of it will cohere and shape themselves into a definite theory in our minds."

"What does Inspector Heather think of it all?"

"I don't know; he only discloses his discoveries to me very much as a lighthouse, with an intermittent flash, throws out a beam into the darkness for the passing ship. I have a vague idea where he is and I suppose he thinks that is quite sufficient for a mere amateur investigator to know."

"Oh, I'm sorry to hear that you've not made better progress. I expected to come down and find that the Scotland Yard people would be able to say that they might be able to discover Lord Bygrave at any moment."

"They may for all I know," replied Vereker. "I wish I could say the same of my own investigations."

Mr. Grierson's face grew grave and he was silent for some moments.

"There is one aspect of the case which has troubled me considerably of late, Mr. Vereker, and it was the chief factor in deciding me to come down here to-day. The more I thought of it the more I was convinced that it was necessary I should come and give you my ideas about the business. Of course you may have considered this aspect yourself. In any case, I couldn't rest until I'd seen you."

"Go ahead, Mr. Grierson. I'm hungry for ideas."

Mr. Grierson smiled wanly.

"Have you considered the possibility that Lord Bygrave may have voluntarily disappeared?"

"I have; but dismissed it long since from my mind."

"Well, well, you may be justified. I myself, not knowing as much as you, have been unable to disregard the contingency. Working on this basis, if you come to a point in your researches which might end in involving his lordship in a grave scandal, I trust you will be diplomatic—"

Vereker glanced sharply up at Mr. Grierson's face; but Mr. Grierson was gazing earnestly at the pattern of the carpet. His brow was deeply furrowed.

"Don't misunderstand me," he continued. "I am not acting on any secret or private information. I am simply trying to obviate anything that would ruin Lord Bygrave's career or dishonour his name. For ten years now I've been his trusted right-hand man officially. I should never forgive myself if Lord Bygrave by any chance could say to me at some future date: 'What the devil were you doing, Grierson? I was relying on you as a man of tact and initiative. In my absence you were my deputy. Why didn't you try and put a stop to this stupid public inquiry as to my whereabouts?' Can you see the position in which I am placed, Mr. Vereker?"

Mr. Grierson looked up, his eyes were brimming with tears. His voice was broken. He was trembling under the stress of a great emotion.

"Mr. Grierson," replied Vereker, impressed by the old civil servant's loyalty to his Chief. "If at any point in my inquiries I discover that Lord Bygrave is alive and well, I shall promptly let the matter end there as far as I'm concerned. As for Heather— well, for him I cannot vouch. But I think you may safely leave it to me—I'll see Heather himself about the matter. If it was a private personal matter of Lord Bygrave's that he should choose to vanish from the world, I should not think that the police will concern themselves as long as it touches no public interest."

"Then I'm heart and soul with you, Mr. Vereker, and I hope you'll prosecute your inquiry with the utmost vigour. Your assurance has taken a load off my mind."

Mr. Grierson extended his hand and shook Vereker's warmly. Glancing at his watch, he found that he had just time to catch a train back to town and promptly took his leave.

He had hardly gone before Inspector Heather returned.

"Well," he asked, "what was troubling old Grierson, Mr. Vereker?"

"I'll tell you all as soon as Farnish brings up that bottle of port. I have just rung for him. I know you won't object to a bottle of '81, Heather, after your day's exertions."

"You know I don't like good port," replied Heather, with a broad grin, as he settled himself opposite Vereker in a comfortable arm-chair.

"Before I tell you anything about Mr. Grierson's errand, Heather," said Vereker later, as he carefully filled two glasses with what he called Falernum Opimianum, "please confide in me the nature of all your telegrams of to-day. You're up to some little game of your own behind my back."

"Oh, nothing much," smiled the inspector broadly. "I've only put another line of inquiry into motion. I ordered young Winslade to be carefully watched some days ago, and one of my men has just been keeping me acquainted with the result of his work and inquiries."

"The devil you have! Well, that's an unfair start. I'm going down to Hartwood to-morrow to see Winslade. As for Grierson— well, he is anxious that we should go cautiously in case Lord Bygrave has disappeared voluntarily. Should we discover that this is the case, he wants us to avoid pursuing a course that would only result in the publication of a scandal that might be diplomatically hushed. You see he's a loyal servant to his Chief. He wants to put up a smoke barrage to hide his lordship from the high explosive shells of the idle mischief-maker."

"H'm," ejaculated Inspector Heather, raising his glass to the light, "is that all?"

"It looks very strange to me. There's Walter suggests a mysterious woman in the case; Farnish is as close as an oyster; Grierson wishes to avoid a scandal. A conspiracy, Heather, a conspiracy—can't you see they are all giving us the gentle hint to leave matters alone for the sake of their master? They are all loyal men—trusted servants—with blameless characters. What do you think?"

The inspector opened his eyes wide. "By Jove, Mr. Vereker, I believe you've scored an inner."

"Merely a light-hearted suggestion, Heather, but it gives a substantial line of inquiry—it's my first generalization to-day. I don't know how many I have already made from the data I have in hand. I have an unbridled passion for generalizations."

"By the way, who's the woman in the case that Walter suggests?" asked the inspector.

"Oh, he has a story of a visit by some veiled lady six months ago. I was quite pleased to hear that there was a veiled lady in the case—I felt all along that she was a sine qua non. Well, she handed in a note for Lord Bygrave. Walter took in the note, which Lord Bygrave opened in his presence. Walter says that Bygrave started violently. An interview followed, and when the lady took her departure Lord Bygrave was in an extremely agitated state. Knowing how imperturbable my friend always was, this information strikes me as significant."

"We must investigate this thoroughly," remarked Inspector Heather, distinctly impressed.

"From the point of time, it's most important," suggested Vereker.

"How?"

"Didn't you say that Lord Bygrave carried out some transaction with bearer bonds six months ago?"

The inspector brought his short, thick fist down on the table with a thud. "You knew all about this lady before I told you of the bearer bonds, Mr. Vereker?" he asked sharply.

"I did, and put two and two together at once. He gave the bearer bonds to the lady."

"Well, I'm damned!" exclaimed the detective. "You're shaping uncommonly well, sir."

"Not well enough to have discovered the lady, Heather, or even her name. It would seem that the correct thing to do now is to discover the lady. Then we could get a move on."

"I wonder why Walter never mentioned the lady's visit to me."

"I've told you, Heather: he doesn't want to start an inquiry which would involve his master in any scandal."

"Just so—that fits in with your idea of a conspiracy. Not an impossible contingency either, Mr. Vereker, not at all impossible!"

Vereker laughed heartily. "I could concoct you a thousand similar possibilities, inspector, but the night's getting old."

"The night's always young when the port's old," remarked Heather, glancing at the bottle appreciatively.

"Brilliant, Heather, brilliant! You couldn't have said that on a poor vintage. By the way, before we turn in there's one little thing I should like you to see."

"What's that?" asked the inspector.

"Oh, something up in the study, come along now."

Inspector Heather rose and followed Vereker up to the study. Having switched on the light, the latter carefully closed the door and led his companion over to the writing-table on which still lay Lord Bygrave's bundles of papers and letters.

"What do you make of it, Heather?" he asked. "You've had a run through the correspondence. Have you discovered anything?"

"No; there was nothing of importance in the correspondence at all. So I thought it a good plan to ask Farnish to tie up all the bundles for me. You see the point now?"

"Excellent, Mr. Vereker, excellent!" exclaimed the inspector. "He has tied up every bundle with a granny-knot."

"It could be argued that Lord Bygrave might have done so in a hurry," remarked Vereker, "but it's almost impossible with such a confirmed tier of reef-knots. The tying of knots is like the tying of a bow tie. Once you have acquired the skill to do it unconsciously, you never deviate even in a hurry from that method. The one occasion on which you might deviate is the one on which you have suddenly become conscious of the actual process or method of tying."

"There's a lot of truth in that," remarked the inspector in a pensive way.

At this moment the telephone bell in the study rang a shrill appeal. Inspector Heather went over to the instrument and put the phone to his ear.

"Yes—yes—all right. I'll tell Farnish. Who am I? A visitor, good-bye."

"Of course," continued Vereker, "this little experiment about knots only tends to prove that Lord Bygrave did not tamper with that one bundle of correspondence. I should say about seventy-five per cent of ordinary people invariably tie with a granny-knot. By the way, who the dickens has rung us up at this time of night?"

"Mr. Sidney Smale, Lord Bygrave's secretary. He's staying in town overnight—will be here for breakfast to-morrow morning."

"The Lord has delivered the Philistine into your hands, Heather. I hope you'll put him through it in your most inspectorial manner. Good night."

"Good night, Mr. Vereker," replied the inspector. "As soon as I have written up some of my notes I shall turn in too."

Chapter Seven

When Inspector Heather and Vereker came down almost simultaneously to breakfast next morning they found Mr. Sidney Smale, Lord Bygrave's secretary, helping himself to a liberal portion of Cambridge eggs from the hot-plate on the buffet. He at once placed his plate on the breakfast table and shook hands with Vereker, whom he had met before.

"It's a perfect morning," he remarked. "I walked over from the station; the nip in the air has given me an enormous appetite."

"Detective-Inspector Heather of Scotland Yard," said Vereker.

"Good morning, inspector—an unexpected meeting I can assure you. I've a crow to pick with you for cutting short my holiday in Paris."

"I'm sorry," replied the inspector quietly, "the situation here demanded your immediate presence," and began to help himself to food.

Little was said during the meal. Mr. Sidney Smale ate avidly, his whole attention centred on appeasing his excellent appetite. His round head covered with fair curls was bent over his plate; his blue eyes, distorted by the lenses in large tortoiseshell-rimmed spectacles, might have been looking anywhere so indeterminate seemed the direction of his glance. His little mouth, though bent in a perfect Cupid's bow, seemed excellently adapted for eating rapidly. Heather, every now and then scrutinizing him furtively, noticed that neither lip nor chin could boast any virile adornment in the shape of hair. He also noticed that Mr. Sidney Smale's hands were diminutive and as chubby as an infant's.

Vereker, who was secretly observing Heather, smiled quietly to himself. He could see that the inspector had taken an immediate dislike to Lord Bygrave's secretary. It was the same feeling of repulsion that he himself had experienced on his first encounter with the man and which had prompted him, in a vein of malicious humour, to misname him Mr. Snail.

Inspector Heather, always economical in the matter of time, had tried at once to broach the subject of Lord Bygrave's disappearance, but Mr. Smale had replied firmly:

"No, inspector, I won't be drawn just now. After breakfast, if you please. It's a principle of mine—think of nothing unpleasant during a meal. Think of nothing, in fact, but your food. Concentrate on it as you would on a work of art. It's the secret to a perfect digestion. Thank the Lord I've got one!"

He rose from his chair, walked over to the buffet, and raised the lids of several dishes.

"Aha, devilled kidneys! I'm passionately fond of them! What a joy an English breakfast is! Thanks, inspector, for recalling me from Paris."

When Mr. Smale had finished eating he lit a pendulous pipe which seemed to add more curves to the almost ludicrous rotundity of his countenance and, clasping his small hands together with an air of complete satisfaction, announced that he was at the service of Scotland Yard.

"You know what has happened during your absence, Mr. Smale?" asked the inspector tentatively,

"Farnish has given me a brief account. Imprimis, let me say, I don't take Lord Bygrave's absence from home very seriously."

"Nobody would, if it were known where he is and what he is doing. You are aware that he was expected back some time ago?"

"I suppose his lordship can take an extension of leave without saying 'please, sir' to his subordinates in a Government office."

"That's not quite the way to put it, Mr. Smale," continued the inspector calmly. "No public servant behaves in the manner you are pleased to suggest. You have probably never been a public servant."

"No, inspector, I have not; I'm sorry if my way of putting it has offended your dignity as a public servant."

"No offence, Mr. Smale, to me. To return to the point, what makes you consider Lord Bygrave's disappearance lightly?"

"Well, you see, I haven't considered it much at all as yet. I haven't shaken off the frivolous atmosphere of my holiday. But, to be serious, Lord Bygrave, as you know, is a very keen naturalist. On this subject I think he is eccentric. I feel sure, if he started chasing a rare butterfly or insect, a Royal command wouldn't bring him to a standstill until he'd captured or lost sight of the prize. Then he'd return and make so nicely worded an apology that he'd turn away all Royal wrath."

"You think Lord Bygrave is eccentric?"

"Is butterfly-chasing a normal pursuit for a man in this year of our Lord?"

"That's his hobby, Mr. Smale."

"It's an extraordinary hobby for a man, inspector. We all chased them when we were boys, but only eccentric men carry their childish hobbies into manhood's estate. I should be very much surprised, for instance, to see you still sucking your thumb."

"I often wish I had a kite," remarked Vereker, glancing out of the window at the breezy sky.

"Is there any other respect in which you think Lord Bygrave eccentric?" continued the detective gravely.

"In several ways: he dislikes strawberries; is extremely uncomfortable in the presence of women, even if he doesn't cordially dislike them; is afraid of spiders, and would rather shoot his grandmother than shoot a rabbit."

"Had he many lady visitors?"

"Very few—practically only his relatives."

"Do you remember the visit of a heavily-veiled lady some six months ago, over which Lord Bygrave seemed unduly agitated?"

For some moments Mr. Smale was silent, as if in an effort to recollect.

"I can't say I do. What was her name?"

"We are trying to discover that."

"You are certain that such a lady called?"

"Yes."

"I was unaware of the incident."

"Now, Mr. Smale, may I ask you what is your position here as an employee of Lord Bygrave?" asked the inspector, suddenly changing the subject.

"I'm supposed—supposed, mind you—to be his private secretary. Lord Bygrave's life seems to leave little about which to be confidential with anyone. Any matter of importance he deals with himself. I merely answer his everyday business correspondence, attend to his gifts to charities, etc. I deal directly with his bailiff or estate agent, because he himself dislikes being bothered about the details of estate management."

"Have you much to do with the financial side of Lord Bygrave's affairs?"

"Only occasionally."

"Do you remember a transaction which occurred six months ago, concerning about £10,000 worth of securities?"

Mr. Sidney Smale puckered his brow; a strange, uneasy look flickered in his pale blue eyes for a moment and then swiftly vanished.

"I can't say I do," he replied slowly, "my memory is not one of the best. Perhaps Lord Bygrave carried out the transaction himself."

"He sold £10,000 worth of registered stock and purchased bearer bonds. You have no idea what happened to those bonds, by any chance, Mr. Smale?"

"I'm afraid I'm unable to enlighten you on the subject, inspector."

"I've only a few more questions to put to you, Mr. Smale. Can you remember the date of your departure for Paris?"

"Let me see—yes—Lord Bygrave left on Friday, the 1st, and I went off on Monday morning."

"Can you tell me what your movements were on Saturday?"

"I went up to town. I had some purchases to make before leaving for Paris. I met some friends and we had a jolly dinner together—bachelor affair you know—a boisterous evening it was!"

"Where did you stay that night?"

"Oh, I say, inspector, does it really matter?"

"It is most important. On that Saturday Lord Bygrave went missing."

"I hope you don't think I'm implicated."

"I'm afraid I must ask for an answer to my question, Mr. Smale."

"I stayed in a little hotel in Soho. I'm blessed if I remember its name now. You see we had had a jolly evening; my recollections are hazy. I sometimes relax, you know, inspector. Life is confoundedly dull down here and as old Horace says:

"'Siccis omnia nam dura deus proposuit, neque mordaces aliter diffugiunt solicitudines.' Please translate, Vereker, for the inspector's benefit."

"Sorry, I'm afraid I haven't got a crib handy," replied Vereker tactfully.

"You stayed in a Soho hotel?" questioned the inspector again, his features showing the faintest trace of anger.

"To the best of my information and belief," replied Mr. Smale airily.

"You signed the usual hotel form?"

"If they insisted on it I probably did. In fact, I have a hazy recollection that I signed my name somewhere; I only hope it wasn't to a promissory note."

"Good, that is something. You returned to Bygrave Hall on Sunday?"

"Certainly."

"Can you remember what you did on Sunday, Mr. Smale?"

"Very clearly. I tried to cure a headache, counted what I had spent the night before and found that I had three shillings in coppers and a few sixpences out of a tenner; packed my trunks and went to bed a wiser man."

"You arrived in Paris on Monday?"

"I did, and put up at the Hôtel des Anglais."

"What salary does Lord Bygrave pay you as his private secretary?"

"Three hundred pounds per annum and my keep. I also take a fair toll of his tobacco and matches. Not so bad, taking it all round."

"You are a member of a night club?"

"I used to be when I lived in town. Can I give you the name of all the ladies I've danced with there?" said Mr. Smale, his face showing its first traces of annoyance during the examination.

"I dare say I know some of them already," replied the inspector bluntly, while Vereker's face broke into an almost imperceptible smile. "Your turf accountant's name is—?" asked the inspector listlessly, as if tired of the bombardment.

"Oh, you know all about him!" snorted Mr. Smale angrily.

"Wasn't there some trouble between you and him?"

"There was; he was a blackmailing scoundrel, and you know it, inspector!"

"I've heard from others, though their opinion may not be worth much, that he is a very trustworthy man," replied the inspector quietly.

"Look here, inspector, I'm not going to be insulted any longer. By what authority are you questioning me like this? Are my private concerns anything to do with you? Damned insolence— that's what I call it!" Mr. Sidney Smale rose quickly from his chair. "If you want any further information from me, inspector, bearing on Lord Bygrave's disappearance, you will kindly put your questions through Farnish. I refuse to see you personally again." With a violent slam of the door, Mr. Smale had vanished.

"What do you think of that, Mr. Vereker?" asked the inspector.

"You fairly put him through it, Heather."

"He asked for it. Two can very easily play at the game of being impertinent. I'll have to look into his story of staying at a Soho hotel. Mr. Smale is evidently a gay young spark."

Vereker vouchsafed no further remark. He was lost in his own speculations. "I'll try a different line of attack," he thought and, rising from his seat, intimated that he would go over to Hartwood before lunch.

"Good, Mr. Vereker. In the meantime, we'll see if Mr. Smale really did stay at a Soho hotel. I'll call at the post office and set my men on the track."

"You know his movements in Paris, I suppose?" asked Vereker.

"Oh, yes, he's a gay young spark is Mr. Smale," replied the inspector as he left the room.

Vereker at once went up to Lord Bygrave's study and there he found Mr. Smale seated at Lord Bygrave's desk, busily attacking the arrears of his work. All trace of his recent anger had left his face and he was whistling cheerfully too himself.

"Hello, Vereker," he said amiably, "is there anything I can do for you?"

"Yes," replied Vereker, "take this matter of Bygrave's disappearance seriously."

"So I do, but that inspector rattled me with his magisterial airs. After all, what have I to do with Bygrave's absence?"

"Of course it's his business to suspect that you may have had something to do with it until you prove you have not."

"I suppose so. That, however, doesn't imply that he's free to browbeat me."

"I have looked through all Lord Bygrave's papers in that bureau; there is nothing there which is of any use to me in trying to trace what has occurred to him. Can you suggest anything?"

"Are you also on the trail?" asked Mr. Smale, looking up sharply.

"I am, for a very definite reason."

"Perhaps Bygrave would rather you didn't interfere in the matter at all," suggested his secretary significantly.

"I have thought of that," replied Vereker, "and, if I see that it is diplomatic to end the inquiry, I shall promptly do so."

"It might be. One never knows. As for my suggesting anything—have you looked in the secret drawer of the bureau?"

"Is there one?"

"Yes, fancy Inspector Heather missing it! I'm delighted."

Mr. Smale rose and crossed over to the bureau. Touching a hidden spring at the top of the bureau, a small drawer shot out at the bottom. It contained one letter which he withdrew and brought over to Vereker.

"That's all there is beyond what you've already seen," he said.

Vereker took the envelope from his hand and extracting a sheet of note-paper discovered that it was a simple receipt for ten thousand pounds worth of bearer bonds. The written address at the head of the note-paper was 10 Glendon Street, W., and the signature, "Muriel Cathcart."

"You knew all along of the existence of this receipt, Smale?" he asked.

"I did," came the laconic reply.

"Why did you hide the matter from Inspector Heather?"

"I'm Lord Bygrave's confidential secretary—you, I presume, are his friend. *Verb. sap.*"

"I see. It's rather risky, you know."

"I don't mind that. What can Inspector Heather do to me?"

"He might make things very unpleasant, Smale. As a matter of fact, he has just gone off to verify your account of putting up in a Soho hotel."

"Has he? He won't find any trace of my temporary sojourn there, Vereker."

"Didn't you put up in a Soho hotel?"

"Not I, Vereker. Now, I'll be frank with you. I met, as I have said before, one or two friends and after a very good dinner and the pouring out of copious libations to the gods, we hied us to a West End gambling den known to me. This would sound very dreadful to Inspector Heather; but, unlike certain wealthy and yet very respectable members of society, I cannot afford to visit Monte Carlo for a little harmless excitement, so I pay an occasional visit to the tables—much nearer home. We played chemmy, trente-et-quarante and roulette and my expenditure for the whole evening, counting my gains and losses, was under a tenner. That wasn't deadly. I wasn't going to give Heather the address of my little casino, so I had to lie, point-blank."

"Indiscreet," remarked Vereker.

"Indiscretion is not a crime," replied Smale. "If I had made Heather my father confessor, so to speak, I should have compromised others. It simply couldn't be done."

Vereker was silent for some moments. "Have you ever seen this Mrs. Cathcart?" he asked.

"I got a glimpse of her when she came here. She only came once, about six months ago. She was heavily veiled and I doubt whether I could recognize her again."

"You don't know if she is still at the London address on that receipt?"

"I know absolutely nothing about her. Bygrave never mentioned the matter to me. It was not my business to be unduly inquisitive."

"I wonder what claim she had on Bygrave?" said Vereker.

"Possibly none at all. Lord Bygrave was very generous in his charity, especially when he came up against a deserving case. He always, however, made a meticulous inquiry into tales of woe. He was no fool."

"Well, I must be off," said Vereker. "But before I go, can you tell me, Smale, if one of the drawers of that bureau had been forced before you left for Paris?"

Mr. Smale started involuntarily, but made a swift recovery of his composure. He rose and walked over to the bureau and carefully examined the drawer.

"It may have been. I can't say I noticed it. However, Bygrave was a perfect artist at losing his keys. He has broken open half the drawers in the house at one time or another."

"Thanks. I'm going over to Hartwood for a day or two. If there's anything you want, let me know. As trustee under Lord Bygrave's will, I'm taking charge."

"Good. I'll expect my orders from you. For the present I suppose I'd better carry on as usual?"

"Just so. Good day."

On the way to the station Vereker met Inspector Heather, who was returning to Bygrave Hall.

"Well, Mr. Vereker," asked the detective, "what do you think of Mr. Sidney Smale for a glib liar?"

"H'm, I'm not quite certain yet, Heather, whether he's a natural or an artificial liar. A natural liar lies because he can't help it, or because he wishes to be interesting; an artificial liar lies to deceive. He's a pretty smart young man, Heather, you must be doubly on the alert."

"I'll see to that, Mr. Vereker. I shall probably join you at Hartwood to-night or to-morrow before lunch. Au revoir."

At the station Walter was waiting on the down platform with Vereker's bag.

"I shall be all right now, Walter, thank you. You won't forget," said Vereker, handing the footman some money.

"I shall not forget, sir," replied Walter, "as soon as I know, I'll wire."

Chapter Eight

As Vereker sat in the corner of a comfortable first-class carriage on the way to Hartwood he swiftly recapitulated in his mind the net results of his labours at Bygrave Hall. Briefly they could be summarized under three heads.

In the first place, Farnish, the trusted servant of the family, was inclined to be secretive and was, according to Walter, behaving in an unwontedly mysterious manner. It was quite possible that it was he who had broken open the drawer in Lord Bygrave's writing-bureau, for some purpose which might or might not be connected with Lord Bygrave's disappearance, Vereker felt uneasy about this matter. In spite of his being able to give no reason for his belief he was, somehow or other, convinced that this incident of the rifled bureau was connected with the whole mystery of Lord Bygrave. He felt that it would eventually fall into its place in the chain of events when their sequence became clear.

Secondly, ten thousand pounds worth of bearer bonds had been given by Lord Bygrave to a mysterious woman, by the name of Muriel Cathcart, who at that time was living at 10 Glendon Street, W. This again might have nothing to do with subsequent events. On the way to the station he had wired to his trusted friend, Ricardo, to make full inquiries about Mrs. Cathcart at Glendon Street and reply to the White Bear Inn at Hartwood as soon as possible.

Thirdly, he had discovered that Smale, Lord Bygrave's secretary, was a gambler, drank, and frequented night clubs. Putting it as baldly as this, it was not a wholesome reputation for a man in a position of trust. Smale, on his own confession, had lied to Heather under the excuse that it was out of loyalty to his employer. He had ostensibly been frank with him, but could any credence be placed in his words? It might be an astute way of misleading both the inspector and himself. Vereker felt that he didn't like Smale, but again this was a prejudice he had entertained long before the disappearance of Lord Bygrave. Smale might, at the worst, only be a young fool. Many good men had passed through a similar phase of sowing wild oats. There was in life such a thing as reaching an age of discretion in which previous experience of the world led to a tolerant attitude towards everyday humanity. *Tout comprendre—*

Taking it all round, the results had been neither very definite nor very encouraging. Still, there had been results. The difficulty of the problem ought not, he felt, to be allowed to dishearten him. He must continue the task with some of the massive imperturbability of Inspector Heather.

On arriving at Hartwood Station he found old Dick, George Lawless's handy man, awaiting him with the pony and trap. The day was gloriously fine, as days in early October can be. Chestnut and oak had strewn the road with russet leaves and shining fruit;

the elms had gowned themselves in pale gold, and every gust of wind blew from them some of their autumn drapery. In the hedgerows, where the sun's direct beams could not penetrate, the light hoar frost had distilled into chill dew—the first icy breath of the coming winter. Vereker's eyes were alight with joyousness. It was the time of the year he loved. The heavy, rounded masses of summer foliage had gone and given place to the airiness of half-naked trees. He had a keen eye for their anatomy and loved to trace the shapes of boles and boughs now half disclosed through the scanty but gorgeous raiment of the waning year. The keen, brisk, buoyant air seemed to drive from his mind all the tenseness and morbidity of his occupation with the Bygrave case, and even the smoke blowing from Dick's disreputable clay pipe, and carrying the odour of strong shag, acquired some of the sweetness of commonplace, healthy humanity, free from all taint of mystery.

"Oh, for a knapsack, my water-colour box and the open road," he thought, "and bread and cheese and beer!"

It was with a sense of returning to a distasteful task that he alighted in the courtyard of the White Bear Inn. As he entered he met Mary Standish, looking radiantly beautiful. She had been busy at her morning tasks and was flushed with hurry and exertion.

"Will you be in for lunch, sir?" she asked in her soft, pleasing voice.

"It will be ready about one, I suppose?"

"Yes, sir. Is there anything you would like to order specially?"

"No, thanks. I'll take the ordinary lunch. I know I shall enjoy it—it's always good—and I'm sure I shall be hungry."

The day was too fine to stay indoors, so Vereker hurried up to his room, changed into an old sports coat, flannel trousers and heavy comfortable shoes. He set off from the inn at a long swinging pace, whirling his ash-stick around in sheer exuberance of spirits. He felt more like his old irresponsible self this morning.

"This business has had a sobering effect on me," he thought as he paced along. "I entered it in the spirit of cap and bells, and before it's over I shall have assumed the gravity of a Divorce Court judge."

He made his way along the road to Windyridge, his eyes taking in the sweeping lines of the rolling country around—lines that seemed to fall into design without any effort on the part of the artist's eye and imagination. He was wrapt in contemplation of a particularly beautiful interlacement of hills and valleys when he heard the cuff cuff of a horse's hoofs on the road in front of him. He glanced ahead at the horseman approaching at a gentle trot. There seemed even at that distance something familiar in the rider's carriage of shoulder and head, and as he came up Vereker recognized him. It was David Winslade. The latter hesitated a moment; then a look of recognition came into his eyes, and he at once reined in his horse. The next moment he had dismounted and was holding out his hand.

"Vereker—what a surprise to meet you out here!"

"I've come down purposely to see you, Winslade. I've been down here once already, you know, but affairs took me away again before I could look you up."

"I heard you'd been at the White Bear and had gone again."

"Of course you've guessed the reason of my visit?"

"Well, I suppose it's all about this strange business of my Uncle Henry." A tense, worried look swept swiftly across Winslade's face—as a cloud shadow sweeps across a sunny upland—and was gone. He struck his leather gaiter with his whip as if dismissing the matter from his mind. "I don't know what has happened. It's a rum business altogether and damned unpleasant for me, I can assure you, Vereker."

"I should like to have a talk with you on the subject at your leisure. You know I'm your trustee in case anything—"

"Yes, I know," interrupted Winslade, and his brow furrowed again.

Vereker was watching him closely. Those boyish blue eyes that he had always remembered for their disarming frankness were glancing uneasily around at anything and everything, but failed to look him straight in the face as had been their wont.

"Well, come over and have some tea with me this afternoon and we'll discuss the affair," said Winslade, after an uncomfortable pause, and next moment he had swung himself easily into the saddle. "I'll expect you about four o'clock," he said as his cob moved impatiently forward, and with a wave of his whip he went clattering off along the dusty road.

Vereker returned to the White Bear by a circuitous route. He was thinking of Winslade as he entered the inn, and at the same moment Mary Standish came out of the dining-room and went into the kitchen. On her way she passed through a beam of sunshine pouring in from a window looking out on to the garden, and a vivid flash of diamonds from a ring on the third finger of her left hand caught Vereker's all-observing eye.

"Hello!" he thought. "So they're engaged! A magnificent ring, too, I should say. I wonder what his Uncle Henry would say if he knew! This is certainly an unexpected turn of events."

Vereker lunched early, and when Mary Standish came in with his food they were alone in the dining-room. It was an opportunity that Vereker felt that he could hardly let escape. As the girl laid the vegetable dishes in front of him he glanced at the ring with a smile and asked:

"Well, Mary, who's the lucky man?"

She blushed deeply.

"Are you very much interested, Mr. Vereker?" she retorted, trying to assume an air of severity, but without much success.

"Very much so."

"That's very kind of you. But do you think that it's any business of yours?"

Vereker's features broke from smiles into laughter.

"In certain circumstances, Mary, it may concern me quite a lot."

"I cannot see that it concerns you in any way at all, Mr. Vereker," replied Mary. She was now looking distinctly annoyed; Vereker's hilarity had quite upset her dignity.

"It all depends upon who the man is. I think I can guess his name. I believe I told you on my last visit that he was Lord Bygrave's heir."

"And you are a trustee under Lord Bygrave's will," she said coldly.

"Just so. You've given me quite a shock. I didn't think you knew."

"I'll give you a further shock, Mr. Vereker. Whatever Lord Bygrave's attitude is to our engagement, and whatever instructions he leaves you as trustee with regard to the disposal of his effects, we—that is Mr. Winslade and I—don't care one rap."

"I came here an ordinary human being, Mary. I'm afraid I shall leave disguised as a pancake. You're so crushing."

But Mary Standish was in no mood to be humoured and, turning on her heel, quickly left the room. For the remainder of the meal another maid attended to Vereker's wants, but Vereker had discovered all that he had set out to discover. The result kept him absorbed in thought for the rest of the afternoon.

At four o'clock Vereker turned into the gate of Crockhurst Farm, and a few steps along a well-kept gravel drive brought him to the house. It was a square, white-walled, old-fashioned farmstead with vigorous climbing roses nailed to its homely front. A green painted wooden portico formed the entrance, and large windows opened on to a well-shorn lawn, which ran to a thick stone wall where in recesses nestled modern, wooden beehives. Beyond the wall could be seen serried rows of orchard trees. As Vereker approached the door a flock of white pigeons settled with a loud rustle of wings on the red-tiled roof, and a quick-eared dog barked from the yard behind. He was about to ring when Winslade leaned out of one of the open windows.

"Don't stand on any ceremony, Vereker. Come in; the door's open and tea's ready."

Vereker walked in and, turning to the left through an open door, entered Winslade's drawing-room. There was a faint odour of potpourri in the air which was infinitely pleasing, and the whole room instilled a feeling of restfulness and quietude which somehow seemed to clash reproachfully with the subject uppermost in Vereker's mind.

"Sit down, Vereker, and help yourself to those potato cakes. They're hot, and Mrs. Rafferty has made them specially in the Irish way—with currants—in your honour. I'm going to be 'mother,' and will pour out the tea."

The words were said in an attempt at a light, jocular mood, but Vereker at once marked the jerky, uneasy manner Winslade displayed. He was feeling distinctly nervous and uncomfortable, and the brow once so sunny and care-free was troubled by an unpleasant furrow.

"I believe I've got to offer you congratulations, Winslade," Vereker remarked, as if the Bygrave case was a subsidiary affair.

"So the news has even reached you, a stranger to the village? Yes, I'm engaged to Miss Standish. Of course you've seen her?"

"Oh, yes. I wrung the admission of her engagement to you from her this morning after seeing her engagement ring. I believe your uncle knew of your intentions."

"Yes, I wrote and told him. He seemed rather disgruntled over the business. You know the line of argument they always take on such occasions—'marrying out of one's social sphere being seldom a success' and all that sort of twaddle. He didn't cut me off with the time-honoured shilling on the spur of the moment. The matter was *sub judice*, so to speak; in fact he was coming down to Hartwood on this last occasion to see 'the lady for myself,' so he said. Really, I thought my uncle would have been too unconventional to play the orthodox heavy to his nephew in such a way, but I suppose he belongs to a theatrical age. In any case it wouldn't have mattered. I'm not beholden to Uncle Henry. I can earn my own living and am certainly going to arrange my own marriage without anyone's interference. The girl he would have chosen for me would certainly never have been one fitted for a hard-working farmer's wife."

"He was doubtless thinking of your prospects as his heir," suggested Vereker quietly.

"Oh, hang him and his money!" said Winslade bitterly. "All the money in the world won't alter my manner of life. I shall still remain a farmer. He never seemed to grasp that fact."

"You've no idea what has happened to him?" asked Vereker bluntly.

"Look here, Vereker," said Winslade, and his face was flushed with rising anger, "I don't know where my uncle is. If I did, why should I conceal his whereabouts? Your inspector fellow—I don't know his name—who is on the business from Scotland Yard, has been annoying the life out of me of late. I've been answering questions to one of his men as to my whereabouts on the day of my uncle's disappearance until I'm heartily sick of it. I suppose he thinks I've spooked my uncle away for the sake of getting my hands on his money?"

"Of course he does," replied Vereker. "It's his business to do so. That's the first thought that enters the criminal investigator's mind. The circumstances in which you are placed with regard to your uncle supply a very strong motive."

"Well, I've given his representative a full account of my movements, and I'm not going to be pestered about the matter any more. You're my trustee, aren't you?"

"I am, if anything serious has happened to your uncle."

"You mean if by any chance he is dead?" asked Winslade, and his eyes looked out of the open window with a strangely disturbed gleam in their depths.

"His death will have to be presumed before his will can be proved," replied Vereker.

"I don't believe for a moment he's dead," came the remark as Winslade stretched his hand for Vereker's empty tea-cup.

"What prompts you to think so?" asked Vereker quickly.

"Nothing—nothing at all. I've not the slightest reason for thinking so. Still, I can't bring myself to think my uncle is not alive. It seems impossible! Nevertheless, this business of his disappearance is beyond my comprehension. I leave it to the inspector and yourself to unravel."

"It's what we've been trying to fathom ever since we feared that it was not altogether innocent," replied Vereker.

For some moments Winslade sat in silence, deep in thought. Then, looking up sharply at Vereker, he asked:

"Do you think the inspector really believes that I've had a hand in my uncle's disappearance?"

"I'm afraid I can't answer your question, Winslade. The inspector suspects anybody he fancies. Of course he bases his fancy on the possible existence of a motive."

"The motive in my instance being that I would benefit by my uncle's death?"

"Naturally."

"It's confoundedly awkward. Moreover, my uncle and I did not see eye to eye over my engagement to Mary Standish. That would be a contributory factor making it all the more necessary that I should get him out of the way—eh?"

"Therefore it's the best thing to be quite frank over every question that Inspector Heather may ask you, Winslade. If you are not, it all goes to supply evidence against you in his eyes. For instance—did you see your uncle on Saturday morning?"

"No, certainly not!"

"Good! Did you see him on Friday night before or after he arrived at the White Bear?"

Winslade rose from his chair to ring for Mrs. Rafferty for more tea.

"No, I did not," he said as he turned his back on Vereker to perform this action. "I've nothing whatever to do with my uncle's disappearance and I don't want to be mixed up in the case at all."

Vereker was silent, but observant. He noticed the uneasy flush that had crept over Winslade's face as he was speaking, and from the look in his eye—for the eye is the last citadel of truth—he felt sure that Winslade was prevaricating. At once all his faculties were alert; there was here something that needed elucidation, but he must probe with the utmost caution. He was sure that Winslade was as yet unaware that he harboured any suspicion as to his being implicated in the matter of Lord Bygrave's inexplicable disappearance, and he felt that he had gone far enough for the present. He therefore changed the topic of conversation to farming, on which subject he found an enthusiastic talker in Winslade and, having thus engendered once more a friendly atmosphere, found that it was high time to take his departure.

Vereker did not return by the direct route to the White Bear Inn. His interview with Winslade had suddenly given his thoughts a new twist, and he desired time and loneliness to adapt his mind to a changed and unpleasant point of view. The unpleasantness arose from the fact that he had been obliged to drag within the circumference of his suspicion a man whom he had always liked. When he had last seen him, he was an ingenuous youth; but that was some time ago. Though he was yet only a young man he had since then passed through the crucial experience of war. What effect might not that devastating period have had on David Winslade? Some strong men it had unbalanced, sending their whole moral outlook unaccountably askew. Winslade had been severely wounded and shell-shocked. Apparently he was again enjoying fairly good physical health, but who could say what mysterious disturbance might not have taken place in those delicate cells man calls the brain?

As he walked along Vereker viewed the matter in every light. Winslade had been blunt enough about the possibility of suspicion falling on himself through the fact of his being heir to Lord Bygrave's money and the subsidiary factor that his uncle had not looked with an altogether favourable eye on his engagement to Mary Standish. Yet this capitulation of the reasons why he ought to be suspect might only be the old ruse of assumed innocence. Why, again, had he made the admission that there had been some friction between his uncle and himself over Mary Standish? Perhaps he was anticipating that it might leak out from Mary Standish and had already prepared the counter move. Should this supposition prove true—for at present the whole was supposititious—it was clear that Mary Standish knew nothing of his connexion with the affair of his uncle's disappearance. Otherwise he would have forbidden her to mention the avuncular distaste for his choice of a partner.

Vereker was still pondering over the subject when he arrived at the White Bear Inn. He found a wire awaiting him from Ricardo with regard to the mysterious lady called Muriel Cathcart. The telegram ran:

Left 10 Glendon Street two months ago destination unknown.

"That's not very helpful," remarked Vereker, and he walked into the coffee-room, where, to his surprise, he found Inspector Heather apparently asleep in a comfortable chair before the fire. The detective, however, was far from asleep. Without even opening his eyes he said:

"Good evening, Mr. Vereker, and where may you have been all the afternoon? Over at Crockhurst Farm, I suppose."

"Quite correct, Heather. I've been over to see Mr. Winslade. He's fed up to the teeth with you and your subordinates. He says he'll brown you and any of your men who dare to interrogate him further as to his movements on the day of Lord Bygrave's disappearance."

"You can tell him from me that we shall not bother him further," replied the detective with a smile.

"You're satisfied as to his innocence?" asked Vereker cautiously.

"By no means," replied the inspector, "but about our further inquiries we'll keep him strictly in the dark."

Vereker sat in silence for some moments. All at once Inspector Heather sat up in his chair.

"You were not quite satisfied with your interview with Mr. Winslade this afternoon?" he asked.

"Not quite," replied Vereker. "How did you guess?"

"You must be more careful in the future when you enter a room containing a sleeping man, Mr. Vereker. Your face was an open book of words to your unpleasant thoughts."

"Cunning old fox, Heather. I shall suspect you in the future. I begin to think you are implicated in this affair. To be serious, have you made sure of all Winslade's movements on Friday night and Saturday morning?"

"Why do you suggest Friday night?" asked the inspector, raising his brows.

"Simply to ascertain if Winslade could possibly have seen Lord Bygrave prior to his arrival at the Inn."

"I see. Well, Mr. Vereker, we have made very careful inquiries, and we have discovered that on Friday he was out all the evening in his new motor-car and did not return till midnight. He has given us the route he followed." The inspector produced an ordnance survey map and pointed out with a thick forefinger the route Winslade had indicated.

"Any confirmation that the story is true?" asked Vereker.

"A Woodbridge constable saw his car making for Hartwood about 11.30, which bears out Mr. Winslade's story in one particular. There is no other corroborating evidence. The only other person who saw a car on that night was the blacksmith at Eyford, who says a car was going towards Fordingbridge as if it had come *from* Hartwood. This is so contradictory that it must have been another car altogether. These country roads are deserted at night. You might go that round after dark and not meet a soul."

"It strikes me he took a long time to do that round," suggested Vereker after some computation.

"The same thought struck me," agreed the detective. "But he says he had a breakdown. Something wrong with the magneto which, being a mystery to a novice, took him an hour to discover. Finally the ignition seemed to right itself and he was able to proceed."

"And on Saturday?" asked Vereker.

"He was at Crockhurst Farm till after lunch, and in the afternoon drove into Castleton. This we have verified fully."

"Friday night seems a bit sketchy," said Vereker to himself, and aloud to Heather: "I think I'll go over his route to-morrow myself. I may glean something from the run."

"You know of his engagement to Mary Standish?" asked the inspector tentatively.

"Yes."

"It proves that Winslade is fairly short of money at present."

"Oh!" remarked Vereker, experiencing some surprise. "How did you figure that out?"

The inspector laughed. "He hasn't paid the bill for that ring outright. We discovered that he bought it at Drake's, the jeweller's, of Barton Ferry. A fair deposit and the rest to follow."

At this moment Mary Standish suddenly entered the room. The inspector glanced uneasily at Vereker and, when the girl had gone, asked:

"Did you hear her approach the door, Mr. Vereker?"

"I'm afraid I didn't, Heather. You ought to be more careful.

"I shall be in future," remarked the inspector and rose to go up to his bedroom.

Chapter Nine

On retiring Vereker strove in vain to sleep. Finally he lit a candle, reached for his coat, hanging on a chair beside his bed, and thrust his hand into a capacious inner pocket for his pillow book. Emerson's essays—"The Conduct of Life." To his annoyance, the book was not there. What could have made him omit to bring with him that trusted companion of his sleepless hours? Much as he loved them, these essays always reminded him of the rush and incessant flicker of the early kinematograph film. Their dogmatism and lively sequence of half-caught and elliptically expressed ideas bore a strange parallel to swift and indistinct visual presentation.

"But they never fail to send me to sleep," he always added to himself with a smile.

What could he do to banish the very unpleasant thoughts that had besieged his brain ever since he had been to Crockhurst Farm that afternoon? The unpleasantness, he was aware, arose from the fact that he was perfectly convinced that Winslade had lied to him about his not having seen Lord Bygrave at some time on Friday night. He had risen and turned his back on him under the pretence of ringing for his housekeeper to avoid lying to his face. And when he had performed this action and returned to the tea-table his cheeks had been deeply flushed and his manner extremely uneasy. Assuming that Winslade had seen Lord Bygrave on Friday night, the whole matter took on a very sinister aspect. Suppose they had quarrelled over the subject of Winslade's proposed marriage—a marriage which his uncle deprecated—there was no knowing what might have happened! Vereker found it extremely difficult to face the probability of Winslade's connexion with Lord Bygrave's disappearance, just as it is difficult for an honourable man to find any motive sufficiently overpowering to account for the committal of a murder. But he felt that because he knew Winslade that was all the more reason why he should harden his heart and face the problem in a cold, analytical manner. He determined there and then that he would probe the mystery thoroughly, regardless of any question of friendship. From various deductions that he had made the whole affair assumed a more puzzling complexion than ever. For, though Winslade's movements on Friday night were rather sketchy, his whereabouts on Saturday had been definitely settled by Heather and his assistants, and those movements were entirely innocent.

"Very strange, very strange!" murmured Vereker. "But it's getting more and more exciting. I wonder what old Heather has arrived at? Personally I feel on the eve of a vital discovery!"

He leaned over to a dressing-table and picked up an ordnance survey map of the district. His eye ran over the route that Winslade had said he had taken on Friday night.

"He picks up his car at Fordingbridge Junction, where it had been garaged for a day or two, takes the road that runs through Eyford, Castleton, Woodbridge, and thence round to Crockhurst Farm."

Vereker paused and pondered for some moments. "I will traverse that route to-morrow, and I'll call at Mill House, Eyford, in front of which he says he had a breakdown, and inquire whether anyone there remembers having seen a motor standing on the road for an hour. It's a sordid business when you have to doubt the word of a friend, but I must doubt everybody and everything now. One lie opens the way to a multitude and disrupts the foundations of confidence."

Vereker sat and gazed blankly at the ordnance survey map for some minutes, but his eyes saw nothing. A curious light of excitement was burning in their depths, for his thoughts had suddenly taken an unexpected turn and he felt more convinced than ever that he was on the brink of a momentous discovery. It might be the first decisive step towards elucidating the mystery of Bygrave's extraordinary disappearance.

"By Heaven!" he suddenly exclaimed. "I believe I'm at last on the right track." With these words he flung the map on his

dressing-table, extinguished the light and lay back in bed.
Sleep, however, was as elusive as a shadow, and when morning
came Vereker had had but fitful snatches of rest. Yet the long
quiet hours of night seemed to have clarified his thoughts and
marshalled them in some order. He rose with alacrity and, having
breakfasted well, took the first train to Fordingbridge Junction.
There he would get a car and run round the route which Winslade
alleged he had taken on the night of Bygrave's disappearance and
see what there was to be discovered.

On arrival at the junction Vereker called at Layham's garage,
where Winslade had put up his car, and, after hiring a Ford,
intimated that he was a private detective and would like to know
certain facts about a Mr. Winslade who had garaged his car there
for some days at the beginning of October.

"Quite willing to give you any information, sir," remarked the
proprietor, "but, bless you, you won't find anything crooked about
Mr. Winslade; he's a gent from top to toe. You're a bit behind the
Scotland Yard folk too. They've been and got all the information a
week ago."

"Thanks; then I'll not trouble you," remarked Vereker, smiling,
and added to himself, "You're a wily old fox, Heather. In future
I'll leave you in the dark too, except for incidents that I feel won't
give you a handicap over me. The tussle is getting exhilarating—I
wonder if you know as much as I do, as far as we've gone."

A few moments later Vereker had passed out of the garage
gates in his hired Ford, and his first stop was just outside
Fordingbridge, where a road turning to the right runs parallel with
the branch line direct to Hartwood.

"This was Winslade's shortest way home," he muttered, "and an
excellent road as far as I can see. I wonder why he chose the long
way round? For the sake of the run, I suppose. There would be no
difficulty about traffic at that time of night in this neighbourhood,
which lies clear of the main routes to the south coast."

He was more perplexed as he ran along the bumpy, winding and deplorably bad road which led to Eyford.

"A novice in driving would hardly choose this jungle track to try a new car on," he soliloquized. "It becomes more and more evident to me that it was not altogether a matter of choice."

A quarter of an hour's further jolting through a beautifully rural district brought him to Eyford Mill, lying in the valley to his left, but clearly discernible from the road. The mill-wheel was revolving and grinding away on the old millstone process as it had done for centuries. Vereker pulled up and surveyed the scene. It might make a nice water-colour sketch was his first thought; but he banished such pleasant projects as painting from his mind and once more started the car.

"Ah, here we are!" he exclaimed when there came into view a house lying on the sloping ground to his right. A high boundary wall flanked the road, and above it a terraced rockery ran up to the dwelling. On the heavy oak gates, painted in white, was the name "Mill House." Vereker pulled up his car and leisurely surveyed the place. It was an old-world house with shingled roofs and hipped gables, and singularly well situated as far as outlook was concerned, for it overlooked the picturesque valley with its mill-stream and dam below. But, though it had been modernized, it bore the unmistakable appearance of neglect, and the presence of a row of yews, bordering the short drive up to the front door, lent a gloom almost inseparable by association from these funereal trees.

"Looks as if I were going to draw a blank," thought Vereker.

He got out of the car and walked briskly up the moss-covered gravel approach. His sharp eye noticed the tracks of a car's wheels made at no distant date on the gravel, but a total lack of movement and the absence of any sound of life suggested that if the place were inhabited its tenants were at present away.

A vigorous tattoo on the front-door knocker brought no response. Vereker glanced at the windows, but it was impossible to look within through the heavy lace curtains, which, from their appearance, had evidently not been changed for many months. An overwhelming curiosity came upon him, and he decided to explore. Making his way round to the right, he passed through a pair of folding gates into a yard containing a garage. Traces of oil and the marks of wheels were symptomatic, but beyond the garage lay a mournful kitchen-garden, overgrown with weeds and devoid of any appearance of recent culture. Vereker wandered idly round the house, tried several doors, peered in at a scullery window and, coming to the conclusion that nobody was about, returned somewhat disappointed to his car.

"I should have liked to verify the fact that Winslade had broken down here," he thought, and added aloud: "I wonder who lives at Mill House?"

But the question was not to be answered by wandering about the precincts of the gloomy old place, so Vereker retraced his steps and, closing the oak gates behind him, boarded his car and ran into the village of Eyford. There he lunched on sandwiches and a glass of beer and, having made about an hour's break altogether on his journey, decided to finish the route without another stop. This would enable him to compare his time with Winslade's.

His further progress gave him food for thought. It was one of the worst roads he had ever driven a car on. What on earth had induced Winslade to take this route? At night, too, it would be dangerous unless the driver knew every inch of his way. Nothing of any importance, however, occurred, and towards three o'clock in the afternoon, having passed through Castleton and Woodbridge on his way, Vereker came in sight of Crockhurst Farm. He met Winslade standing at the gate, and pulled up.

"Hello, Vereker; where did you get that tub from?" he asked, eyeing the Ford car critically.

"Hired it at Fordingbridge from old Layham. I thought I'd have a run round in the fresh air. I came by Eyford and Castleton along the most execrable road that I've ever covered."

An uneasy glance from Winslade was the result of this information.

"Were you making for Hartwood?" he asked. "If you were, you could have taken the direct road parallel with the railway line. It has a really good tar-macadam surface."

"I saw that," returned Vereker with satisfaction; "but I wanted a run, and I'd heard that the old mill at Eyford would make a charming watercolour drawing. You know my passion for messing about with paints."

"It's a lovely spot," agreed Winslade.

"By the way, Winslade, do you know if the Mill House is tenanted?" asked Vereker, carelessly lighting a cigarette.

With the tail of his eye he saw that Winslade involuntarily started, but recovered himself at once.

"I couldn't say," he replied. "It's a tumbledown old place, low ceilings, stuffy little rooms and no damp courses, as far as I know. You're not thinking of taking it?"

"No, I haven't got as far as that. I had a look round the grounds this morning. I thought what a charming place it could be turned into with the expenditure of a little money."

Winslade pulled out his watch. "What are your plans?" he asked, as if eager to change the conversation.

"Oh, I'm going straight back to Hartwood."

"You won't stay and have some tea?"

"No, thanks; I must get back. I've a good deal of work to do and several letters to write. Au revoir."

"Cheerio," returned Winslade as Vereker's car, with a throb and a jerk, started off on the way to Hartwood.

Vereker was smiling. He felt that he had sailed dangerously near the wind, if he had not indeed roused some suspicion in Winslade's mind as to the object of that journey. He would have liked to cast a glance back; something personal, almost magnetic, nearly caused him to do so. He would have given a lot to see the expression on Winslade's face, but second thoughts counselled discretion. He must not startle the quarry; it might elude him if forewarned of his approach. The journey had not been altogether fruitless: it had confirmed some of his conclusions of the night before and convinced him that his research was proceeding along lines which would yield definite results.

From Crockhurst Farm Vereker bounded along until he reached the White Bear. He was anxious to get back because he was eager to ask Mary Standish a very personal question. Her answer would possibly strengthen a theory. He had long since formed a theory which as time passed seemed to him more and more to embody the salient facts of the Bygrave mystery. Running the car into the courtyard of the inn, he left it in the hands of Dick and hastened into the inn. He ordered tea and went into the large dining-room to await its arrival. Mary Standish brought in the tray a little later and, after some preliminary conversation, Vereker suddenly asked:

"I wonder could you tell me, Mary, if you remember what Lord Bygrave had for breakfast on the morning of his disappearance?"

"Quite well, sir. Two boiled eggs, toast, butter and marmalade and coffee."

"Thanks," replied Vereker with suppressed excitement, "that's all I wish to know."

When Mary Standish had left the room he could no longer contain himself. Bringing his hand down on his thigh with a resounding slap he exclaimed:

"Well, I'm damned!"

He was so agitated that he wanted to talk things over with Inspector Heather at once, but the latter was out and would not be in until dinner, so that he had to exercise his patience until the officer returned.

Retiring to his room he took a sheet of foolscap from his case and put down on paper all the surmises that were surging chaotically in his brain. This cold examination of the facts rid his mind of all details not germane to his main theory. Every now and then he glanced at the ordnance survey map, and when he had grasped the significance of that network of roads more thoroughly his eye lit with enthusiasm. Brick after brick seemed to be dropping into place in the construction of his edifice. He felt that the foundation was sound and was gleefully rubbing his hands together when the dinner gong warned him of the hour.

"That infernal signet-ring only points to one very grave conclusion," he exclaimed, as he descended to the dining-room, and his features assumed a seriousness that was seldom seen on the face of Algernon Vereker.

As he entered the room he saw Inspector Heather seated at their usual little table, waiting for dinner to be served. His brow was puckered and he was lost in a brown study. Vereker's entry brought him at once to the world.

"Well, Mr. Vereker," he said when the latter had taken his seat opposite to him, "has your run round the route disclosed anything of value?"

"Yes," replied Vereker, "it disclosed that you had already tapped Layham at Fordingbridge for information, and I dare say I'd not be far wrong in saying you had already covered the very ground I've gone over to-day."

The inspector laughed heartily. "I won't deny it, Mr. Vereker. If we compare notes perhaps something important may divulge itself. In the first place, I know you will have wondered why Mr. Winslade took such a rotten road to get to Crockhurst Farm."

"I did wonder, and could come to no conclusion," replied Vereker guardedly.

"You have no theory on the matter?"

"Oh, yes, I've many theories, but what we want is significant facts. I've got a strange piece of information for you, inspector—much more important than theories."

"What's that?"

"Lord Bygrave had boiled eggs for breakfast on the morning of his disappearance."

"I hope they were good," remarked the inspector as he helped himself to vegetables.

"Now that I am serious you are beginning to assume a jocular vein, Heather."

"I can't quite hatch those eggs," replied the inspector, looking hard at Vereker.

"I hardly expected you to, although you're broody. But to me they're significant, more than significant—they're conclusive!"

"Of what?"

"That Lord Bygrave never arrived here on Friday night," said Vereker impressively.

"Explain, Mr. Vereker."

"Lord Bygrave hasn't eaten boiled eggs for years—they are almost poison to him. You know how some people are upset by certain kinds of food. For instance, I cannot touch honey. Though I like it, I suffer almost agonizing pains after consuming even a spoonful. Some people daren't partake of strawberries, others of rhubarb. The man who ate those boiled eggs for breakfast on that Saturday morning was certainly not Lord Bygrave!"

Heather was distinctly impressed. "This is most important," he remarked, "but there are one or two facts we have to clear away before accepting your theory as conclusive. In the first place, Mary Standish and George Lawless have identified this photograph as the man who arrived here on Friday night. It is a portrait of Lord Bygrave."

Vereker took the photograph from the inspector's hand and closely examined it. "That is Lord Bygrave, but it was taken some years ago," he said, "and it's not a good photograph at that. It is just possible that Mary Standish and Lawless have made a mistake. As you know, people are hopelessly unobservant and identification is, with the majority of witnesses, an altogether inconclusive business. Women have identified strangers as their long-lost husbands. Inspector, you surely cannot have forgotten the facts of the famous Tichborne case."

"That is so. Let us say for the sake of argument that we have removed the first obstacle to your theory. Number two requires the elucidation of the mystery that Lord Bygrave left his signet-ring here on Saturday morning. You are convinced that it is his ring?"

"I believe it is his ring," replied Vereker gravely, "and it drives me to a very serious conclusion that the man who arrived here and impersonated Lord Bygrave—for I assume this for the present— had by some means, fair or foul, obtained possession of his ring. There is one thing, however, about that ring that puzzles me. It seems to be a somewhat larger ring than I thought it was. It may be a duplicate; it may have worn away to such an extent that it now slips easily on and off my finger. Once upon a time it fitted me very tightly, for I tried it on my finger years ago and had great difficulty in removing it."

"Have you any more facts in support?" asked the inspector, with kindling enthusiasm.

"Several. You remember the dottle of tobacco I found in the fender on our examination of Lord Bygrave's bedroom?"

"Distinctly."

"That was not the same tobacco as was contained in Lord Bygrave's tin. The dottle contained latakia. Bygrave only smoked a certain Civil Service Stores mixture which contains no trace of latakia. Again, Bygrave was supposed to have drunk whisky before retiring. He may have done so, but I have never remembered him to touch spirits all the time I have known him. Once more, you see this key-chain. It is undoubtedly Bygrave's, but it has been detached so violently that the leather buttonhole on the tab has been torn, and, as I pointed out before, there was no reason for Bygrave detaching this keychain, unless he had changed his clothes. Miss Standish, however, has informed us that he wore a dark suit all the time he was here, and, as you know, the only other suit he had was a light one. To sum up, inspector, the man who stayed here on Friday night and left early on Saturday morning never to return was not Lord Bygrave, in my humble opinion."

Inspector Heather could not resist expressing his admiration. "Mr. Vereker, you are shaping uncommonly well—uncommonly well for an amateur," he said patronizingly. "My own investigations bear out your theory—a theory which I myself have entertained for some time. For instance, the porters at Hartwood Station cannot remember Lord Bygrave arriving by the train he is supposed to have arrived by. This is very extraordinary, because very few people ever return to Hartwood by the last train from town. But, granting that you have discovered that it was not Lord Bygrave that stayed at the White Bear on Friday night, the next difficulty is to find out who impersonated him."

Algernon Vereker smiled: he thought that his discovery would have startled the inspector, and he was secretly amused that Heather was quietly professing to have arrived at the same conclusions, without disclosing his reasons.

"Yes, that is the next difficulty, Heather, and I'm counting on you to make the matter look quite simple. My efforts have rather exhausted me and it's your turn now for some hard work."

"I shall go back to London to-morrow," said Heather quietly. "The centre of gravity of the mystery has moved to London. It's my opinion that Lord Bygrave never left London."

"What makes you think that?" asked Vereker, with some surprise.

"Certain investigations we have made point to the fact," replied Heather with solemn satisfaction.

"I'm afraid you're wrong, inspector," replied Vereker carelessly.

"And what makes you think that?" asked the detective, with a keen glance.

"Other investigations that I have made," retorted Vereker, with a broad smile.

At this moment Mary Standish brought in a telegram for Vereker. He tore open the envelope, read the message without displaying any emotion and thrust it into his pocket.

"Another important discovery?" asked Heather tentatively.

"Not in the least, inspector. Merely a message saying I've got to return to London to-morrow. I shall probably only stay there for the day and return at night."

"I made a discovery to-day," continued the inspector, lazily puffing his pipe.

"Oh!" exclaimed Vereker in a non-committal way.

"Yes. Our young friend Smale is a liar. He stayed at no hotel in Soho during the week-end that Lord Bygrave disappeared."

"I guessed as much," remarked Vereker. "I tell you, Heather, you'll have to keep a skinned eye on Smale. He's a particularly clever young man."

"We're watching him very closely, Mr. Vereker."

"You know I took a dislike to that clever young man from the very first."

"Purely prejudice, inspector. I'm surprised at your making such an admission. I thought such a privilege was reserved for thoughtless and inexperienced beings like myself. Well, if you're determined to watch Smale, I'm going to keep young Winslade under observation."

Inspector Heather laughed loudly.

"You'll be wasting your time," he said confidently.

"Well, that's my own and not worth much, Heather," replied Vereker and, complaining of having had a tiring day, he went up to his room. There he drew from his pocket the telegram he had received earlier in the evening and read it again. The message ran:

9.15 train from Fordingbridge tomorrow—Walter.

Chapter Ten

On reaching his room, Vereker rang for a strong coffee and, filling his pipe, sat down in the wicker-chair at the foot of his bed. He was not yet ready for sleep.

"As Heather has put the matter very concisely, we have now to ascertain who impersonated Lord Bygrave," he said to himself, and sat for some time lost in thought. "In the first place it must have been some one who bore some physical resemblance to him," he added, "the question of make-up I think we can temporarily leave out of the discussion—though it must not be recklessly discarded. Again, the impersonator must have been fairly well acquainted with Bygrave's affairs, and known two things especially. First, that Bygrave had not been to the inn for some years, for if Lawless had remembered Lord Bygrave's appearance the impersonation would have been detected at once. Lawless had evidently been deceived, but that was not a supremely difficult matter. As for Mary, she would scarcely have known Lord Bygrave by sight unless she had seen a photograph of him, and even the photograph which Heather had obtained was a very old one. Secondly—"

At this point in his soliloquy Vereker halted. He had encountered a remote possibility—that of collusion between Lawless, Mary Standish and David Winslade. It was not a point to be lightly set aside, though the motive for such a deception was not strikingly obvious. He would bear it in mind and keep all three under suspicion. Vereker racked his brains to remember anyone in any way concerned in the case who could possibly impersonate Bygrave, but could think of no one without the concomitant idea of collusion. Temporarily he gave up the problem and decided to get to bed. A night's sleep would refresh his tired brain and to-morrow—well, there was work in hand to be done. He would travel up to London by the 8.15. Walter's telegram might open up another line of inquiry and lead to a fuller phase of understanding.

Next morning, Vereker rose early and made an elaborate toilet. The elaboration consisted of trying to disguise his rather well-marked features without the disguise being palpable. A heavy moustache gave him considerable trouble and after innumerable attempts he discarded it with the words:

"Too much of the walrus about it—its pessimistic droop would reduce me to melancholy before the day was out—this business is depressing enough without artificial aids."

He finally adopted a nicely-waxed, impertinent type hovering airily above an imperial, and having fixed these adjuncts to his satisfaction descended to breakfast. Heather was the sole occupant of the coffee-room at the hour and on seeing Vereker he promptly burst into loud and unrestrained laughter.

"What are you laughing at, inspector?" asked Vereker.

"Your face, Mr. Vereker," was all the reply the detective could make as he shot helplessly down another cascade of hilarity.

"I thought you'd address me as Count Antoine de something, inspector. You've got a hard heart and offer no encouragement to a mere tyro at your own game. I hope I shan't get any yolk of egg on this imperial. Perhaps I'd better stick to fish for breakfast."

Inspector Heather wiped the tears of merriment from his eyes.

"It won't do, Mr. Vereker—you remind me of that man, what's his name, who played Captain Kettle."

"Then be helpful and suggest some other facial lie, Heather. I must do something to obliterate Algernon Vereker for the day."

Inspector Heather pulled out a notebook, tore a leaf from it and wrote some words thereon. "Go to that address, Mr. Vereker, and I think they'll put you right. You must be a curate for the day, it suits your frank cast of countenance. Show them that note and old Jacobs will make you a work of art."

When the 9.15 train steamed into Charing Cross Station that morning Algernon Vereker, in clerical garb, was standing under the clock ostensibly reading a morning paper. He was actually watching every passenger who had come by the 9.15 train from

Fordingbridge file past the ticket collectors at the platform gate, and could hardly repress the excitement he felt. Every one seemed to have emerged, and a look of disappointment and annoyance passed across Vereker's face. The collectors were about to close the gates, but they hesitated and impatiently glanced up the platform. There was still another passenger. At length he burst into view—it was Farnish, Lord Bygrave's butler! At once the morning paper eclipsed Vereker's face from any direct scrutiny and he waited until Farnish had passed through the western exit of the station before swiftly following him. Vereker had a taxi in readiness should Farnish decide to drive, but Farnish had evidently no taste for such luxuries and wended his way on foot, at a medium pace into the Strand. Crossing the Strand he passed into Trafalgar Square and up the Haymarket, with Vereker following at a discreet distance.

"He is evidently going to make the journey on foot—his destination cannot be very distant, thought Vereker, and at that moment he came face to face with his friend Ricardo. "Hello, Ricky, you're about at an early hour!" he exclaimed.

"Good Lord, Vereker!" replied Ricardo, after gazing in bewilderment at his friend. "You've not taken Holy Orders?"

"Not quite good enough for that yet, Ricky. This is only a disguise; I'm shadowing a man in front. Look here, take this key, it's the key to my flat; meet me at five; have some tea ready; you'll find the key to the commissariat attached to my easel. Au revoir, I've no time to waste on you just now. By the way, get some fodder for tea—cheerio!"

"Right-o, padre! I'll get some kippers for tea and have 'em ready. Five o'clock sharp."

The next moment Vereker was striding with quickened gait after the disappearing Farnish. The pursuit wandered farther west and came at length to a street of the poorer class chiefly devoted to the letting of apartments. Vereker glanced up to see its name and with an electric thrill of excitement read Glendon Street W. Farnish was some twenty to thirty yards ahead of him, glancing

first at one side of the street and then at the other, evidently
looking for a number. Vereker cautiously slackened his pace to
let the butler increase the distance separating them, and shortly
afterwards stopped and gazed with apparent absorption at a row
of tinned salmon in a small provision dealer's window, all the
while keeping his eye on Farnish. The butler finally appeared to
have found the number he sought for he quickly halted and at
once mounted the steps to a front door on the left-hand side of the
street. He was well in view of the vigilant Vereker, who noted the
door by the cleanly whitened steps and polished door-knocker. He
could see it was a boarding-house of a poor but respectable type.

I'll disappear diplomatically and return later, thought Vereker,
but a sudden wild impulse seized him to continue his way up the
street and pass Farnish while he was still waiting for the door
at which he had knocked to open. Pulling his clerical hat well
down on his head to screen his face as much as possible from
observation, and crossing to the opposite side of the street, he
hastened forward. He had hardly advanced a dozen paces when
the door opened and a prim lady wearing an early Victorian mob-
cap appeared and spoke to Farnish. Now was the time to pass him
closely. The conversation lasted some seconds and in that brief
period became rather heated, for portions of it reached Vereker's
acute ears very distinctly.

"I tell you he is not here—he has been gone some days now. Do
you doubt my word...?"

Farnish's reply was inaudible, but from his general attitude
seemed argumentative. Vereker hastened his footsteps in order to
pass the house while Farnish was still engrossed in controversy.
As he reached a spot directly opposite the door he heard the butler
remark: "But, Mrs. Parslow, he must be here; he's expecting me.
Will you kindly let me go up to his room?"

"I tell you, sir, he's not here; he left some days ago... no
address... I'll send for police..."

Vereker quickened his pace and, reaching a street running off Glendon Street to the north, turned up it, casting a glance backwards before he was completely out of view of No. 10, where Farnish had called. The prim lady of that house had closed the door with a slam in the butler's face and Farnish was slowly descending the steps with an air of disappointment and hesitation. The next moment Vereker had turned the corner and Farnish was walking dejectedly back the way he had come. Vereker made his way northwards until he reached a shopping thoroughfare, and turning in at a Lyons tea-shop ordered coffee. Pulling out his morning paper from his pocket, he lit a cigarette and glanced cursorily at the day's news. A brief paragraph notified that Lord Bygrave was still missing, but that the police had stumbled upon new clues which promised to lead to a swift unravelling of the mystery. On another page a leader called attention to the alarming number of recent crimes the perpetrators of which remained undiscovered, and demanded in a peremptory manner a better co-ordination between the police organizations of rural districts and the more experienced staff of the Criminal Investigation Department at Scotland Yard. Having finished his coffee and cigarette at his leisure, Vereker rose, paid his bill and turned his steps once more towards Glendon Street.

The excitement of the chase was in his blood and the remarkable coincidence that Farnish had called at 10 Glendon Street, the address at which he remembered the mysterious and elusive Mrs. Cathcart had stayed, intrigued him.

"The skein is unravelling," he muttered to himself and quickened his pace. Arriving at 10 Glendon Street he knocked and the door was opened by the same lady who had confronted Farnish. She had now, however, divested herself of her cap and was looking tidier and primmer than ever. At sight of his clerical garb she at once asked Vereker in, and led him to a cosy little drawing-room the window of which overlooked the street, but was fenced against any intrusive gaze from without by a magnificent aspidistra in a large, blue, earthenware bowl. Vereker opened the conversation by saying that he had heard of the address from a Mrs. Cathcart who had stayed there, and asked if he might rent a room for a few weeks, during his stay in London. Evidently Mrs. Parslow was impressed by Vereker's manner and garb, for she immediately confided in him that she had a room which had just been vacated and after which there had been several inquiries. One had been from a young lady on the stage and another from a similar young lady, stylishly dressed and a colonel's daughter, who was engaged in the moving picture business, but, as Mrs. Parslow added: "Not that theatrical people aren't respectable, sir, but I'm not partial to them. They may be good enough in their way, but being a widow (and mark you, sir, I've seen better times and was born and bred a lady) I have to earn my living and pay my way. These stage people are always in and out of situations, and of course are therefore not always regular in their payments—"

"I quite understand, Mrs. Parslow," interrupted Vereker, "on the financial side I don't think we'll have any difficulty. I always pay for my rooms in advance."

"Thank you, sir. You'll excuse my being particular about money, but the very last gentleman who had my room, a Mr. Henry Parker by name, he left without paying his bill. Fortunately for me he had only stayed a few days before he went."

"H'm, iniquitous!" exclaimed Vereker, suppressing his excitement with difficulty. "Strangely enough, the name seems familiar to me, Mrs. Parslow, probably one of the parishioners I've met in my wanderings. I can't just place him at present. Of course he didn't say where he had gone?"

"No, sir, he evidently didn't tell even his friends. A gentleman called here this very morning for him—an aristocratic looking gentleman he was too—and when I told him Mr. Parker had left he doubted my word, sir; had the audacity to say he didn't believe me and said he must see Mr. Parker at once. I threatened to call the police."

"Persistent fellow!" exclaimed Vereker with simulated and sympathetic indignation. "Had he any other callers?"

"Another young gentleman, sir, a Mr. Winslade by name, but Mr. Parker wouldn't see anybody, and much to my shame, sir, for I hate lying, I was obliged to tell him that Mr. Parker was out, but if he had any message to leave I should be pleased to give it when he returned."

"Do you know, I believe I can trace all these gentlemen. I may be of some use to you later on in the way of getting your money for you for Mr. Parker's stay here."

"Thank you, sir, it would be very kind of you, and now would you like to see your room?"

"I should, Mrs. Parslow," replied Vereker, rising as his new landlady led the way from the drawing-room.

"I must warn you, sir, that the room hasn't yet been tidied up since Mr. Parker left. I haven't had time, as my sister living further down the road has not been very well and I've had to devote all my spare time to looking after her affairs."

"That doesn't matter, Mrs. Parslow, I can quite understand. I'm afraid you'll find me a most untidy occupant when I'm here."

The room to which Mrs. Parslow led Vereker was on the next floor and, to his joy, overlooked the street. It was a comfortable and spacious apartment, spotlessly clean, though at the moment littered with odd newspapers, brown paper and string, and bearing unmistakable evidence of the hasty departure of its last tenant. Even the bed in which he had slept had not yet been made, and Vereker's roving eye noted the depression in the pillow made by the departed lodger's head. An ardent desire for a thorough examination of that room at once seized him and he wildly sought for some excuse to rid himself of Mrs. Parslow's presence for even a few minutes.

"A very comfortable room, Mrs. Parslow, I am sure I shall be very happy here—a home from home, so to speak," he said, and hoped the sentiment of the last phrase would find a responding chord in her heart.

At this juncture a young woman's voice called up from below:

"Mother, are you there?"

"Yes, dear, what do you want? I'm engaged."

"I won't keep you a moment, mother—it's most important."

"Excuse me a minute, sir," said Mrs. Parslow, turning to Vereker.

"Certainly—don't hurry on my account. I'll just take this easy chair and rest for a minute. I'm absolutely tired out hunting for rooms. I've been on my feet all morning."

"Shall I make you a cup of tea, sir?" asked the landlady as she reached the door.

"You're a brick, Mrs. Parslow!" exclaimed Vereker with enthusiasm, and the compliment brought him a motherly smile as she left the room.

On her departure the overtired Vereker sprang with alacrity from his chair, and made a rapid but exhaustive search of the room as quietly as possible. Noticing some torn paper in the waste-paper-basket he rapidly filled his pockets with the fragments. The returning footsteps of Mrs. Parslow quickly recalled the well simulated look of fatigue to Vereker's face, and he was comfortably ensconced in a wicker arm-chair when she entered the room with a cup of tea.

Over that cup of tea Vereker augmented the goodwill that Mrs. Parslow had already shown him. He asked for her terms for a month and handed her a roll of Treasury notes considerably over the amount demanded, with the excuse that as he was a most untidy "paying guest," and was erratic in his comings and goings, it was only fair.

"You see, Mrs. Parslow, I'm an extremely busy man and have all sorts of friends to visit. If I am here one day and absent for the following week you mustn't be alarmed. I shall not have been run over by a bus—at least the odds are against it—and if I don't leave definite instructions you must not be annoyed with me."

"I shan't worry, sir, now that you've told me beforehand," replied Mrs. Parslow, her eye beaming as it fell on the notes in her hand.

Having completed his arrangements for arrival and occupation within a few days, Vereker took his departure. Now that he had lost the first fierce excitement of having struck a strong scent he began to feel uncomfortable in his clerical garb, but came eventually to the conclusion that the disguise must be suffered until he had completed his investigations as far as 10 Glendon Street was concerned. It was a nuisance, this masquerade, but inevitable. He must give the better-known thoroughfares a wide berth—the less his friends knew at present about his adventure in the domain of criminal investigation the better. He could not, however, resist lunch at a well-known little restaurant in Jermyn Street, where the food was an artistic delight, and later dropped into a picture gallery where there was a temporary exhibition of old English water colours. At five o'clock sharp he turned up at his own flat and on Ricardo admitting him was assailed by the odour of grilling kippers.

Ricardo had temporarily donned one of Vereker's painting overalls and, with sleeves rolled up and red face, was doing his best to play the rôle of cook.

"Interesting smell, Ricky!" exclaimed Vereker.

"Nothing to beat 'em, Algernon, my boy, only they want a lot of watching, you know. Another fraction of a second and we're ready. Oh damme! I've forgotten to heat the plates."

"Boiling water's the quickest method," suggested Vereker.

"Then lend a hand and do the needful. The water won't be quite boiling yet, because I made the tea without putting any tea in the pot and had to go back to the starting-post. But, if you'll saw a few chunks of bread and butter, I'll see to the tea."

At length the tea was ready and laid on a rickety table in Vereker's studio in front of an easel on which stood a canvas with a rough charcoal sketch.

Vereker's glance wandered to that sketch and he almost sighed. It took him back to times untroubled by mystery except by the mystery of beauty. Ricardo noticed his expression and turned round to look at the canvas.

"I suppose you'll finish it?" he asked. "What's it supposed to be?"

"An industrial landscape, Ricky. Just near Bricklayers Arms Station, a yard with oil barrels by the score, all shining wet on a drenching winter's day. One of the most heartlessly depressing scenes imaginable, but visually exquisitely beautiful. I'm going to call it 'Civilization'—if I can just capture that light and atmosphere and overwhelming sadness."

"Sounds morbid," suggested Ricardo. "Give me a jolly old picture post card with hollyhocks and a thatched cottage and roses and a girl with a Dolly Varden hat. Something wholesome, you know. I count these first-class kippers, don't you?"

"They're excellent."

"Of course it's the cooking. You'd have spoilt 'em, my old sky-pilot; but tell me all about this sleuth-hound business you're wasting your time at. I guessed it was over the Bygrave affair, but didn't know you were playing an important character part."

Vereker sketched the matter as briefly as he could to Ricardo and, when they had finished tea, cleared the table and promptly emptied his pockets of the contents of the waste-paper-basket that he had stuffed into them at his newly-found lodgings.

"By Jingo, it sounds awfully exciting," exclaimed Ricardo, as he watched his friend deftly sort out the pieces of paper and arrange them on the table until they fitted into their original entities.

"This is absolutely splendid," exclaimed Vereker at last. "Mr. Henry Parker, otherwise Lord Bygrave if I'm not mistaken, leaves a track behind him like an elephant on soft ground."

He sat for a long while examining the writing and comparing it with that of a letter produced from his pocket-book.

Ricardo was looking over his shoulder and wondering what was the cause of his friend's undue excitement.

"What would you say about the writing on the envelope and label that I have just pieced together when compared with that on this letter, Ricky?" asked Vereker at length.

"I suppose I'm to make you shine in the Watsonian manner, Sherlock, eh? I don't bite, old man."

"No; be serious, Ricky. What do you think?"

Ricardo gazed earnestly at the specimens of writing and after some hesitation remarked:

"I'm no expert, but it looks as if the writing on the envelope and label which you have reconstructed is an attempt to disguise the actual handwriting as seen on the letter. From which I deduce by a process unknown to anyone but myself that Lenin and Trotzky—"

Vereker smiled.

"An excellent guess, Ricky. It looks very much like that to me. We don't want your esoteric deductions. More important still is the information conveyed. On the label is the address, 'Mill House, Eyford,' which probably means nothing to you beyond an ordinary address. To me it is most significant. On the envelope is another address, 'Mrs. Cathcart, Bramblehurst, Farnaby, Sussex.'"

"Lord! that's the lady about whose address I inquired some time ago on your behalf. I'd quite forgotten her. Well, you've found out that much, anyway. Who is she, by the way?"

"Looks as if she's going to be the lady in the case," remarked Vereker, and added, "This has been a most fruitful day's work. It's too late to get down to Farnaby to-night, but I must make a point of seeing Mrs. Cathcart before she takes it into her head to change her address once more."

"I believe she's an extremely pretty woman, or rather has been, so Mrs. Parslow told me," mused Ricardo.

"Her looks don't concern me, Ricky. What I want to know is who she is, what she does, what she has done?"

"Futile questionings. If a woman's good-looking what does the rest matter? Don't you remember once quoting your musty old Emerson to me, 'Beauty is the form under which intellect prefers to study the world? Measuring up with that rule, Vereker, I find I'm something like pure intellect."

Vereker was obliged to laugh. "Fancy your remembering that, Ricky!" he exclaimed. "You're a freakish youth!"

"Heavens! I must be off!" exclaimed Ricardo, glancing swiftly at his wrist watch. "Kippers and crime and a dash of the philosophy of beauty are entertaining enough, but I'm taking Molly to dinner to-night. You haven't met Molly yet—she's a peach!"

"I know, and she'll be a pumpkin in about a fortnight's time—good-bye, Ricky. When this case is done with you must accompany me to France. I'm going to have a long holiday in Provence. We shall be troubadours."

"Accepted, Vereker. I love a Romaunt," replied Ricardo, and the door of Vereker's little flat slammed noisily as he vanished.

Vereker donned the overall that Ricardo had flung over a chair and picked up his brushes. He stood for many minutes before his easel lost in a reverie over that scene at Bricklayers Arms. At the moment of conception the significance of the picture had been overwhelming, it carried more than its visual beauty of colour and light and mass and composition. Underneath lay the impersonal tragedy of modern industrial life binding together the whole in a forceful unity. But now! No, he was not in the mood. He flung palette and brushes listlessly down on his table and pulled a chair over to the glowing gas fire. His meeting with Ricardo had been an interlude, a sudden thrust of his normal life into his present absorbing work. He must now return with redoubled ardour into the atmosphere of the mystery of his missing friend—for the moment it must be the Bygrave case and nothing but the Bygrave case!

Chapter Eleven

For over an hour Vereker sat gazing into the orange glow of his gas fire, turning over in his mind the facts of the Bygrave case from the very beginning to the point reached by his recent discoveries at 10 Glendon Street. Those discoveries had finally convinced him that Lord Bygrave had disappeared of his own volition, whatever might be the motive for that disappearance. That Farnish and Winslade were secretly acquainted with the facts of the case was apparent from their clandestine visits to Glendon Street, in the hope that they might see Lord Bygrave on business known only to themselves. Certain facts swung as satellites to this central theory. They might be intimately connected, but at present they moved obscurely.

There was the strange behaviour of Mr. Smale, Lord Bygrave's secretary who, whatever he knew, was discreet enough to refuse to disclose that knowledge. There was the mysterious Mrs. Cathcart, with her unknown history and her receipt of £10,000 worth of bearer bonds from Lord Bygrave. Still unexplained and refusing to fall into any scheme of things was the fact that a drawer had been forced by a screw-driver in Lord Bygrave's study and some paper or papers extracted from one bundle of letters. These were probably significant facts, but the difficulty lay in discovering their orientation.

Lastly, who had impersonated Lord Bygrave at the White Bear Inn? Could it be Farnish? Vereker had thought deeply over this possibility. There were many facts in its favour. Farnish was about the same age and height; he assumed that aloof and reserved mien which his master wore by nature; he had access to his master's clothes; he knew Lord Bygrave's affairs and habits, he alone could have managed to secure the loan of Lord Bygrave's ring for the purpose of creating the belief that Lord Bygrave had actually stayed at the White Bear. The egg breakfast and tobacco were a lapse in cunning, but a pardonable lapse with a man unacquainted with the clever criminal's habit of avoiding glaring mistakes when removing his traces or creating fictitious ones. It was a possibility not to be lightly dismissed.

The underlying motive, however, of all this mystery floated beyond Vereker's ken—that motive could only swim into his vision by the discovery of further facts. He rose suddenly from his chair and crossing over to the table on which lay the reconstructed envelope and luggage label examined them once more. The altered handwriting was pregnant, it was a very ordinary ruse to hide a clue to the writer's identity. Vereker was obliged to smile when he thought of his friend, Henry, descending to these subterfuges. It pointed to the fact that the necessity was urgent, the consequence of discovery calamitous! In no other way could it be explained when taken in conjunction with Lord Bygrave's known probity and upright, almost Puritanical character.

Vereker glanced again at the label. The name was not there, but the address, Mill House, Eyford, fell in with his previous deductions so neatly that the conclusion was inevitable—Winslade had called at Mill House on that memorable Friday night to see Lord Bygrave or had even taken him there from Fordingbridge Junction. In further corroboration Heather had practically proved that Lord Bygrave had not arrived at Hartwood by train. Vereker once more pulled out his ordnance survey map and glanced at the network of roads from Fordingbridge Junction down to Hartwood.

"It seems pretty definite to me now!" he exclaimed. In any case, I hope to prove it within the next few days.

A loud knock at his door startled Vereker from his reverie. Quietly picking up the label and envelope from his table, he walked over to a bureau and thrust them into a drawer containing some unfinished sketches, and then opened the door.

"Come in, Heather, come in!" he exclaimed, as he caught sight of his visitor. "I was just wondering where you had vanished to."

"Oh, I've been poking about town, Mr. Vereker. I had an hour to spare and thought I'd look you up. I felt you'd be here."

Vereker closed the door, ushered the inspector into a comfortable chair and produced whisky, soda and glasses.

Heather glanced inquisitively round the room, and his eyes finally alighted on the easel and canvas.

"Gone back to the old love, Mr. Vereker?" he asked, jerking a thumb in the direction of the sketch.

"No, not yet, Heather. I can only return when I've finished with the present job."

"How are you getting on?"

"Still in a maze, Heather, and yourself?"

"Sure but slow," remarked Heather quietly. "I had a rather startling piece of news this morning. You'll be interested in it, I'm sure."

"You've discovered Lord Bygrave's whereabouts?" questioned Vereker, with sudden excitement and not a little misgiving that he had been beaten in the game.

"Not so rapidly as all that, Mr. Vereker. But we have discovered a rather important factor. Mr. Sidney Smale has suddenly left Bygrave Hall, and at present we've got no trace of him. It looks fishy."

Vereker whistled.

"Farnish is still there?" he asked quickly.

"Oh, yes, Farnish is there. I don't think there's anything wrong with Farnish. But Mr. Smale's quite another proposition. It won't be long before we lay him by the heels. A man doesn't fling up a comfortable, well-paid job without some very good reason. What do you say?"

"But I thought you had decided that the centre of gravity of the Bygrave case had unaccountably shifted to London!" asked Vereker, with a smile.

"So it has, Mr. Vereker."

"Then this discovery about Smale is just a piquant bit of news solely intended for my edification or distraction, Heather?"

"You'll grant it's interesting, Mr. Vereker?"

"Oh, quite, but it points nowhere."

"It may."

"That's possible, but off with the motley, Heather, what have you been discovering in London that's really vital?"

"Ah, now you're treading on forbidden ground. There are certain things we don't disclose even to a promising amateur like yourself," remarked Heather pompously.

"I think I can make a fair guess, Heather. Let me try just for the fun of the thing. Now when you came to the conclusion that Lord Bygrave had not stayed at the White Bear—"

"I didn't come to any such conclusion," interjected Heather, lighting his pipe.

"Well, you were driven to it by my brilliant deductions. I grant I had a big advantage over you because I was intimately acquainted with Lord Bygrave, but that is neither here nor there." Vereker joined in Heather's loud amusement.

"Well, proceed, Mr. Vereker," continued the inspector.

"Having been driven to the conclusion that Lord Bygrave had never put up at the White Bear, you promptly decided to work on the assumption that he never left London."

"Quite true: it's a possibility if not a probability."

"Agreed. Then you directed your inquiries again as to when he left his office, who was there when he left, where he went after he left. What train he caught to Hartwood, etc., if— But, no, in your opinion he never caught the train to Hartwood."

"He never *arrived* at Hartwood," remarked Heather, emphasizing the words with a gesture of his pipe.

"I agree with you in that particular. However, you've searched the whole office, you've gone into his papers, you've tried to find out the relations existing between him and his subordinates, you've inquired about all callers prior to his disappearance—in fact, you have covered every inch of the ground that I as an unmethodical amateur have omitted to cover. But you've omitted to examine one very important particular."

"What is that?" asked Heather, without displaying the vaguest emotion.

"Have you examined the waste paper furnace in the basement of the Ministry offices?"

"I've made a very careful examination of that furnace, Mr. Vereker."

"Splendid, Heather, you are shaping uncommonly well for Scotland Yard. Do you know that that furnace would incinerate a body in a very short space of time."

"What about the odour?" asked the inspector, looking up suspiciously.

"Who could detect that odour? The resident clerk lives on the top floor of the building; the night-watchman would not go down to the basement till ten o'clock at night. They are the only people in the building after six o'clock at the latest. It's a closed furnace with a terrific draught and, after all, I should say roast humanity differs little from roast beef as far as odour is concerned. If the night-watchman on the ground floor detected it he would promptly ascribe it to the resident clerk's kitchen efforts."

"Quite so, and then—?"

"And then you come to the inevitable deadlock. There are Messrs. Grierson, Murray and Bliss—immediate subordinates of Lord Bygrave's. Civil servants of many years standing and unquestionable probity. Now, if Lord Bygrave had been using an economy axe on the Government officials' salaries there would have been reason, and ample reason, for their knocking him on the head and using the furnace as a crematorium; but he wielded no such provocative weapon. Who had any cause for removing his lordship?"

"There's the rub, Mr. Vereker. Now, you have deftly outlined some of the investigations I've made, I'll let you into a little secret. The nightwatchman is an ex-service man, who for over a year after the war was in a lunatic asylum. He was placed there for a violent and quite inexplicable assault on a complete stranger. Investigation into his case brought to light the fact that a shrapnel wound in the head had unhinged the poor fellow's brain. He made a rapid recovery, however, and was then set at liberty. It is possible that the man may have had a recurrence of his homicidal mania.

But there, I shan't tell you any more. I've just given you sufficient information to pique your curiosity. If you're wise you'll inquire into the habits of that night-watchman. I must be going now."

"Well, good night, Heather. You can keep your night-watchman with the homicidal mania. I've no more use for him than you have. He is not the kind of pet I keep. Let me know if you track down Mr. Smale; his sudden disappearance is rather more interesting to me than the propensities of a combative night-watchman. I have still got a niche for him in my mental museum of possible criminals."

"Good night, Mr. Vereker," laughed the inspector.

A few moments afterwards Vereker watched him walking along thoughtfully down the street until he vanished in the dusk. He then resumed his own seat by the fire.

"I wonder just how much Heather knows?" he soliloquized. "He's as impenetrable as a bit of armour plate. Once upon a time I thought I could pull his leg with some grace and a suspicion of humour. Now he is too nimble for my grasp, and actually attempts to pull mine. His visit to this place to-night is probably only the result of his insatiable curiosity to know exactly what I'm doing. His methods are characterized by an amazing thoroughness and an appalling, almost destructive common sense. No flights of imagination for old Heather! To quote my friend Emerson, 'Relation and connection are not somewhere and sometimes but everywhere and always; no miscellany, no exemption, no anomaly but method and an even web; and what comes out, that was put in.' It's the most reliable method after all, I suppose, but there are many ways of solving a problem. The answer's the thing! Strangely enough, he never once mentioned Winslade's name! And as for myself, my chief interest is centred in Winslade—he knows a lot, if not all. He is certainly deeply implicated. Heather has surely not left that line of inquiry untouched? But, then, he's not going to tell me his greatest secrets—instead, he tries to fill me up with some bunkum about maniacal night-watchmen!"

Vereker could not restrain a hearty laugh. He glanced at the clock on the mantelpiece which Ricardo had evidently wound up and set right. It was late and early next day he must get away down to Farnaby to see Mrs. Cathcart. She might be able to throw some light on his darkness.

Vereker rose at six o'clock and, having bathed and shaved, consumed a simple breakfast of porridge and milk, toast and marmalade and tea, rushed off to Waterloo Station and caught the seven o'clock train southwards. He changed at Willow Tree Junction, where he had an hour to wait, and then embarked on the train running down the single line to Farnaby. On the way, his thoughts were unavoidably centred on Mrs. Cathcart. He found himself trying to imagine the type of woman she might be, and somehow or other he could not avoid picturing her as a faded widow, battered by a hard world, and shrivelled into the narrowness and cynicism that accompany ill-usage at the hands of circumstance.

"It's only those who can feel their strength in their struggle with their fellow men who manage to retain the bloom of courageous youth," he thought, and came to the conclusion that this was a feeble generalization. His thoughts got inextricably involved on the difference between moral and physical courage and the retention of youth, and then he suddenly remembered that he was quite unaware what age Mrs. Cathcart might be. Thence his musings flitted to the question of the relation in which she stood to Lord Bygrave. Was it a case of generous help offered on his part to a stranger after being convinced of her hard experience of life— or had she some closer and secret claim on him for pecuniary assistance? Well, he would soon know. His plan of campaign he had already settled. He was going to come straight to the point with regard to the payment to her of £10,000 in bearer bonds. It might be a private affair, but the secret must be divulged in the ordinary course of the solution of the mystery of Lord Bygrave's disappearance. It would not be difficult, on her part, to prove that

that payment had no connexion with subsequent events and once proved the matter could be promptly and discreetly dropped.

On arrival at Farnaby, he lunched at the village inn and somewhat early in the afternoon made his way to Bramblehurst, the location of which he had learnt very circumstantially from the landlord of the inn, who owned the cottage. As he came into view of the place he was struck by the peace and serenity of the surroundings. It was exceptionally warm for an October day, the sun beat down out of a cloudless and beautifully azure sky and a warm south wind came over the land like a passionate caress of the parting autumn. In the garden a riot of colour from dahlias and golden glow and chrysanthemums gladdened the eye and cheered the heart. It was a charming spot. Some one in the cottage was playing a piano. Vereker stopped and listened; it was Chopin's Study in C major, and exquisitely played. His knock at the door put an end to the music, and was answered by a girl of some seventeen years of age, of distinctly prepossessing appearance.

"Is Mrs. Cathcart in?" asked Vereker.

"Yes, but I cannot say whether she will see anybody. I'm rather afraid she's busy and doesn't wish to be disturbed."

"You might plead for me; I've come down from London on rather important business expressly to see her. I'm Lord Bygrave's executor and trustee—my name is Vereker."

"Oh!" said the girl, unable to conceal a start, and vanished. In a few minutes she returned and led Vereker into a tastefully furnished and cheerful little drawing-room.

"Mrs. Cathcart is sorry to keep you waiting, Mr. Vereker," she said pleasantly, "but she will be with you in a few minutes. Pardon my leaving you."

Vereker hoped that this vision, so radiant in appearance and easy in her manner, might stop and beguile the few minutes of his waiting, but he was disappointed. He heard her light footstep on the gravel of the garden path outside and discreetly watched her progress down the garden until she vanished. A few seconds later he heard her footsteps once more now bounding along the path as if running for dear life. Glancing out of the window he caught a momentary, flashing glimpse of a lithe, muslin-clad figure running at top speed followed by a beautiful red setter leaping along delightedly at her flying heels.

"Talk about Atalanta's race!" exclaimed Vereker to himself, and was still eagerly watching those vivid examples of youth and grace when the door opened and Mrs. Cathcart entered.

"Good afternoon, Mr. Vereker; you're admiring my garden, I see," she said diplomatically.

"Well, I had gone further than that, Mrs. Cathcart—I had begun to admire your beautiful Irish setter."

"He is lovely, isn't he? I suppose Lossa has taken him out for a run," she replied.

Delightful name, thought Vereker; it seemed to fit its beautiful owner in the unaccountable way that names generally do. The faintest glimpse of merriment in Mrs. Cathcart's eye told him that she had understood his appreciation of the red setter with that fiendish intuition which the majority of women possess when the admiration of their own sex is in the air. Vereker felt slightly uncomfortable; he disliked to be caught and turned inside out so deftly.

"I hope I've not disturbed you, Mrs. Cathcart," he said, to ease matters for himself, "and I hope you'll forgive my descending on you in this way, but my business is urgent."

"Well, I had told Lossa I was not to be disturbed. You see, I'm busy writing up reminiscences of my chequered career in the hope that I may some day find a publisher. I'm afraid I'm not a practised literary artist and any interruption seems to dry up the fountain of memory—I was going to say inspiration, but that'll hardly do with reminiscences."

"Inspiration helps, Mrs. Cathcart, if the reminiscences are to be more interesting than truthful!" laughed Vereker.

During this preliminary conversation Vereker's eyes had
never left Mrs. Cathcart. He tried swiftly to sum her up, and came
to the conclusion that her age was about thirty-five. She was an
extremely comely woman. The poise of her head was a joy to an
artist and her whole carriage bespoke that agility and acquired
grace of movement which he knew belonged in a superlative
degree to one profession only, that of the stage. Either she was
an actress or a dancer. Her intuitively chosen movements in
crossing to a settee where she could recline with grace and yet be
near enough for conversation told him that it must be the stage.
His glance wandered discreetly from the shapely feet to the even
more shapely hands and thence to the vivacious face, with its alert,
sympathetic eyes, showing every varying colour of her thoughts.
His first resolve on this discovery of her almost magnetic beauty
was to throw up a mental bulwark of defence against her powerful
equipment of feminine charm; it is so easy to acquire bias when
dealing with a fascinating woman. He felt also that he must waste
no time in coming to the business which had been the object of
his excursion to Farnaby, but was already at a loss to know how
to begin. All along, since his first discovery of the presence of a
Mrs. Cathcart in his investigation of the Bygrave mystery, he had
mentally misplaced her. In his mind's eye she had always been a
woman who had sought and obtained pecuniary assistance from
Lord Bygrave, and this conception without any explanatory detail
had in some subtle manner utterly distorted his imaginary portrait
of her. He had conceived a being inclined to shrink from the world
on account of some inability to grapple with it through lack of
mental or physical strength, or both.

Here was a woman radiantly beautiful with a manner
assured yet not provocative; her face alight with quick feminine
intelligence, her attitude full of the quiet well-being that is born
of confidence and lack of cares. He had been prepared to pity and
had been constrained to admire. The discovery necessitated a
quick and complete change of plan on his part. The frontal attack

had to be discarded or carried out in a manner suitable to the changed circumstances. Vereker cursed himself for his utterly unwarranted preconceptions and determined to profit by this discomfiture in future work. As these thoughts flashed swiftly through his mind he glanced up at Mrs. Cathcart. She noticed his hesitation and came swiftly to his rescue.

"Lossa mentioned, Mr. Vereker, when she came up to my room just now, that you were a trustee under Lord Bygrave's will."

"That is so, Mrs. Cathcart, and I'm presuming you know all about his mysterious disappearance."

"Well, I know nothing more than I have read in the daily papers. Naturally, I've been terribly excited about the whole business because I once knew Lord Bygrave extremely well. Have you any news of him?"

"None whatever. It is now some time since his extraordinary disappearance and we are very little nearer discovering what has occurred to him than we were on the fateful day."

"The police, of course, are making inquiries?"

"Oh, yes, and I, as trustee to his estate, am also making certain subsidiary investigations. To come to the point, that is the reason of my call on you to-day. I wonder if you can assist me in any way?"

"I shall be only too glad to do so, Mr. Vereker, if you will let me know how I am to set about it."

"Well, I think the simplest way would be for me to put you through a sort of catechism."

"Before you go any further, Mr. Vereker, I may tell you frankly that there may be some of your questions which I shall flatly refuse to answer."

Vereker glanced up quickly and saw the light of battle in a pair of flashing, brown eyes, and a chin and mouth the set of which disclosed an unexpected strength of concentration and will. She had flung down the gage of combat early in the interview and he felt that a little diplomacy was necessary.

"Well, Mrs. Cathcart, I trust you will give me all the information possible in reply to my questions. My visit to-day may save you any further unpleasant police interrogatory. You must try and meet me half-way when I tread on dangerous ground. An exercise of tact on both sides may evade a heap of subsequent annoyance."

"But, surely, Mr. Vereker," exclaimed Mrs. Cathcart, and her face had assumed a sudden air of anxiety, "the police do not think I am in any way connected with Lord Bygrave's disappearance?"

"They certainly do not, at present," replied Vereker quietly, "but your name has cropped up in the course of their inquiries and they would naturally like to be satisfied that you are not concerned."

"I see. Well, I suppose the situation must be faced, though as far as I can see it's going to be most annoying. Please go ahead with the catechism, Mr. Vereker, and I'll reply to the best of my ability."

"When did you first meet Lord Bygrave, Mrs. Cathcart?" asked Vereker, taking out his memorandum pad.

"Exactly twenty years ago. I was then seventeen and he was about twenty-six."

"Did you know him well or was he merely an acquaintance?"

"We were lovers: I'm afraid it implies that we knew nothing of one another at all." A shadow seemed to flit across the woman's serene brow and vanish as quickly as it had appeared. She looked at Vereker, and a charming smile chased the shadow.

"You subsequently knew one another better?" asked Vereker tactfully.

"We thought we did, and parted. You see, I had just decided to take up singing as a career and we disagreed very thoroughly on the subject of the stage as a suitable career for a woman."

"Have you kept up your friendship during these twenty years?"

"No, the rupture was final. I went to America and earned my own living there and I never saw Lord Bygrave again until the early part of this year."

"Have you been in England long?"

"No. I only came a month prior to my calling on Lord Bygrave."

"Now, Mrs. Cathcart, I feel I'm approaching the forbidden ground. May I ask why you called on Lord Bygrave?"

For a fraction of a second Mrs. Cathcart seemed to Vereker to hesitate, and then she replied somewhat casually.

"Well, it's difficult to give any definite reason. Things of the heart, of memory, of sentiment, are not very easily definable. You can understand, perhaps, that I wanted out of sheer morbid curiosity to rake among the ashes of a past fire.

"Yes, I can," replied Vereker quickly, "I feel that I am sentimentalist enough to comprehend."

"Good! Well, I wanted to see Henry again; to see how he looked, to see how he compared with the man I had once loved—"

"And you have not seen him since, Mrs. Cathcart?"

"No, I have not; before I called on him I felt that it would probably be the last time I should see him. I did not go there with the intention of resuming a friendship or a love affair."

"Has he written to you since?"

"No, but I have been in communication with his secretary, Mr. Smale, on a matter the nature of which I'm afraid I cannot divulge. In any case, it is of no importance to anyone in the world but ourselves."

"Well, we'll leave it for the present, Mrs. Cathcart, but I may just refer to it again in connexion with a further inquiry. Could you identify Lord Bygrave's handwriting if I showed you a specimen?"

"I think so."

Vereker produced from his pocket-book the envelope addressed to Mrs. Cathcart that he had gathered from the waste-paper-basket at 10 Glendon Street, and handed it to her. He keenly watched the expression of her face as she read her own name and address and noticed a swift blanching of her cheeks as a look of sudden fear entered her eyes.

"Yes, that is Lord Bygrave's writing. But how did he get to know my present address and how did you come by this envelope,

Mr. Vereker?" she asked, as with trembling fingers she passed it back to her visitor,

"Well, Mrs. Cathcart, I can't tell you how he discovered your present address. It was this envelope which made me ask you if you had heard from Lord Bygrave since your interview with him some months ago. It was through this envelope I discovered your whereabouts, and I found the envelope in a room in 10 Glendon Street."

"Good heavens! is Lord Bygrave staying there?" asked Mrs. Cathcart, aghast.

"No—not at present—he left there some days ago and now we've lost all trace of him again. By the way, you yourself have stayed with Mrs. Parslow at Glendon Street, Mrs. Cathcart?"

"Yes, that was another sentimental visit of mine. When in England in the early days of my struggle to get a footing and a hearing on the stage it was a well-known lodging-house for female members of our profession, and I returned to renew its acquaintance. What puzzles me now is how on earth Lord Bygrave got to know my present address; I took good care on leaving Glendon Street to let nobody know my destination."

"That I can't say. Of course Lord Bygrave knew you had stayed at Glendon Street?"

"Oh, yes, that is where his secretary, Mr. Smale, came and interviewed me."

"To revert to a former question, Mrs. Cathcart, may I ask if that interview concerned money matters?"

"It had absolutely nothing to do with money matters, Mr. Vereker," said Mrs. Cathcart precisely, and once more the fire of combat lit her eye.

The challenge on this occasion piqued Vereker and, cost what it might, he decided to accept it. Producing her receipt for the bearer bonds from his pocket, he handed it to her and asked:

"It had therefore nothing to do with this particular transaction, Mrs. Cathcart? Kindly forgive my referring to it, but as Lord Bygrave's trustee and executor I have naturally to probe into these matters."

"What's the meaning of this?" asked Mrs. Cathcart, aghast. "A receipt for £10,000 of bearer bonds purporting to be signed by me. It's an impudent forgery! I have never in my life received £10,000 worth of bearer bonds from Lord Bygrave," and before Vereker could prevent it she had torn the receipt into fragments and flung them angrily in the fender. Rising from her settee she stamped a neat but vicious foot on the floor. "How dare you insult me, sir?" she asked.

"Mrs. Cathcart," said Vereker quickly, "I have not the slightest wish to offend you in any way. Please try and understand my position. I am striving to elucidate the strange mystery of my friend's disappearance, and during my investigation I have been obliged to go through all his papers. This receipt I came upon in Lord Bygrave's bureau. Instead of handing it over to the police I have taken a considerable risk in keeping it to myself and inquiring clandestinely whether it had any connexion whatever with Lord Bygrave's disappearance. As an intelligent woman who knows the world, you can clearly see why I took this line of action. That the receipt proves a forgery reveals to me that I must pursue my investigations in quite a different direction. I am delighted to find that it is so and that I shall not have to trouble you further in the matter."

"I trust you'll forgive me, Mr. Vereker," replied Mrs. Cathcart, her anger vanishing as swiftly as it had arisen. "I have a most devilishly hasty temper and I couldn't control myself in the face of that outrageous lie." She glanced at the fragments of the receipt in the fender and suddenly kneeling down began to pick them up carefully.

Vereker's appreciative eye took in at a glance the suave, graceful curves of that kneeling figure; he beheld for a moment the snowy nape of a beautifully modelled neck; with the jet hair swept and caught above by some discreetly jewelled comb; it was an unforgettable pose. The next moment he was on his knees too.

"Let me pick them up, Mrs. Cathcart," he said, "please don't you trouble. I can manage it."

By some chance, for which Vereker could never afterwards account, her hand touched his and it seemed to him that the contact thrilled him through and through. To his immense relief Mrs. Cathcart at once arose and, placing the fragments of paper she had gathered from the fender on an occasional table, sat down in a chair. Vereker gathered up the remaining fragments and placing them in an envelope returned them to his pocket-book.

"Have you any idea, Mr. Vereker, who could have perpetrated such a cruel forgery as that receipt?" asked Mrs. Cathcart calmly.

"I think I have a shrewd suspicion, Mrs. Cathcart," replied Vereker, "and I shall at once give it my attention."

"I trust it won't bring me into any publicity."

"I don't see why it should."

"Because I have a very cogent reason why I should not in any way be connected with Lord Bygrave. You have given me your trust, Mr. Vereker, over the matter of this receipt; you have clearly shown me that you believe me, and I am going now to reciprocate your trust. May I?"

"I shall be glad, Mrs. Cathcart."

"Well, to begin with; you wanted to know exactly why I visited Lord Bygrave on my return to England. I'm afraid I didn't tell you the whole truth, but I will do so now. At seventeen years of age I was married to Lord Bygrave in the little church here at Farnaby. As I have told you, we couldn't see eye to eye on the subject of my trying to fulfil my ambition as to a stage career—preferably in opera—and before many weeks we had quarrelled and parted. Perhaps it was my fault. I am very self-willed and I know I have an unpardonable temper. In any case I went to America and forgot all about Henry, and I presume he consigned my memory to a similar oblivion. I carried out my intention with regard to a career and made a tolerable success as a singer in the States, where I was known as Ida Wister."

"I have heard of your fame, Mrs. Cathcart—you made more than a tolerable success of your career. You were a star; but I'm interrupting."

"Well, having made sufficient money to retire on, I determined to return to England and enjoy life quietly; for the career of a singer is no sinecure and is really one long series of self-restraints and gruelling efforts. I am by nature a slacker, I'm afraid, and once the flame of ambition died I saw no further wisdom in mortifying the flesh for the sake of money, for that was the logical conclusion of continuing my work. I had reached my full powers and knew I could go no further in the way of achievement."

"Have you no duties to your fellow-creatures, Mrs. Cathcart? Your voice was a gift to you," interrupted Vereker in his old vein.

"I'll think of that when I have finished my reminiscences, Mr. Vereker, and now I am going to tell you why I called on Lord Bygrave. I did not do so to get financial assistance in the way of £10,000 worth of bearer bonds. I went to ask him if I might divulge in my memoirs the fact of our early marriage. He begged me not to do so and I gave him my word of honour that I would respect his wishes. There the matter ended and I have neither seen nor heard from Lord Bygrave since that day."

At this moment the sound of light footsteps on the gravel path outside signalled the return of Lossa and her red setter.

"Your daughter, I presume, Mrs. Cathcart?" asked Vereker.

"No; merely an adopted child," replied Mrs. Cathcart, and rose as if to signify that the interview was terminated. "Mrs. Cathcart is merely an assumed name. I do not wish to be recognized at present as Ida Wister, so please do not give me away."

"My lips are sealed," replied Vereker, smiling, and took his leave.

On reaching the corner of the lane in which Bramblehurst stood he chanced to glance back and saw Mrs. Cathcart at an upstairs window evidently seated at her writing-desk. She caught that backward glance of Vereker's and gaily waved her hand in adieu. Vereker raised his hat in salutation and the next moment he turned the corner.

"Algernon," he remarked to himself, "you're a damned impressionable fool—and she knew you would look back, you simpleton. She's spun you a nice little yarn, I bet."

When he reached Farnaby Station, however, his thoughts had temporarily taken another turn, for he was thinking to himself that of all the young cads he had ever met it appeared that Sidney Smale aspired to the questionable honour of being the worst.

Chapter Twelve

As Vereker travelled back to town that afternoon he found, in spite of himself, that his thoughts continued to alternate between those that were distinctly annoying and those that were strangely intoxicating. The source of his annoyance was the unpleasant personality of Sidney Smale, for that personality had, in an unexpected way, thrust itself with a jarring lunge into a delicately framed edifice of theory about the Bygrave mystery. And he had appeared in a most sinister garb, especially in the light of Heather's recent information as to his sudden disappearance. That Mrs. Cathcart had not received those bearer bonds Vereker was inclined to believe. The difficulty was that he could not be certain.

"Now let us be frank," he soliloquized. "You have been most favourably impressed by a very beautiful woman. She has denied receiving any money from Lord Bygrave, and you are averse to thinking that this prepossessing lady is capable of lying. Perhaps you are biased by some early habit of associating beauty with goodness. You must thrust this habit from you when dealing with criminal investigation. Especially as an amateur. The lady, in spite of the impression made by her charms, may be a most unreliable character. The anger she displayed might have been assumed: such an assumption would be the easiest thing in the world to a woman of great dramatic talent, as undoubtedly she was. Yet, again, even though she had prevaricated about the £10,000 worth of bearer bonds, she might be entirely innocent of any connexion with Lord Bygrave's disappearance. But how had he discovered her address at Farnaby? Why had he desired to write to her again! She was his wife!"

This last piece of information had come as a lively shock to Vereker. Intimate as he had been with Henry Darnell, he had never been allowed to peep into the cupboard containing that skeleton! Vereker laughed at the word "skeleton" as it passed through his mind. She was an altogether delightful skeleton even though her temper had been incompatible with a lifelong domestic association with Bygrave. Vereker, as he thought of her—he called her by her professional name of Ida Wister to himself—could see very clearly what a wide abyss separated her vivacious, self-assured, volatile temperament from the diffident, grave and studious Bygrave. And what a beautiful head and neck she had! And hands and feet! How he would like to hear her sing! After hearing her, he felt it would be more difficult than ever to credit her with anything evil. He must avoid hearing her sing! Really fine art would bias his mind hopelessly in her favour. Then his thoughts oscillated swiftly to Mr. Sidney Smale. Could he possibly have appropriated that £10,000 worth of bearer bonds and, when the moment was favourable, disappeared? The receipt was, according to Mrs. Cathcart, a shameless forgery. Could Smale have perpetrated that forgery? If Lord Bygrave had discovered that forgery and taxed Smale with it—the assumption pointed to a possibly grave conclusion! Why had he surrendered the receipt? It was a risky, if bold move in a game of bluff. The matter was bewildering. No, it was useless to try and fit these pieces into the picture at the present. They must be laid aside; perhaps they were odd pieces from some other puzzle that had nothing to do with the Bygrave case proper. It looked suspiciously like it at a first glance. So much for that!

When Vereker reached his flat that evening he returned to the garb and name of the Rev. Passingham Patmore and made his way to Glendon Street, carrying with him some drawing material to pass away the time of his sojourn at that address. He knew that otherwise the sojourn meant a species of incarceration for some days with time hanging heavily on his hands. On arrival he at once retired to his room and wrote a letter to David Winslade asking him to call with regard to matters concerning Mr. Henry Parker, and signed it with his assumed name—he felt that the ruse offered a chance of a dramatic meeting—and, with a quickened sense of excitement, walked to the pillar-box at the corner of Glendon Street and posted it. On his return Mrs. Parslow was busy in his room laying the table for his supper. He soon discovered that Mrs. Parslow was a woman ever ready to enter into conversation and obstinately slow to desist from it once it had commenced. Hers was a clear mind which held tenaciously to the main subject, though continually slipping down explanatory by-ways. Before he retired that evening he had discovered that there was only one other fellow-lodger in the house, an American, Drayton C. Bodkin by name, who had arrived the morning after Mr. Henry Parker had so suddenly left.

The following day hung heavily on Vereker's hands. It was a dull pause in the very midst of the most exciting part of a game. He ventured out of doors only to get a supply of tobacco, and during the afternoon pottered about with some drawing, but could not get deeply absorbed in it owing to the distraction of expected events.

In the evening Mr. Drayton C. Bodkin asked if he might come and smoke a pipe with him. Vereker willingly acceded to the request and passed a very pleasant evening with the American. Mr. Bodkin was a journalist who was intent on writing an intimate book on London and Londoners for the edification of his compatriots. He was not going to live in the orthodox way of Americans in England. He was out to discover things for himself and not allow the hospitality of Englishmen to pull the wool over his eyes. From his own account, Vereker was informed that Mr. Drayton C. Bodkin was neither a bone-head nor a mutt nor a hike, but had something lively always doing in the cocoa. Most of his compatriots, at least in his own profession, were dead from the knees upwards. That sort of state was the least desirable one in the world for a journalist, who must be right there from the word "Go."

Vereker was in a mood to listen and thoroughly enjoyed Mr. Drayton C. Bodkin's information about himself and the world, couched in his vivid and arresting phraseology. He wondered as he listened how long it would take to get tired of that continual straining after the explosive in language, and whether Englishmen could ever get over their culture of reticence to stomach easily American gush and genial vulgarity. Perhaps the world's future depended upon an emulsion of these two antagonistic ingredients. It was late when Mr. Bodkin, after finishing his last whisky and averring that he was lit up like a cathedral, bade Vereker good night and good-bye. He was going next morning; stagnation was impossible for a man who liked to see a "chemical hustle in the grey-matter."

Next morning, after breakfast, Vereker watched the departure of America's representative on his voyage of discovery in the land of racial characteristics, and wished him good fortune and the divine blessings of an understanding mind and a kind heart. Shortly afterwards Mrs. Parslow handed him in a wire which came from David Winslade and stated that he would call at four o'clock. The result was a sense of excitement tempered with a feeling akin to shame.

"The fly is going to walk into the spider's parlour," he said to himself, "but I'm afraid, in spite of its necessity, the action of the spider is not morally alluring. However, it's got to be done."

The time between ten and four o'clock was going to flit on leaden wings; of this Vereker was confident; to counteract the perception of its tardiness something was to be done. He would

pay a visit to the National Gallery, lunch at the grill room of the
Grand, stroll through the Mall and get back to Glendon Street at
the pace of a lazy camel. He was on the point of setting out and
was about to descend the flight of stairs from his room to the
ground floor when he heard the booming of a now very familiar
voice. He was at once startled and amused and perplexed. Quickly
going downstairs, he was on the point of acquainting Mrs. Parslow
with his plans for the day when that lady emerged from the
drawing-room with Detective-Inspector Heather. At sight of the
latter Vereker could not restrain a hearty laugh.

"Hello, Heather; our courses seem to be running parallel."

"Good heavens, Mr."—he deftly omitted the surname—"what
on earth brings you here?" asked the detective, with a look of
astonishment.

"I wanted a quiet little retreat where I should not be disturbed
by callers and, knowing of this address, I decided to put up here.
And you? What wind blew you to these shores?"

"Oh, only the ordinary course of business. I see you are just
going out."

"Yes, I'm going down to the National Gallery for inspiration
about the Bygrave case."

Heather smiled. "Well, I'll come along a little of the way with
you, if I may."

"By all means, Heather," replied Vereker genially.

The two men sallied forth. As they passed out of Glendon
Street Vereker again returned to the question of Heather's visit
to No. 10. There was something so unexpected in the inspector's
sudden appearance at that address that Vereker was distinctly
piqued.

"Now, Heather, be frank about this ordinary course of
business which brought you to Mrs. Parslow's. What on earth did
you want there?"

"I thought that would prick your curiosity, Mr. Vereker.
Well, I came to see if I could find a Mr. Drayton C. Bodkin, who

purports to be an American citizen. Unfortunately he has already taken his departure."

"You don't mean to say he's involved in the Bygrave case?" asked Vereker abruptly.

"Well, no, I can't say that he is. You must remember that the Bygrave case is not the only mystery with which we have to deal at Scotland Yard. Now, did you see this American gentleman?"

"Yes; I had quite a long conversation with him. He is an American journalist, and came up to my expectations of such, for I have never met one in the flesh before. He was shrewd, quick to form a facile generalization, vivid, ready to exaggerate in an overpowering desire to be interesting to the average listener, a good fellow, genial, not easily deterred by any rebuff, ambitious and as curious as a child—that's a sketchy portrait of him, but, I think, a fairly good likeness."

"You wouldn't credit him with being a continental crook wanted by the police of France, America, Italy, Austria and few other nations thrown in?" asked Heather quietly.

"Good Lord! You don't mean to tell me, Heather, that my estimate of a man can be so far from the mark as all that?" exclaimed Vereker with some surprise.

"Well, Mr. Vereker, a man who can hoodwink two continents is not going about among his fellow men with a character that can be read like an open book, eh? It's quite within the bounds of possibility that he has deceived you as well as the two continents."

"Quite neatly put, Heather! I like the undercurrent of sarcasm; it's a shade heavy, but let that pass. On the other hand, seeing that Mr. Drayton C. Bodkin is so clever, how is it that the C.I.D. know so much about him?"

Heather burst into loud laughter.

"That's simply told, Mr. Vereker. We've got all our information from the French and American police. I don't know what we'd do without these wonderful foreign detectives, but this is in strict confidence." Inspector Heather perpetrated a portentously heavy wink and added, with a smile. "I rely on your reverence not to give our incompetence away to the public."

With this last sally he left Vereker musing with some perplexity as to just what Mr. Drayton C. Bodkin was wanted for, and entertaining a distinct suspicion that once again Inspector Heather had managed to effect that delicate operation known "leg-pulling."

Just before four o'clock in the afternoon Vereker returned to his room at Glendon Street, and it was with a heightened sense of excitement that he awaited Winslade's arrival. Punctually at four he heard the front door bell ring and, glancing out of his window, saw that his expected caller had arrived. Mrs. Parslow, who had been asked to show him in without delay, answered the bell, and soon his firm tread resounded on the creaking stairs of the old house. Vereker casually met him at the door of his room and extended his hand.

"Come in, Winslade, come in," he said.

For a few moments Winslade looked with hesitating curiosity at Vereker, and then turned suddenly pale.

"You, Vereker!" he stammered uneasily. "What the devil are you doing here? What's the meaning of this?"

"Sit down, Winslade, and let me explain matters. At present I'm masquerading as the Rev. Passingham Patmore. As you know, I have been endeavouring for some time past to elucidate the mystery of your uncle's strange disappearance, and I eventually tracked him to the present address. I believe you were aware that he came here subsequent to that disappearance."

For some moments David Winslade failed to reply. His face was a study in annoyance, and that annoyance arose out of a keen sense of shame, for had not Vereker found him out in some unequivocal lying? He paced up and down the room with flushed cheeks and tightly pressed lips.

"Well, Vereker," he said at length, as if with some feeling of relief, "I'm not going to lie about the matter any more. You have already detected me in some departures from the truth, and I feel it will ease my conscience to make a clean breast of things and let you know all that is to be known. The only condition of my speaking, however, is that I must enjoin the very strictest secrecy on your part. The action I have so far taken in this extraordinary business has not been of my own choice. What I have done has been done in the interests of Uncle Henry. You can imagine that the reason for my conduct has been an extremely urgent one, for though I have never claimed to be a rival of George Washington I certainly have an aversion to being called a disciple of Ananias."

"I can quite understand how distasteful your prevarication must have been to you, Winslade," said Vereker, "and I feel that the affair must be a very grave one to drive you to such a course as far as I was concerned."

"It was a matter of life and death, Vereker. It was impossible for me willingly to divulge my secret to anyone. Besides, I'd given a pledge to my uncle. I was between the devil and the deep sea."

"I don't think your uncle, who was my friend and who trusted me implicitly, would have minded your confiding in me, Winslade."

"Perhaps not, Vereker, but he gave me no instructions on that point. From his silence I could only infer that he felt that too many people were already privy to the whole ghastly affair. Even now I'm afraid you are not alive to the seriousness of the situation as far as all of us who know anything about it are concerned. Can I ask you before I speak that you will not use any information that I may give against my uncle?"

"I am one of his greatest friends," replied Vereker calmly. "You must let me know the facts of the case. In any circumstances is it likely that I would consciously do anything to injure your uncle?"

"Well, to put it as briefly as possible, Vereker, he has killed a man—and is anxious to keep out of the clutches of the law."

"Good God, you don't mean to say so!" exclaimed Vereker, overwhelmed with the suddenness and seriousness of the news.

"It's impossible, Winslade, impossible! I can't believe it. There must be some awful mistake—an accident. Why, Henry Darnell could never kill a beetle, much less a human being!"

"I'm afraid that is the terrible truth, Vereker. The man he killed was a damned scoundrel, if that's any justification for taking a human life, but let me tell you everything from the beginning and leave you to judge for yourself. As you are aware, Uncle Henry set out on the evening of the 1st of October on a brief holiday, which he intended to spend at Hartwood. One of the principal reasons for his visiting our neighbourhood was to see Miss Mary Standish, for from the first he was hostile to our engagement owing to the disparity between our social positions. I am reminding you of all this, though you probably remember that I have told you it all before."

"I remember quite well, Winslade; but proceed.

"Well, a few days before his intended visit to Hartwood he asked me to meet him at Fordingbridge Junction and motor him round through Eyford and Castleton to his destination. He had arranged, as you are aware, to put up at the White Bear Inn."

"And you took him to the Mill House at Eyford on your way, I presume," commented Vereker quietly.

Winslade looked up sharply.

"You have found that out?" he asked.

"It was merely an assumption. You remember you told me your car broke down opposite the Mill House. I assumed that this was camouflage in case anyone had seen your car on the road at that spot. It was unreasonable to think you chose that appalling route without some definite purpose. The rest was a wild guess on my part."

"It was a very shrewd guess, Vereker," replied Winslade. "To resume. On meeting my uncle at Fordingbridge he informed me that he wished to stop at the Mill House because he had an important appointment with the occupant, and from the general tone of his remarks I gathered that it was going to be a none too pleasant function."

"Who was this occupant of the Mill House?" asked Vereker.

"I know nothing whatever about him. From subsequent but extremely guarded inquiries I learned that he went by the name of Twistleton—a Mr. Twistleton. He was only in the place a week, but the villagers gathered even in that short space of time that he was a solitary sort of man who lived entirely alone and looked after himself."

"Did he run a car?" asked Vereker, remembering the wheel tracks up the drive.

"Not to my knowledge, but let me proceed. After I had met my uncle at Fordingbridge I had to go and get my car out of Layham's garage. As you know, it is at the other end of the village and, instead of accompanying me there, my uncle said he would walk on and let me overtake him. I picked him up about half a mile out of Fordingbridge, and we ran without any stop to the Mill House. He asked me to pull up about a hundred yards from the gate, because he did not wish it to be known by Mr. Twistleton that he was accompanied. This I did and, with the parting remark that he would not be long, he disappeared."

"What, in your opinion, Winslade, was Bygrave's general state of mind at the time? Was he calm or much perturbed?" asked Vereker.

"I could see he was ill at ease; though, as you know, it took a great deal to ruffle my uncle's serenity. Before arriving at Mill House he spoke as if the matter was one of those unpleasant interviews that are the lot of nearly all of us from time to time. Of the object of the interview he did not tell me until afterwards. I waited about an hour at the point at which we had halted and, remembering his remark that he would not be long, I grew uneasy."

"Did you remain in your car the whole time?"

"Practically. I had a thermos flask of tea and some sandwiches with me, and passed some of the time in refreshing myself. I had had a light lunch, and a busy afternoon had prevented my having tea at the usual time. My housekeeper had, however, put the sandwiches and tea in my car in the morning, knowing that at times it is difficult for me to return home regularly for meals. At the end of an hour my uneasiness verged on anxiety, so I thought I would look into matters. I drove the car quietly up to the gates of the house and waited there for a few minutes."

"You heard no cry or loud conversation?"

"Not a sound; so I got out of the car and walked up the drive—if it can be called a drive—and approached the house. The front door was wide open. This surprised me at the moment; I don't know why, but I suppose by this time my nerves were getting jumpy. The very place was enough to give any man a fit of depression: the dark yews, the gloomy facade of the old building and, in the air, a damp musty smell betraying a garden sheltered from freshening winds—you know the odour of moss and wet undergrowth! I stood at the door and listened, and thought I heard the dull thud of footsteps in the upper part of the house. Straight in front of me, running up from the small hall, was a flight of stairs which terminated in a landing. Thence the staircase swung round spirally to the right and was lost to view. On the wall just above the landing was fixed an ordinary kerosene lamp with a pear-shaped funnel and a reflector—one of those old-fashioned lamps now only seen in remote country villages. It had evidently been placed there to light up the staircase—but only seemed to accentuate the general gloom. As there seemed to be nobody about downstairs, I took the liberty of stepping into the hall, and had barely done so when I heard the sharp slam of a door upstairs, and footsteps came hurrying down the first flight of steps to the landing above me.

"It was my uncle. On reaching the landing he uttered a low cry and promptly extinguished the oil lamp on the wall. 'Is that you, David?' he whispered hoarsely. 'Yes. What's the matter, Uncle Henry?' I asked anxiously. 'For God's sake keep quiet!' he said and came noiselessly and rapidly down the last flight of steps into the hall. There he caught me by the arm, and I could feel that he was trembling violently. 'For Heaven's sake get me away from here,

David!' he gasped. 'I've killed him—the blackmailing swine. Good God, what shall I do?'

"I could only just get the sense of his words; he was speaking in an undertone and jerkily, for he was shaking with agitation and horribly unstrung. I tried to get him to sit down and calm himself, for such a stupendous crisis requires the utmost control of mind and nerves, 'Look here, Uncle Henry,' I said, 'collect yourself. We've got to look at matters calmly. We must come to a quick decision as to what you are going to do. Remember I'm willing to stick to you right through this matter—if you make one false step we are both undone.' 'Get me away quick, David,' he repeated, 'there's not one moment to lose. We'll think things out later— later—not now."

"With these words he ran out the door and down the drive with me following at his heels. Opening the gate he looked round and, seeing nobody about, he jumped into the rear portion of my four-seater and flung himself in a huddled heap on the floor of the car. 'Drive on to the White Bear Inn at Hartwood,' he whispered as I took my place at the wheel, and next moment we were off at top-speed. For some time I drove in silence, thinking of nothing but putting space between us and the Mill House, and thanking Fate that there was not a soul on the road. As we approached Hartwood, just where the road bends round and then bifurcates near the old cow-pond—"

"I know exactly," interrupted Vereker. "There is a short cut across the fields from that point to Hartwood which comes out near the White Bear Inn."

"Quite so. Well, as we approached that point my uncle spoke again, and now in more natural tones, for he had had time to pull himself together. 'Drive slowly, but don't stop,' he said. 'Tomorrow I shall be at 10 Glendon Street, West. Post me some money there. Address the letter to Henry Parker, but don't try to see me. I want to be alone for a day or two to think things over and make my plans. Remember, 10 Glendon Street.' And before I had time to realize what was happening he had leaped off the car and vanished into the darkness. I pulled up and shouted after him, but there was no reply. Thinking I heard a footstep coming along the road behind me, I started off again at a slow pace and, further up the road, halted once more and pretended to be attending to my engine until the late wayfarer had passed. But evidently I had made some mistake, for no one passed; and, though I listened with every faculty on the alert, I heard no sound on the road. Now, for the first time since we had left the Mill House, I had leisure to think calmly and, taking my seat in the car, began to look the whole horrible business in the face.

"The more I thought of it the more was I impressed with the gravity of the affair. Knowing the fine pitch to which detection of crime has been brought by our Criminal Investigation Department, I was convinced that if we made the slightest slip or left a single clue behind us detection would inevitably follow. At the same time the unpleasant truth dawned on me that I might be considered an accomplice, and with this realization my nerves seemed to steady themselves in a flash and I began to think rapidly and coolly. I felt I was now inextricably involved in the affair and that I must do everything in my power to cover up my uncle's tracks, for on his safety depended my own. On looking back this seems a selfish point of view, but after all the instinct for self-preservation seems to blossom out luxuriously in a crisis. I thought of all that the discovery of my uncle's deed implied. I thought of his ruin and degradation; of my own; of Mary, to whom I was virtually engaged. I must act, and act quickly. In the first place, had my uncle left any personal trace of his visit to the Mill House? In his perturbation he might have forgotten gloves, stick—anything. One clue and all was up with him. I must go back, and, though the step was one fraught with all manner of risks, I decided that it was the wisest move in the circumstances. I would return, make sure that not a trace of his presence had been left behind and then make for home at top-speed.

"Turning my car, I fairly hogged it back to the Mill House and was within a hundred yards of the place when I became aware that there was some one on the road in front of me. I could hear voices speaking in loud tones, and the speakers seemed to be standing together at a spot that I judged was right in front of the Mill House gate. I cursed their unexpected presence and die away. Good—my luck was holding. You cannot imagine what a relief I experienced! Running the car off the road into a vacant space where stones were usually stored, I put out the lights, hared it to the Mill House and ran up the drive. The place was in darkness and not a sound was to be heard. Pulling out a flash lamp which I always carried, I found the front door open as we had left it, and promptly entered. I determined to make a swift and thorough examination of the place, and decided to commence on the upper floor, for it is a two-storied building.

"I mounted the stairs and entered the first room on the landing. It was a bedroom. One glance round sufficed; it had not been occupied. A bed-spread covered the bare mattress; every piece of furniture was in place and undisturbed. Systematically I visited the other rooms, with a similar result. I had come to the last room! I opened the door with a heightened sense of excitement, for I knew it must be the room containing the body of the dead man! Flashing my electric torch round I discovered that this room had been furnished as a library: book-shelves lined the wall; a table with a thick, dark, chenille table-cover stood in the centre of the room; a blotting-pad with an inkstand and pens lay on the table. A slight odour of tobacco still pervaded the air, betraying its recent occupancy. One of the pens lying across the heavy cut-glass ink-bottle was still moist with ink. Two chairs were drawn up at the table, and these I presumed were the chairs on which my uncle and his blackmailing acquaintance had sat. All this, which I took in at a glance, was of minor interest to me at the moment. I hurried round to the other side of the table and flashed my lamp over the thickly carpeted floor—to discover an overturned chair, the only evidence of any recent haste or violence in the room. Where, I asked myself in consternation, was the body of the man whom my uncle averred he had killed? There was not a trace of it!

"A great sense of relief at once surged over me. I promptly came to the conclusion that the man could only have been stunned and, having recovered his senses, had decamped. But on second thoughts I felt this was a hasty conclusion; he must have staggered into some other room and died there. Ah! I had forgotten the bathroom. After a final glance round the library I hastened thither; but the result was the same. There was no body there! What on earth could be the solution of this mystery? I thought of my car standing by the side of the road to be observed and noted by any passer-by, and with that thought I became conscious that every moment of delay was dangerous and bore on its swift wings the risk of discovery. Hastening downstairs, I made a rapid but thorough search of all the ground-floor rooms—in vain! Quietly closing the front door of the house, I departed, hastened to my car and drove speedily home."

"H'm," interrupted Vereker, quietly lighting a cigarette. "There's just one point that intrigues me, Winslade. Do you remember, when you first arrived at the Mill House, whether the gas-lamp just outside the gate was alight?"

Winslade's brow wrinkled with thought. He hesitated as if in doubt, and then his face lit up with recollection.

"It was. I remember distinctly observing my foreshortened shadow flung on the rising gravel path. It struck me at the moment, in my excited state, as something rather grotesque. Strange that you should have asked the question."

"Can you say whether it was alight when you and your uncle left the house together?"

For some moments Winslade was buried in thought, striving to recall all his observations during those critical moments.

"No," he said, shaking his head with a gesture of weariness, "I can't remember. My thoughts were entirely centred on getting my uncle away from the wretched place. I can't even bring to mind whether it was alight when I returned by myself."

"That's unfortunate—so much depends upon this seemingly trifling point," remarked Vereker, his gaze wandering idly to the strip of azure sky visible above the roofs opposite.

For some moments there was silence. Vereker seemed utterly buried in his own speculations. Winslade sat with his hands clasped and his eyes fixed expectantly on the shrewd face of the man in front of him.

"When your uncle left you near the cow-pond he presumably took the field path across to the White Bear?" asked Vereker casually.

"Obviously. He stayed at the inn for the night and then incontinently vanished, as far as the world is concerned. As you know, he came here."

"Yes. What did you do about money?"

"I sent him fifty pounds in Treasury notes next day by Farnish, who thrust them through the letter-box."

"How did Farnish get to know he was here?"

"I told Farnish. I was obliged to let him into my confidence for one very good reason. On thinking matters over, I came to the conclusion that this man, Twistleton, must have written to my uncle fixing the appointment to meet him at the Mill House. Where was that letter? If it was at Bygrave Hall among his papers I must get hold of it and destroy it. It would have proved a most informative clue to the police had Mr. Twistleton's body been subsequently found."

"Now I understand why one of the drawers of Lord Bygrave's writing-bureau was forced."

"Farnish was the culprit," remarked Winslade, with a wan smile. "You can imagine his relief when he discovered Mr. Twistleton's letter in the first bundle of papers he opened."

"You destroyed it, of course?"

"You bet your boots!"

"A pity; but still you took a safe course. By the way, you haven't seen your uncle since?"

"No. He left here some time ago and I'm still waiting to hear from him. He left word with Mrs. Parslow that he would write to me when opportunity and circumstances permitted." With these words Winslade glanced anxiously at his watch. "Good Lord," he added, "how the time's flown! I must be getting back to Hartwood. I promised to meet Mary this evening."

Vereker rose from his chair.

"Don't let me detain you, Winslade, if you want to catch a train. I must say your story is an amazing one. Naturally, I shall keep the whole matter entirely to myself. There are several points about it that completely puzzle me at present. I may want to discuss certain details with you over again; in that case, I'll come down to Crockhurst Farm and see you when you are disengaged."

"I'll be at your service at any time, Vereker."

"Thanks. Meanwhile, should you be interrogated further by the police, stick grimly to the statement you have already made. You and Farnish and I are the only persons who know the somewhat baffling facts of Bygrave's disappearance and, come what may, we must shield old Henry in this dreadful trouble."

"By Jove, Vereker, you don't know what a relief your words have given me! I should have told you everything long ago, but I didn't know how you would take matters and thought I'd better keep the secret to myself until I saw clearly how things stood."

"I quite understand, Winslade," replied Vereker, as he warmly gripped the young man's hand. "After all, we may be over-estimating the gravity of the affair. From what you have told me I should feel inclined to prophesy that—Mr. Twistleton is at this moment very much alive."

"I hope so in all conscience," remarked Winslade, picking up hat and gloves, and added: "Should I hear from my uncle I will let you know."

"Do so at once, but I'm afraid the chances are against your hearing from him for the present. He will be too cautious," said Vereker.

A few moments later Winslade was hurrying down to Charing Cross to catch the 5.30 train to Hartwood. Unknown to him—but now in his ordinary garb, for he had changed swiftly at his flat on the way down—followed Vereker, who managed to enter one of the rear coaches of the same train just as it began to move slowly from the platform.

Chapter Thirteen

On the journey down to Fordingbridge Junction—for that was Vereker's destination—he sat in a corner of a first-class carriage apparently asleep. He was, in fact, very much awake, his alert brain swiftly analysing the details of David Winslade's story. Once again had his chain of reasoning received a dislocating jolt. He thought almost ruefully of his deduction that Lord Bygrave had not himself visited the White Bear on that Friday night. The clues from which he had arrived at this conclusion had seemed irrefragable: they had apparently satisfied even the cautious and experienced Heather.

That theory seemed utterly at variance with Winslade's assertion that Bygrave had undeniably passed the night at Hartwood. If Winslade's assertion were true, that theory fell to the ground. But was Winslade's assertion true? He had lied in the first instance when he disclaimed all knowledge of Lord Bygrave's whereabouts. That would justify the assumption that, on being cornered at 10 Glendon Street, he would lie again to save himself. Yet his story fully explained the mystery of Lord Bygrave's rifled drawer. Again, Bygrave had undoubtedly come to Glendon Street, for even Mrs. Parslow's description of Henry Parker bore out the truth of this statement. Moreover, there was the startling fact that he had from this boarding-house addressed an envelope to his wife—an envelope which had proved so useful in the discovery of Mrs. Cathcart's whereabouts.

"What about that boiled-egg breakfast?" soliloquized Vereker with a wry smile. "Perhaps I've been under-estimating old Henry's astuteness all the time. It has been a great mistake, now I come to ponder over the matter. Henry has as fine a brain as any man living. In difficult circumstances, as I know from experience, it can rise to an extraordinary height of alertness—and he's as supple as an eel!"

At, this moment the train ran into Fordingbridge Junction.

With some trepidation Vereker leaped from his compartment and hurried through the station gates, glancing anxiously back to see that Winslade had not left the train. Satisfied on this point, he hastened to Layham's garage and once more hired the Ford car. Without stopping he drove straight to the Mill House at Eyford and pulled up in front of the gate. A few moments later he was knocking loudly on the door. Receiving no response to this summons, he knocked again and listened intently to any sound of movement within, but not a sound disturbed the almost oppressive silence of the place.

"He hasn't returned here," he soliloquized, and for some moments stood on the whitened doorstep uncertain what to do. At this juncture something prompted him to try the handle of the door and to his amazement he discovered that the door was not locked.

"Hello! this is rather unexpected," he exclaimed to himself, and silently entered.

"Anyone in?" he shouted, but his query remained unanswered. A strange sense of eeriness, and an unaccountable fear came over him, and for some moments he hesitated whether he should make a further examination of the house or return to the car. Upbraiding himself for being unnecessarily nervous, he decided to pursue his investigations, and was about to ascend the stairs leading direct from the hall when the front door closed with a sharp slam. In a flash Vereker was on the defensive, his hand instinctively clutching the automatic pistol that of late he had carried in his hip pocket. But his alarm was groundless, for the door had been closed by a sudden gust of wind sweeping through the hall.

"Ah, that's symptomatic," he said, and smiled at the sudden start he had received. "It bears out my little theory."

Without further delay he quickly ascended the stairs and made a swift examination of the rooms, following the order that Winslade had taken. In the library he lit the gas and seated himself at one of the chairs drawn up at the table, his observant eye glancing leisurely at every detail of the furnishing. Here was the overturned chair, the blotting-pad, inkpot and pen just as Winslade had described them. The book-shelves were all neatly stacked with books which looked as if they had remained untouched for years. Beyond the overturned chair not a vestige indicative of any struggle or violence was to be observed; but one fact which Winslade had not mentioned seemed to hold Vereker's attention with an all-absorbing interest—an open window.

"Very remarkable," he exclaimed, as he lit a cigarette. "It explains many things—the slamming of the front door for instance."

He rose quickly, walked over to the window and very carefully examined the catches, the frame and window-sill. Thrusting out his head, he glanced down into the old cobbled backyard below.

"Just what I thought," he murmured and, swinging his legs through the open window, dropped down into the yard, a distance of some twelve to fourteen feet. "H'm," he murmured, as he glanced upwards at the open window, "that points to one very definite fact."

Passing out of the yard gate he returned to the front door of the building, retraced his steps to the library, and shut the open window.

"There's nothing more to be learned from this room," he said, as he passed out of the door and descended the stairs to the first landing. There he drew from his pocket a box of matches and lit the kerosene lamp affixed to the wall. Standing with his back to the light, he peered down the stairs into the hall and tried to imagine just where Winslade had stood when Lord Bygrave had turned out the lamp on the night that he had killed the blackmailing Mr. Twistleton. As he did so, he uttered a sudden exclamation of surprise and rapidly descended a few steps to examine a broken rail of the banister. The light on the staircase was now so feeble that he was obliged to strike a match to observe the fracture of the wood more clearly.

"That's quite recent," he muttered. "I wonder if Winslade remembers whether it was done previous to his visit. It's a point I must remember to ask him. I'm rather astonished that he failed to acquaint me with two such important facts as the open window and this broken banister rail."

Extinguishing the lamp on the landing, Vereker passed down into the hall with a strangely bitter look on his curiously handsome face. Something that he had deduced from his search had evidently disturbed his usual equanimity, and his short, rapid steps betokened that he had suddenly picked up some unexpected thread and was eagerly following it up. Without any further examination of the house he passed out, closed the door behind him, and walked straight across to the rock-garden, which stretched from the circular gravelled space in front of the house to the stone wall dividing the grounds from the road. The light was fast waning and it was with difficulty that he made his way over the tangled plants, stepping on the boulders projecting through the growth. All at once he halted and struck a match to examine a displaced stone. Carefully raising it, he pushed it back into the socket from which it had been moved, and noted the bleached appearance of the rock plants on which it had been resting.

"Good, good!" he exclaimed to himself, and made his way rapidly to the wall at the point where it terminated at the front gate-post. Seating himself on the coping of the wall, he found just below him the top of the gas-lamp illuminating the road. Leaning forward, he extended his hand to see if the lamp was within reach and in so doing his wrist touched the scorching hot frame of the lamp and was rather severely burnt. With a stifled oath he quickly withdrew his hand, and the sudden movement, throwing him out of equilibrium, sent him hurtling into the rock-garden behind him. The back of his head struck a sharp boulder and for some moments Vereker was too stunned to move. Gradually, however, his senses returned, and picking himself up he scrambled on to the gravel drive and passed out of the front gates on to the road. Clambering up the standard, he made another careful examination of the gas-lamp, especially the side facing the boundary wall of the Mill House garden, and, having satisfied himself on a certain point, descended and entered his car. Without further delay he drove straight into Hartwood and put up once more at the White Bear Inn. George Lawless, in his brusque way, seemed pleased to see him again, and even ventured on conversation.

"No more noos of his lordship, sir?" he asked.

"No, Lawless, none so far, but of course at any moment Scotland Yard may let us know what has happened—they keep us in the dark at present for very good reasons no doubt."

"My candid opinion, sir, is that his lordship is wandering about somewhere, having lost his memory. It seems to be the rage just now to lose the memory, though it never were when I was a boy."

Having thoroughly agreed with Lawless in his theory, Vereker ordered some supper before retiring, and when Mary Standish brought in the meal he was quick to notice a worried and detached look on her face. He at once inferred that she suspected, if she was not thoroughly acquainted with David Winslade's connexion with the strange disappearance of Lord Bygrave. Her curt manner also declared that she was none too pleased to see Vereker back at Hartwood, whereupon he deduced that any reference to the subject would fail to elicit any information that might prove useful. He smoked a cigarette after his meal, and retired—but not to sleep. As was his wont when absorbed in any subject, he lay awake with eyes closed and quietly pondered over his recent experiences and discoveries. His mind reverted again and again to the details of the story that Winslade had told him, and the more he analysed it the less credible it seemed. Told as it had been either with actual or well-feigned sincerity, it had at the time seemed extraordinarily strange, but probably true. Now, under close and cold examination, it appeared to Vereker as almost impossible.

In the first place it seemed to him contrary to all his knowledge of Lord Bygrave that the latter would resort to physical violence in a moment of fury. In unusual circumstances, however, there was no saying what any man might do, but even were this possible with regard to Henry Darnell, it was highly improbable. Secondly, what could have happened to the body of the man he was supposed to have killed. If there were no accomplice that body could not have been removed. No, this portion of the story was sheer nonsense. The only deduction he could draw, if Mr. Twistleton had actually been killed, was that Winslade had disposed of the body and was for some reason or other lying on this point. Yet another theory presented itself. Could Bygrave have framed this story for some hidden purpose of his own, and deceived Winslade? Finally, the whole story might be a fabrication on the part of Winslade to cover up his own tracks and gain time by keeping Vereker inactive. He finally fell asleep troubled in mind, for once again the threads of mystery which he had picked clear seemed to have become irretrievably tangled.

In the morning, when he awoke, he resumed his speculation and as he was buttoning his collar his face brightened, and he suddenly exclaimed:

"A ray of light, a ray of light!"

He finished dressing hastily and without waiting for breakfast left the inn on foot and walked briskly across to the cow-pond, the point at which Lord Bygrave had left Winslade.

"Exactly ten minutes walk," he soliloquized, glancing at his watch and, taking a seat on the stile, lit a cigarette. On throwing down the match, his eye caught sight of a small shining disc in the morning sunlight. Thinking it was a coin he stooped to pick it up. It was merely a trouser button, but on that button was something which momentarily startled him. It bore the inscription, John Wilkes, tailor, Bond Street, W.

"Bygrave's tailor!" he exclaimed with suppressed excitement. "This is surely more than a coincidence! Apparently he lost it when crossing the stile."

Placing the button in his pocket, he walked quickly back to the White Bear, and with an air of briskness, which always betokened with Vereker a sense of satisfaction, ordered his breakfast. After breakfast he took leave of Lawless, and on entering the yard where his car was garaged he met Mary Standish. A glance at her face showed that she had slept ill, and her eyes bore the red and swollen appearance of recent weeping. It flashed through Vereker's mind that she might possibly wish to speak to him; but in this surmise he was mistaken, for on seeing him she turned aside and hurriedly disappeared into the kitchen. Without further delay he took out his hired car and drove back to Fordingbridge. Having returned the car to Layham's, he discovered that he had an hour to wait for a train to London. A sudden thought struck him that he had sufficient time to see a doctor about his badly burned wrist, which, owing to the friction of his cuff, was becoming severely inflamed. Some liniment and a bandage sufficed to relieve irritation and, catching his train with some minutes to spare, Vereker ensconced himself in a corner seat and fell fast asleep.

When he awoke again he glanced at once out of the carriage window, only to discover that he had been asleep for a very short time and that there was now another passenger in the carriage fast asleep, with a felt hat pulled well down over his face to exclude the light from the lamp overhead. Vereker glanced casually at the man's burly figure and discovered to his surprise that it was shaking in an unaccountable manner. Then the felt hat seemed to be thrust further forward by a backward motion of the head and fell on the floor, disclosing the face of Detective-Inspector Heather, who was shaking with laughter.

"Well I'm damned!" exclaimed Vereker, laughing in turn. "You again, Heather. I really believe you are shadowing me now."

"Hardly that, Mr. Vereker," replied the detective genially, "but there's such a thing as the convergence of two parallel lines if we are to believe the latest theories of people who wish to put Mr. Euclid in his place."

"I'm too conservative to believe any new theory, Heather. Euclid was always good enough, I might say too good for me. By the way, have you laid hands on Mr. Drayton C. Bodkin yet. I bear him a distinct grudge for having deceived me so thoroughly."

"Ah, yes, Mr. Drayton C. Bodkin, we've got him all right."

"Good, how did you catch him, and where?"

"Well, to let you into a very great secret, Mr. Vereker, we never lost sight of him for a moment."

"Splendid, Heather, there are no flies on Scotland Yard, to use one of Mr. Bodkin's own phrases. Where did you run him to earth?"

"He came right to Scotland Yard after leaving 10 Glendon Street."

"What an ass!" exclaimed Vereker.

"Not by any means. He's one of our brightest men. I don't know what I'd do without him."

"Very little, I should say," remarked Vereker with supreme sang-froid, "but he errs on the side of inquisitiveness. Did he tell you I was a very informative young man?"

Inspector Heather smiled wryly. The only thing he could tell me about you, Mr. Vereker, was that you kept as nice a drop of whisky as any man he knew.

Vereker burst into loud laughter. "He was the thirstiest detective I've ever played host to."

At this juncture the train ran into Waterloo Junction, where Inspector Heather, after a warm handshake, was about to leave

Vereker when his eye suddenly caught sight of the bandage around his burned wrist.

"Hello!" he exclaimed, unable to conceal a look of surprise. "What on earth have you been doing to your wrist?"

Vereker was at once on the alert. Had Heather guessed by any chance how he had come by his injury? It was impossible, but nevertheless he was determined to disclose nothing to the astute inspector.

"Oh, merely a sprain," he said carelessly.

"How did you manage that?" asked Heather, with what appeared to be inordinate curiosity.

"Oh, one of Layham's old cars backfired when I was starting her," lied Vereker glibly.

"Well, good-bye for the present. We shall meet again shortly, no doubt," said the detective, and departed with a strangely puzzled look on his face.

"Now I wonder what's pricked old Heather's curiosity about my injured wrist?" asked Vereker of himself when alone again, and for some moments he gazed at the bandage and pondered. Then, with a sudden start, he exclaimed: "Good Lord, fancy my having forgotten! But it's impossible—there's no connection, no motive. Yet it's a strange coincidence; no wonder it intrigued Heather!"

Vereker was lost in thought. It had been revealed to him in a flash how keenly observant the detective officer was and how little escaped his marvellous memory. He was so absorbed in reverie that it was some time before he was aware that the train had arrived at Charing Cross Station.

Chapter Fourteen

Before returning to Glendon Street, Vereker was obliged to visit his flat to resume once more his disguise of the Rev. Passingham Patmore that he had so rapidly discarded before catching the train to Fordingbridge Junction. He felt, however, that it would now be unnecessary to play the rôle of a cleric much longer—this indeed might be the last occasion. He would call again at Mrs. Parslow's, get the few things he had taken there, pay his bill and return once more to his flat. He felt there would be little else to do at Mrs. Parslow's. Farnish would hardly call there again, and, to a certain extent, he had placed Farnish and knew fairly well the extent to which the trusted old butler was involved in the Bygrave case. Nor did he think that Winslade would venture to visit Glendon Street in the hope of meeting Lord Bygrave. Winslade would, as he himself had said, make no further move without hearing from his uncle, to whom he looked for future instructions.

As Vereker strolled lazily westwards his mind reverted to David Winslade with increased uneasiness. The shaky story he had retailed gathered further sinister significance from Mary Standish's attitude and distressed frame of mind. Vereker would have given something to know just how much she was cognizant of with regard to her lover's connexion with the disappearance of his uncle. Enough indeed to perturb her unduly. And why tears and depression without some very grave reason? All along Vereker had had, in spite of his former belief in Winslade, some haunting suspicion that he might be inculpated. In every crime there was motive, sometimes unintelligible to the normal mind, but still a motive. Of all the persons connected with the Bygrave mystery, Winslade was the man who would benefit most by his uncle's disappearance. Vereker had hastily thrust this from his mind during the initial stages of his investigation, but gradually every other line of inquiry had broken down under his keen inspection and flung him back ruthlessly on the one which was most distasteful to him. For, in spite of himself, he liked Winslade and could not readily bring himself to believe that he had had any hand in the disappearance of his uncle against the latter's will.

The difficulty now was to pursue this line of inquiry. Winslade had been trapped into a visit to Glendon Street, and had on the spur of the moment concocted a story which cleared himself and branded his uncle as a murderer. If it had not been deliberately thought out beforehand it seemed a clever impromptu fabrication. There were two methods which Vereker felt he might pursue. He must either try to discover what had become of the body of Mr. Twistleton, if he had been killed, or Mr. Twistleton alive. In his own mind, from certain deductions he had made after his visit to the Mill House, he was convinced that Mr. Twistleton was alive. Should he discover Mr. Twistleton he would soon arrive at the true part played by David Winslade in the perplexing drama. If Winslade and Twistleton had acted in collusion to ensure Lord Bygrave's disappearance the problem would then be solved. The second line to pursue was to keep a very guarded eye on Winslade, and through him discover Lord Bygrave's whereabouts.

There were, however, many little facts which pointed to a much more complex solution of the mystery, but for the time being he chose to keep them in reserve. Those facts would not sufficiently cohere to give him a definite conception of the whole business, but as every day passed he seemed to acquire a clearer view. One or two links were missing in the chain of deduction; should he alight on them, he felt that he could swiftly bring matters to a head. There was nothing for it but perseverance and unlimited patience. On arriving at his flat he was surprised to find that some one was in occupation. As he thrust his latch-key into the lock he heard the sound of movements inside, and on opening the door a pronounced odour of frying steak and onions assailed his nose.

"Who's that?" came a voice from the studio beyond.

"Who the devil are you?" asked Vereker, a smile flitting across his features, for the voice was familiar to him.

"Look here, Vereker, it's most inconsiderate of you to turn up like this! I'm afraid I can't put you up in your own flat at present— there's no room; you'll have to go to an hotel. Will you kindly come to Mahomet, for Mahomet can't come to you; he's busy with a steak and onions. I wouldn't spoil them for a ransom—my reputation as a cook— Damn the fat, it scalds like the devil!"

Vereker passed into the studio to find Ricardo, enveloped in his painter's overall, busy over the stove with a frying-pan.

"Lord, what a stench! By the way, how did you manage to get in, Ricky?"

"Got the key from Stimson—spun him a yarn that I had your permission and so forth. I'd have written to you, but didn't know just where you were."

"Have you been kicked out of your digs in Oliver Street?"

"No, my dear old landlady has retired on her ungodly profits; given up the house and gone to live by the wild waves."

"I suppose there's some difficulty in finding a new place nowadays?"

"One unsurmountable difficulty: I've no money until the governor sends me my monthly cheque. It was a bit of luck my meeting Aubrey Winter yesterday. I hovered about the door of his club about tea-time, and indirectly he bought me this steak and onions. It's a ghastly world for a literary genius."

"You're an improvident devil, Ricky. I suppose your last bean was swallowed by the peach you were raving about the last time I met you."

"Molly Larcombe, do you mean? Ah, well, *de mortuis nil*—" replied Ricardo sadly.

"Good heavens, you don't mean to say she's dead!" remarked Vereker with surprise.

"No, not in the accepted sense. Only she's dead as far as I'm concerned. After I'd taken the trouble to fall madly in love with her and proposed, she'd the callousness to tell me that she couldn't possibly marry a man who hadn't at least a thousand a year. I believe she's fond of me, but as she put it, rather unkindly, I think, it wouldn't be quite fair of me to expect her to wait until the twenty-first century. Lord, but I wish I had that wrist-watch I bought her in a moment of bewildered infatuation!"

"Unromantic thought, Ricky."

"Perhaps; but look at the pabulum it represents. A man must have food. At present I can do without romance as represented by the modern young woman. Henceforth I'm a cynic, Vereker. No more calf-love for me. The chrysalis that might have burst into an amorous poet shows a grave disposition to become a mere degraded, case-hardened man of the world. I shall write novels in the French manner yet."

"Never, old son, never; you're incurable. How long do you intend to stay here?"

"Until the financial horizon clears, Vereker. I can easily make myself a comfortable bed in the studio; I've got two overcoats, and my portmanteau makes quite a serviceable pillow. Do you think I'd be in your way?"

"In my way, Ricky? You know me better than that, old man. Make yourself at home; there's an army camp-bed and bedding parcelled up in my dressing-room. We can feed together if you'll give a hand at the cooking. When we get tired of our own culinary efforts we'll go down to Jacques. Are you doing any work?"

"Writing like a popular novelist—at a godless pace. Will you share this steak and onions?"

"No, I'm going to lunch out. I have to go to 10 Glendon Street. I may be back this evening."

"Ah, Mrs. Parslow's—that reminds me. Do you know, I believe I saw Lord Bygrave leave 10 Glendon Street yesterday evening when I called—only to find you had gone."

"Impossible, Ricky!"

"I don't think I'm mistaken. You know I only saw Bygrave once, but I've got a wonderful memory for faces."

"I know you have; but I feel certain you've made a mistake."

"No, Vereker, the more I think of it the surer I am that it was Bygrave. I was terribly excited about the business; so much so that I was quite at loss to know what to do—so I went and had a drink."

Vereker stood as if petrified. "That beats creation!" he exclaimed. "And to think that I could not have been gone more than an hour or so when he called! Well, I'm going to Mrs. Parslow's at once. If I don't return to-night don't be surprised. Stock the larder, Ricky. Order the comestibles at Wharton's Stores; I have an account there. So long for the present."

"God bless you, old horse! By the way, do you like tinned lobster? Because I do."

But the remark remained unanswered, for Vereker had retired to his dressing-room and closed the door. When he emerged again, dressed as the Rev. Passingham Patmore, he found Ricardo ravenously devouring his fried steak and onions.

"I'm going, Ricky—take the helm while I'm away, and don't starve yourself. Also try and do some work: you've been playing too long, you know."

"True, oh, padre—bye-bye. If you don't return by evensong I'll know you're not coming back. If you do there'll be lobster mayonnaise Ricardo for supper."

On leaving his flat Vereker took a taxi at once to Glendon Street. Ricardo's story of having seen Lord Bygrave calling at that address had excited him more than his appearance disclosed, or than he would have cared to admit. Again and again he cursed his luck that he had not been in. Still, he would question Mrs. Parslow and get every scrap of information out of her that was possible. At last he seemed to be nearing the conclusion of his long and baffling quest, and the thought seemed to instil into him new enthusiasm and spur him on to fresh effort. So eager was he to reach Glendon Street that the inevitable delays at the congested street crossings irritated him beyond measure: never had a taxi journey seemed such a sluggish affair. At length he arrived and, having paid his fare, shot up the steps two at a time. Mrs. Parslow was in and seemed glad to see him.

"Any news while I've been away, Mrs. Parslow?" he asked.

"Yes, sir; good news as far as I'm concerned. Mr. Henry Parker arrived last night to see if anyone had left a letter for him. He seemed very disappointed that a Mr. Winslade, whom you know, hadn't left some word for him."

"Quite so, Mrs. Parslow; I understand. Did he leave any address to which his letters might be forwarded?"

"No, sir. He said he had no fixed address at present and could easily write to Mr. Winslade if he desired to."

"Ah, I wish he had left his address."

"He didn't seem to remember you, sir, when I mentioned your name. I told him that you were in the Church and knew him. He tried hard to recollect, but said he thought you must have made some mistake."

"Perhaps I have, but his name seemed very familiar to me. I hope he paid you, Mrs. Parslow, for his board and lodgings. I think you told me he had left without doing so."

"Well, sir, I did, and it just shows you how slow you ought to be in judging people harshly. He remembered it quite well and settled up his account. In fact, he said that was the principal reason why he had come back. He suffers very badly at times with his head and is shockingly absent-minded."

"A terrible complaint, Mrs. Parslow. I feel quite sorry for him. However, all's well that ends well. I shall be leaving you to-day, but I should like to keep on my room for another month if convenient, so that I might come and stay here at any odd time should I wish. Of course, if you get another applicant, don't hesitate to let me know, and I'll make way for him. On the other hand I'm quite willing to pay you as if I were having full board here while I am away. Would that be convenient?"

"You shall have the room, sir, as long as you choose. I'm a respectable lady and I like to have real gentlemen in my house, sir. One never knows how some young gentlemen are going to behave, well-educated though they may be..."

Mrs. Parslow continued at some length, and retailed the story of one of her former lodgers, the nicest young gentleman, just down from Oxford, who used to climb in at his window at two and three o'clock in the morning, and who, to annoy an irritable old gentleman next door, hired four organ grinders to play simultaneously beneath his window. Vereker was apparently listening intently to Mrs. Parslow's story, but in reality his thoughts were elsewhere. He was wondering what move he should make next in his quest of Lord Bygrave. One thing was fairly certain: Bygrave had called for a letter from Winslade which he expected would contain money. It was this factor of money which in the end would certainly give a clue to his address—for he couldn't possibly go on without means. Rising from his chair, Vereker bade good-bye to Mrs. Parslow and took his departure. He decided to return to his flat and drop Winslade a line letting him know that his uncle had called again at 10 Glendon Street. On arriving he was glad to discard his disguise and get into a comfortable old lounge suit. He found Ricardo seated at a table with a sheaf of manuscript in front of him, rolling cigarettes.

"Glad to see you busy on the magnum opus," commented Vereker.

"Please don't interrupt the flow of imagination, Vereker. I've no time for idle conversation just now. Let me see—let me see. Wroth must put an end to this low fellow's baboonery. One straight from the shoulder ought to hand him the dope tablet, although it would be easier to kick him on the shin— No, that won't do. We must harass the gentle reader by letting Silas have Wroth down for a count of eight about four times, and then Wroth, gathering every ounce of failing strength, puts in a bone-crushing right swing to the ear. Pop goes the weasel with Silas— he's dead—Wroth's a murderer—Beryl breaks off the engagement. Silas not at all keen on the quiet of the tomb—very much alive—"

"Shut up, Ricky, I'm trying to think."

"Wroth wandering in the never-never land—water-bottle lost in the bush—dying of thirst. Silas passes by on horseback and waves a flask of the best in his face with the words: 'Die of thirst, you dog!'"

"Will you shut up, Ricky!" exclaimed Vereker. "Can't you see I'm trying to write a letter?"

"Letter—letter—ah, Vereker, that brings me back from thrilling dreams to sordid reality. A letter arrived for you by the midday post. You'll find it behind the clock. It's a good place to put anything. One has to wind up a clock, and there you are, elementary mnemonics without moans."

Vereker continued his letter to Winslade without further interruption. It was a difficult letter. Henry Darnell would undoubtedly write to Winslade for money, with the request that it be forwarded to a certain address. Winslade was not in a position to meet repeated demands for money. As Bygrave's executor and trustee, Vereker felt that he might take a hand in the matter without undue offence to Winslade. The strange part of the affair was that Bygrave had not sent some word to him about money matters through Winslade. The more he thought of it the stranger it seemed. Winslade, should he consent to his proposal with regard to furnishing funds for Bygrave, could hardly refuse to let him know Bygrave's address. And then—well, that could all be settled in due course. If Winslade chose to be secretive about the matter, that would put a very sinister complexion on the part he had played—it would be tantamount to a very damning admission. Things were travelling apace. He finished the letter with a sense of satisfaction, for he felt that it would scarcely fail to elicit some new information, sealed it up and rose from his writing-desk.

"The letter behind the clock is in a feminine hand," remarked Ricardo as he wrote furiously.

"Oh," said Vereker with some surprise and, glancing at the postmark, saw that it had come from Farnaby.

"From Mrs. Cathcart," he thought. "I wonder how she got my address? Directory of course."

He tore open the envelope and glanced at the contents:

Dear Mr. Vereker,

I shall be very glad if you will come and see me as soon as you can find a convenient opportunity, or, if more suitable, I will call on you. I am here (should you run down to Farnaby) at any time. There is something I feel I must tell you before I leave England, for I have suddenly decided to go abroad. The matter has been very much on my mind since I saw you and might be of considerable interest to you.

With kind regards,

Yours sincerely,

Ida Wister

Vereker read the letter carefully several times and then, folding it up, thrust it into his letter-case. Sitting down, he strove to discover what might be the matter disturbing Mrs. Cathcart's conscience. Surely she was not going to make a confession about those bearer bonds after her furious declaration that the receipt for them in her name was a forgery. That did not seem likely— though he could see no other subject on which she should wish to unburden her mind. At length he gave up the conundrum with the thought that it was just like a woman to make a mystery about a probably trivial affair.

"Ricky," he suddenly remarked aloud, "you're a connoisseur as far as the feminine mind is concerned. I'm going to put a simple question to you. If a woman tells you there's something on her mind which she wishes to tell you about before she leaves England, and you haven't the vaguest notion about the nature of that something, what inference would you draw?"

Ricardo solemnly laid down his fountain-pen and faced Vereker. Without giving the matter a moment's consideration, he replied:

"That's a most serious symptom, Vereker, my boy, a most serious symptom. You must walk warily; there are pitfalls ahead, or rocks—whichever you prefer. Of course with your limited experience how can you be expected to know, poor old soul? But it's just at this critical moment in your life I can render you a signal service as some small recompense for the kindly shelter of your roof and the generous provision of food. Even a man of genius cannot write on an empty stomach. You know the story of dear old George Gissing—the woeful product of an ill-nourished brain can never be a best seller."

"Get to the point."

"I'm getting—though my mind may seem to move in a mysterious way—it's too large to move in a bee-line. Bee-lines for bee-minds is one of my brightest apophthegms. The lady— By the way, what's her Christian name?"

"Ida."

"And surname?"

"Wister."

"That makes matters simpler. Miss Ida Wister merely wishes—"

"She's a Mrs., Ricky: so be careful."

"Good Lord above! A widow?"

"Probably."

"I should take the trouble to find out."

"It's immaterial."

"Then I may assume she's a widow. She merely wishes to tell you that the problem that troubles her is whether you're sufficiently in love with her to marry her."

"You think so?"

"Most indubitably. The going abroad wheeze is the oldest arrow in the female quiver. If you're in love you'll have to make a forced march, so to speak, to attain your objective. It also suggests that if you don't wish to attain the objective she's going to forget the tragedy by having a merry old time on the Riviera, or Deauville, or wherever they go to flirt at this time o' year. Should anyone else wish to attain the objective, they can wait until she returns. In short, you're the odds-on favourite. Go and 'win in a common canter.'"

"Thanks, Ricky. Your knowledge of woman is simply invaluable. Let's go and dine at Jacques'."

"But I've got all the materials for a tinned lobster mayonnaise."

"You can sup on that alone. I never eat anything after dinner."

"I've also managed a bottle of wine. I—I was going to make it a sort of supper in honour of—of—let's see, what does the calendar say? Ah, Jean Jacques Rousseau died—no, that was yesterday. The sun rises at 8.30—well, that's an excellent reason. I didn't see him rise, but it's a comforting assurance in this climate."

"Barbera—good—bland—genial—generous—inexpensive."

"You'd better have that for your supper too."

"Splendid. I'm sorry you don't care for Barbera. Then let's hie us to Jacques'. You shall order any dinner you like. I can eat and drink anything that the Fates provide."

"Well, Jacques plays the part of the Fates very satisfactorily."

"I don't know his 'eat emporium,' as the Americans call it, I believe. You're not going to dress, I hope, because Uncle has my dinner-jacket suit in his strong room at present."

"No—it's a very Bohemian place; I like the easy atmosphere. I'm just going out to post a letter; on my return we will go."

"Righty-o. I shall have settled the fates of Wroth, Beryl and Silas by the time you return."

Vereker, having dispatched his letter to Winslade, turned into Oxford Street and then sauntered leisurely down Regent Street. It was his favourite stroll before dinner; but on this occasion he pursued his way almost automatically. His eyes were unobservant, his mind on other things than the ever-absorbing throng of passers-by intent on reaching home after the close of the day's labour. He turned into Piccadilly, thence wandered up Bond Street, and arrived back at his flat in Fenton Street about a quarter to seven. He found Ricardo busy with a bottle of his fountain-pen ink and a camel-hair sky brush; he was inking his heel where it peeped through a hole in his black woollen sock just above his shoe.

"Rather a good way of darning," suggested Vereker.

"I was just thinking that your paint-box will make an excellent assortment of wools," replied Ricardo. "Now, there's a hole in my grey socks—I couldn't mend that with Swan ink. After all, this studio of yours is rather a handy place. Are you ready?"

"Quite. Come along."

Together they walked along at a brisk pace towards Jacques' restaurant in Soho, Vereker quietly intent on certain street effects that pleased his painter's eye; Ricardo chattering incessantly in his ebullient, boyish way, heedless whether his companion was listening or not. As they passed into Greek Street Vereker suddenly came to an abrupt halt. There was a look of surprise and excitement on his face, for not ten yards ahead of him he saw the unmistakable figure and gait of Mr. Sidney Smale.

"What's up, Vereker?" asked Ricardo.

"The man in front of us is a certain Mr. Sidney Smale, once Lord Bygrave's secretary. He disappeared a week or so ago, much to our surprise, and hasn't been seen or heard of since. Now I've caught sight of him I'm not going to lose him. We must follow."

"*You* must follow, Vereker. I'm not the least bit interested in him; I'm too hungry."

"Come on, Ricky, give me a helping hand. I shall need your assistance. This will be your first attempt at shadowing—it may prove useful if you ever attempt a detective yarn."

"I can imagine that without much effort, Vereker. I can't imagine I've dined at Jacques'; but give the word of command and

I follow to the death—probably from exhaustion due to lack of nourishment. What am I to do?"

"You must follow him. He knows me too well, so I shall make myself scarce. Run him to his lair and then come and report to me. I shall return to the flat."

"After dining at Jacques', I presume?"

"No; I'll go back and prepare the lobster mayonnaise for supper."

"I say, Vereker, look—he has actually turned in at Jacques'."

"Well, here's some money. Go and sit at the next table. Follow him wherever he goes."

"Right. Count on me. Au revoir," and Ricardo hurried on and vanished into the comfortable little French restaurant, leaving Vereker to retrace his steps to Fenton Street.

On returning to his flat Vereker discovered Detective-Inspector Heather in the act of pressing the electric door-bell.

"Hello, Heather; what a pleasant surprise! Come in and have a chat over a whisky and cigar."

"Thanks, Mr. Vereker; I've quite a lot to talk about."

"Going to pull my leg again?" asked Vereker, as he pushed the burly detective into the most comfortable arm-chair and placed a decanter and glasses between them.

"No, it's getting rather too serious for any more fooling," replied Heather gravely. "I think we're getting to the bottom of the Bygrave case at last. I'm afraid we shall see no more of your friend."

"You mean Lord Bygrave?"

"Yes. From all I have gathered I'm coming swiftly to the conclusion that he has been got rid of."

"Who's the culprit?" asked Vereker quietly.

"Everything points to his nephew, young Winslade, being deeply concerned."

"I have been thinking that myself for some time now," remarked Vereker, with a grave shake of the head, "but the indications are none too convincing."

"Well, let's be frank about the matter," said the inspector, as if discarding for the time being his usual attitude of professional secrecy and discretion. "We both agree on the point that he is the one man mixed up in the case who benefits most by his uncle's disappearance.

"Materially, Heather, yes. But I'm inclined to view these matters from a psychological point as well. I do not believe that Winslade is much concerned one way or another about his uncle's money."

"He's short of money, as I've discovered," continued Heather imperturbably.

"Yes; but he has been short of money for many years."

"He's engaged to be married."

"To a woman quite accustomed to hard work and little enough luxury."

"Just so, but that doesn't kill the desire for luxury."

"That's a point to you, Heather. I quite agree."

"He was the last man known to be with his uncle on the Friday night of his supposed disappearance."

"But he is supposed to have disappeared on Saturday morning," argued Vereker.

"You maintain that you have disproved that Lord Bygrave visited the White Bear on Friday night. You surmised or deduced that some one had impersonated Lord Bygrave; isn't that so?"

"I did, but I'm in a quandary about the point just now. Let's leave it in abeyance for a moment, Heather, and return to it later. I think you have gone a shade too rapidly for my complete comprehension. How did you discover that Winslade was the last man to have been with his uncle on Friday night?"

"He was seen driving him towards Eyford by a villager working in the fields between Fordingbridge and Eyford. This villager happened to have once worked on Lord Bygrave's estate and knew both the men."

"Ah, that's satisfactory. Where did they part?"

"That's the one point I wish to discover. I should say at the cow-pond near Hartwood, where there is a short cut across the fields right to the White Bear. That, of course, is presuming that Lord Bygrave *did* stay at Lawless's hostelry on Friday night. It is just at this very juncture that there is room for some clever work on the part of Winslade. Did he assume the rôle of his uncle? Lawless is a most unobservant man. Mary Standish, the only other person who saw his lordship, is engaged to Winslade. She is an astute and very discreet woman. It's not likely that she would give her lover away should there be any question of his being involved in the case. In fact, she would tell us just what Winslade would teach her to tell us. She is at present very greatly distressed. Winslade himself is behaving in a strange manner, and is nothing like the man he used to be before this matter occurred. That signet-ring was a master stroke on Winslade's part—presuming this theory to be correct."

"Winslade's disguise would be an extremely risky venture," suggested Vereker, lighting a cigar. "You know, Heather, I've thought out very carefully what you have just sketched. I also came to the conclusion that between Fordingbridge Junction and Hartwood was a vital time in the affair, but I couldn't quite convince myself that Winslade played the rôle of his uncle. I wondered if there might be an accomplice."

"You discovered that they drove together towards Hartwood?" asked the detective with a shade of surprise.

"Oh, yes. That was not a very difficult matter. Winslade admitted it to me."

"Ah, that's most important. You remember, he denied it at first. It looks very fishy."

"It does; but he told me that he did so to cover his uncle's tracks. He says that Bygrave left him at the cow-pond, and that he hasn't seen him since."

"But what was the reason for all this mystery?"

"Perhaps he'll tell you," remarked Vereker guardedly. "Perhaps at this moment you know. But to return to the question of whether the person who stayed at the White Bear was Lord Bygrave, what do you make of this?"

Vereker handed the inspector the trouser button that he had picked up at the stile near the cow-pond. Heather examined it carefully and returned it.

"It means little enough to me," he remarked, "in its isolated state. What story does it tell you?"

"That button is one of Lord Bygrave's," remarked Vereker. "I found it at the stile near the cow-pond. It looks as if Lord Bygrave actually left Winslade's car at that point and in hastily crossing the stile lost it. That's the name of his tailor. Strange coincidence, if it's only a coincidence, that some one in Hartwood should also patronize a Bond Street tailor."

"It can hardly be a coincidence," remarked the detective, lost in thought.

"I'm perfectly convinced that it is one of Lord Bygrave's buttons," said Vereker and returned it carefully to his purse.

"So," said the detective with a non-committal air. "And tell me, Mr. Vereker, did you discover the reason for Winslade taking such a time over his journey from Fordingbridge to Hartwood? Of course we need not believe the story of the breakdown of his car unless we choose to do so."

"I didn't choose to do so. He stopped at the Mill House, Eyford, where he alleges that his uncle paid a call on a gentleman called Twistleton."

"Good. I can verify that much. Two yokels on the road saw a car stop near the house. They, however, maintain that the car was coming from the Hartwood direction, and they only noticed one gentleman enter Eyford Mill House."

"Winslade remarked to me that he had seen two yokels, but they were in a stage of beery mirth. Now, Heather, I wish you could find out just where this Mr. Twistleton is, and who he is, and why Lord Bygrave should call on him."

"You don't know anything about him, Mr. Vereker?" asked the detective, with a sly glance.

"I don't, beyond the fact that Lord Bygrave called on him with regard to money matters, and that the interview wound up in a violent quarrel; that Lord Bygrave struck him, thought he had killed him and promptly vanished, believing himself to be a murderer."

"A sufficient reason for making a hasty disappearance, of course. Lord Bygrave was quite certain that he had killed him?"

"He was. Winslade promptly drove him, after this fracas, to the stile at the cow-pond, left him there and hasn't seen him since. Winslade returned to the Mill House to verify the story, but found no trace of the defunct Mr. Twistleton. That accounts for the direction in which the car came when Winslade was seen by the two yokels."

"Have you examined the Mill House since?" asked the inspector.

"Very carefully. I found the window of the library—the scene of the altercation—open, and I dropped from the window into the back-yard, which contains the garage."

"And you deduced that Mr. Twistleton must be an active young man to jump from the window and bolt before anybody—say, Winslade—could return from the gate with Lord Bygrave and continue the little altercation?"

"That's the exact inference I drew, Heather. If an old man had dropped from the window it would have shaken him up pretty badly."

"And do you believe this cock-and-bull yarn of Winslade's?" asked the inspector with some impatience.

Vereker blew a smoke ring into the air and with some deliberation replied:

"In the main it's perfectly true."

Detective-Inspector Heather greeted this remark with a loud guffaw of laughter.

"My dear Mr. Vereker, really this is too bad. I have never heard such balderdash in my life. I begin to see that we shall shortly have to arrest Mr. David Winslade. If not the actual criminal, he's an accessory."

"Ah, well, I must leave all the arresting to Scotland Yard. Later on, however, I may have some very important information for you. I feel that matters are coming to a climax."

"Well, I'll look you up again very shortly," said Heather, and rose to go. "By the way, how's your sprained wrist getting on?" he asked on reaching the door.

"Oh, progressing very favourably," replied Vereker, carelessly thrusting the injured wrist more deeply into his trouser pocket, and mentally cursing the inspector's inquisitiveness.

"A burn takes some time to heal, doesn't it?" remarked the detective, smiling broadly as he hastened away.

For some moments Vereker stood at the threshold of his flat with a slightly chagrined look on his face. He was just trying to measure the depth of Heather's last remark.

"Now, how did the devil find that out?" he exclaimed as he closed the door and re-entered his room. "I really believe the wily old hound has got on the scent too. I must hurry up or he'll forestall me."

Chapter Fifteen

Returning to his easy chair on Detective-Inspector Heather's departure, Vereker sat with legs extended, his elbows resting on the comfortably padded arms, his hands clasped together in front of him. It was an attitude he always unconsciously assumed when he was engrossed in thought. Every now and then he would jump to his feet and pace the room with short, quick steps, a curious smile on his lips, his eyes alight with excitement, his glance swiftly, restlessly roving over the pattern of the red and blue turkey carpet. It seemed as if the detective's last remark had fired a train of thought, the materials for which had lain dormant in his mind awaiting the inflammatory touch.

"So much seems clear," he soliloquized, "so clear that I wonder why I haven't assembled the apparently disconnected fragments before. And Heather must know a good deal, that's patent from the significance of his last remark. I scarcely think he was merely drawing a bow at a venture."

He glanced at the clock on the mantelpiece. The hour was late and as yet there was no sign of Ricardo's return.

"I wonder what has happened to Ricky!" he exclaimed with some impatience. "I hope he hasn't run his head into any trouble. It would be just like him to get mixed up in some imbroglio."

Vereker yawned with the weariness of his vigil and then, going into his studio, prepared himself a pot of hot coffee. With this he returned to his drawing-room and picking up a volume of Tchekov's short stories he settled himself down to read them over a pipe. He read on until weariness—sheer boredom of their naked primitiveness—overcame his attention, the hand holding the volume fell listlessly on to his knees and his head lurched forward on to his breast. He was awakened at length by the persistent ringing of an electric bell followed by a booming tattoo of the knocker on the entrance door to his flat. He jumped from his chair and hastened to open the door. A white and weary Ricardo entered listlessly, emerging into the brilliantly lit hall from the twilight of the landing like some dejected apparition.

"You look tired, Ricky, what on earth kept you so late?" asked Vereker with gentle concern.

"Fagged out, old man. I guess you knew what sort of a job shadowing a man like Smale would be. I shan't deputize for you again on such an errand for the price of a dinner at Jacques'."

"I'm sorry you had such a rough journey. Here, have a whisky and soda, it will buck you up."

"Ugh, whisky and soda—not just now, thank you. I've just eaten a quantity of sausages and mashed and drunk a pint of coffee at a questionably clean coffee-stall amidst a band of apparent cut-throats."

"Can I offer you anything?"

"Sympathy, Vereker."

"Won't you try your tinned lobster?"

"Don't, Vereker, don't. You might as well whisper boiled pork to a seasick passenger. Let me sit down and in a few minutes I'll relate my lurid adventures."

Ricardo flung himself into an easy chair, loosened the laces of his shoes, decided that perhaps after all whisky and soda might be piled on top of inferior sausages and mashed as a corrective, and began his story.

"When I left you, Vereker, I followed your man into Jacques' restaurant and, taking a small table behind him, I ordered a sumptuous repast. I did the thing properly, you know—it's impossible to be careful with other people's money, and I assured myself that you wouldn't countenance any niggardliness on my part when on such an important errand as your proxy."

"Naturally—I expected you to do yourself proud, Ricky."

"It wouldn't have mattered in any case. When I see a menu with all that choice, mouth-watering French I simply throw discretion to the four winds of heaven. I cut loose with the knife and fork and fairly tear leaves out of the wine list. I'd use Trust funds if anyone were so foolish as to trust me with anything; that is—I press the point—if I had no money of my own."

"Well, and what about our friend Smale?"

"I didn't give him a thought at the moment. By Jove, the fish was excellent, you know—grilled sole, and the wine accompanying it was Chambertin. I've tasted better, but not much. Then old Jacques possesses a Burgundy fit for Olympus. I got through a bottle of that—I couldn't help it. The sweets were good of their kind, which is saying a lot for me, for I rarely touch sweets. I did the dessert justice with a port of delightful quality—a really estimable wine."

"And Smale, what about Smale?" asked Vereker with a faint show of impatience.

"I capped it all with a Corona. I say, they do know how to distil a drop of majestic coffee at Jacques'. Liqueurs are poison—I abhor them. How people can ruin the carefully built edifice of a good dinner by drinking liqueurs!"

"Did Smale indulge in them?" asked Vereker.

"Damned if I know," replied Ricardo. "I wasn't looking at the brute, and when I did look up to see how he was getting on, what do you think?"

"I don't," replied Vereker, glancing at his friend apprehensively.

"He'd gone!"

"Oh, Ricky, you don't mean to say you lost sight of him," queried Vereker dejectedly.

"Most indubitably. He'd gone—vanished like a spook. I was staggered—I mean apart from the copious libations I had poured out to the gods—'This is a pretty kettle of fish,' I said and, seizing my hat and coat, I simply shot out into the street to see if I could get a glimpse of him."

"Not a vestige of him did you see, I suppose," commented Vereker resignedly.

"Not a vestige, but I was tapped gently on the arm and reminded by one of the waiters at Jacques' that I hadn't paid the bill. This fairly put the lid on matters. Instead of dashing around at once and picking up the trail I had simply to go back into Jacques' and waste time by paying a footling bill: really a detective shouldn't be asked to pay bills at critical moments. You can imagine how I swore, using every known term of the vocabulary of bad language to little purpose. It failed to relieve me and only incensed the waiter. Once again in the street I glanced round. No sign of Smale. I might as well have looked in the gutter for a golden sovereign. A feeling akin to real grief overcame me—I was sorry for you, old man, for having leaned so stoutly on a broken reed like myself. I thought how foolish it was of you to have trusted me so implicitly with money and a task at the same time. My dazed eyes flitted around in a glassy stare, seeing nothing clearly until they alighted on the words 'saloon bar' on the opposite of the street. This brought me to a rational frame of mind; those words admirably matched the texture of my thoughts, and offered me purpose instead of weltering indecision. What more fitting than to drown grief and blow the rest of your cash; never had the offensive words 'saloon bar' seemed so imbued with a sense of ministering comfort—they caught some shadow of the divine—"

"And you promptly went in and stayed there till closing time," added Vereker with a suspicion of curtness.

"Don't descend to bathos like that, Vereker. I've had an adventure and if I unconsciously compose in the narration it is simply instinctive. The true inwardness of events has lit up my imagination, every moment of my evening has been touched with the magic of a certain sublime inevitableness—Fate, you may call it—which has put its very commonplace incidents on a plane which is rarely visited even in moments of the highest artistic exaltation."

"It wasn't the wine, I presume?"

"Wine—no, certainly not. It wasn't wine that led me into the saloon bar of Billy's opposite and brought me shoulder to shoulder again with Mr. Smale!"

"Good Lord, was he in there too?"

"He was. Mere chance, eh? A blundering and careless Ricardo is thus waited on by that inscrutable thing we call chance."

"You followed him up this time?"

"I did. I was closer to him than his shadow. I followed him until he disappeared into some mean purlieu of Soho, where he disappeared down into an unsavoury den where human faces appeared inhuman—they were the faces of fauns. From this I was promptly ejected by a super-faun who said I was not a member of the club. I feigned intoxication and blundered back to decency."

"So you lost him there. Do you remember the street?"

"I didn't lose him there. Remembering that I had been once favoured by the capricious goddess, Chance, I was not going to beg at her feet again in a hurry. I patrolled that street until Mr. Smale once more emerged. I was remorseless; I was cunning; hours mattered not to my firm resolve. Had he journeyed to Cathay I would have trudged unflinchingly after him—the Polar wastes would not have sheltered him. As a matter of fact it took just five minutes to reach his digs. They were round the corner of the same street. I know them well—pal of mine suffered there for over a year."

"Good, Ricky. Well, that's an accomplishment—by Jove, we've got him."

"The balance out of your money is elevenpence halfpenny, old man, and I'm off to bed."

Finishing his whisky, Ricardo rose from his chair, sought out a heavy khaki overcoat, relic of his army career, and disappeared into Vereker's studio with a somnolent "Good night, Sherlock."

"Good night, Ricky," replied Vereker with a faint smile, "I'm greatly indebted to you for the night's work."

Flinging the butt of his cigar in the fire Vereker sat thinking over his plans for the morrow.

Chapter Sixteen

It was with some difficulty that Vereker roused the somnolent Ricardo at seven o'clock next morning; but once awake his irrepressible friend was soon busy helping to prepare breakfast, or rather taking the onus of that operation entirely on himself. Over the meal Vereker ascertained the exact whereabouts of the lodging-house into which Smale had retreated on the previous night and, leaving Ricardo busy rolling cigarettes and drinking strong coffee, paid an unusually early call on Lord Bygrave's secretary. It was with a considerable feeling of suppressed excitement that he informed the maid who answered his ring of the object of his visit. Would Smale, he wondered, resort to the subterfuge of being absent or inaccessible? He might take such a course and create a rather difficult situation for the time being.

To his surprise the maid returned with the information that, though Mr. Smale had not long since risen, he would be pleased to see Mr. Vereker. Ushered into a tidily furnished and scrupulously clean little drawing-room, Vereker was met by Smale attired in his dressing-gown and looking fresh and roseate after a hot bath. There was no touch of uneasiness in his cherubic countenance, no hesitation or awkwardness or hint of annoyance in the manner of his reception of Vereker.

"Good morning," he began, "I'm afraid you've caught me before I'm quite ready to face the world, Vereker, but, if you don't mind, I'm sure I don't. How on earth did you dig me out? I didn't know you were acquainted with my address."

"I happened to find it out quite by accident," replied Vereker. "In fact, I saw you enter by sheer chance. As I had something about Bygrave's affairs on which I wished to consult you, I took the opportunity of calling on you first thing this morning. You must pardon the hour."

"I'm glad you did, as I'm only staying here temporarily and might be off again to-day. I'm waiting to hear from my people with regard to my going abroad and expect to have an interview with the guv'nor to-day on the subject, an interview to which I do not look forward with pleasure. Having once settled the business, I was going to drop you a line privately and let you know that I was relinquishing my post at Bygrave Hall."

"We wondered what had become of you," remarked Vereker quietly. "You left without letting anyone know your destination or plans."

He shot a keen and challenging glance at Smale; but that glance, which Vereker hoped might prove awkward in its frank provocativeness, was answered by a cheerful, gurgling laugh.

"I bet you did some thinking, Vereker," he replied gaily. "Put all sorts of sinister constructions on my behaviour, ascribed damning motives to my perfectly innocent actions, eh? Ah, well, you can't be an amateur detective without acquiring the private inquiry agent's mind; a cesspool of suspicion. If there's anything you want to know I'm at your service."

The tone of Smale's reply nettled Vereker: it was exasperatingly confident, either from a consciousness of superior astuteness, and an ability to measure swords favourably with his antagonist, or from a knowledge of his innocence. Vereker had been so convinced that Smale's sudden disappearance from Bygrave Hall had been intimately connected with the matter of the bearer bonds, the receipt for which Mrs. Cathcart had alleged to be a forgery, that he was considerably shaken. Not for a moment, however, did he disclose by facial expression anything that was passing in his mind, and with characteristic resilience he met the situation with reciprocal urbanity.

"Well, Smale, I can assure you my thoughts weren't too flattering at first, but after pondering the matter I came to the conclusion that I must see you and get some explanation before condemning your action in any way. It's on this very subject I have come to see you this morning. You can possibly give me the information I'm seeking and set my mind at rest on the whole business forthwith."

"Only too glad to do so, Vereker, but it's entirely a personal matter, and I must ask you to treat what I tell you as strictly confidential."

"Certainly."

"Well, I suppose you want to know, in the first place, why I left Bygrave Hall without giving any information as to my destination or intentions? I can do so very briefly; but, as I have said, the matter is a private and rather unpleasant one for me. It has nothing whatever to do with Bygrave."

"You may count on my treating the information confidentially," interrupted Vereker.

"I'm sure I may," added Smale, "and I shall not hesitate to let you know the inner truth of what I may call a crisis in my life. I am in serious trouble."

"Financial, I suppose?" commented Vereker.

"Well, that has been a concomitant of all my earthly worries, and I am so used to it that it troubles me no more now than harness does a horse. No, it is more poignant than a question of the wherewithal to live—it's a matter of the heart. I'm an unlucky man, Vereker. Let me compare life for a moment to a revolving door. You cannot negotiate a revolving door except by taking a compulsorily uniform step—the 'everybody's doing it' method. A hop, skip and a jump, though admirable in themselves, would end in disaster. Now, though I have never wished to get through this revolving door in any but the orthodox method—the civilized step, if I may put it so—I've stumbled and got mixed up badly with the contraption. A year or so ago I was still idealist enough to fall desperately in love with a barmaid. I made all sorts of foolish protestations and promises. If she had been a good woman I should doubtless have carried matters through, but she is an utterly worthless woman. Having acquired a little discretion of late I have not the slightest intention of marrying her. She threatens to sue me. I have tried to buy her off; but no—she's tired of working, and wants a husband to keep her and supply her with money to have a good time on. She knows I have prospects and she is banking on that fact. Having no desire for combat, for I'm a man of peace, I have come to the conclusion that the best way of meeting the situation is by running swiftly away from it. In the words of an old music hall song, 'I've made up my mind to sail away.' As a matter of fact, I intend to leave by aeroplane—but that's a mere question of despatch. You have my story in a nutshell."

For some moments Vereker sat silent and pensive. Passing his long fingers across his brow he suddenly looked up at Smale to encounter a pair of frank, blue eyes from which he had temporarily removed the distorting lenses of his spectacles. The latter he was meticulously wiping with a silk handkerchief.

"I see the difficult situation in which you are placed, Smale. Having had little experience of the crises which arise in the affairs of the heart I must run mute, so to speak. Naturally, I had no cognizance of this secret trouble of yours, and you will have to pardon me for ascribing your sudden disappearance from Bygrave Hall to a vastly different cause. This was inevitable in the circumstances. Now, I am going to be brutally frank with you as to the reason of my call on you this morning. It is no use my mincing matters. I have here in my pocket the receipt, now in fragments, which Mrs. Cathcart gave Lord Bygrave for the £10,000 worth of bearer bonds and which you found for me in the secret drawer of his bureau. I confronted that lady with the receipt and she angrily proclaimed it an impudent forgery. In a paroxysm of rage she tore it in pieces. She tells me she had an interview with you at Glendon Street which doesn't quite conform with your story to me that you had only seen her once and that for a few seconds only. Will you be utterly frank, Smale, and tell me what was the nature of that interview and how came Lord Bygrave by this receipt for £10,000 worth of bearer bonds."

Smale drew himself upright in his chair and his face, now deeply flushed, bore an air of perplexity.

"H'm," he muttered, "it is difficult for me to know where to begin and how much I ought to divulge of this matter. In the first place my interview at Glendon Street was with regard to a furnished bungalow at Shoreham which Lord Bygrave offered to the lady rent free during her stay in England, and which she refused. As you know, Vereker, I was Lord Bygrave's confidential secretary, and have felt all along that my lips ought to be sealed with regard to his private affairs. I feel much in the same position as a doctor or priest called upon for evidence. It's against my principles—I have little conscience left, but still a few principles—to reveal anything about Lord Bygrave's hidden life, on which I have been honourably paid to keep silence. You see my position?"

"The present circumstances, I think you will agree, Smale, warrant your departing from those principles. It may be a very serious matter for you not to do so."

"Yes, yes. I have weighed all that up long ago, and don't feel the least bit afraid of any consequences on account of my reticence, or even prevarication, provided I do my duty to Bygrave."

"I know, of course, that Bygrave was married many years ago to the present Mrs. Cathcart, if that removes an obstacle in the way of your revealing to me more of the matter of this receipt," interrupted Vereker bluntly.

Smale gave an involuntary start at this information.

"The devil you do!" he exclaimed. "I suppose she told you so?"

"She did," replied Vereker.

"And she says this receipt for the bonds is a forgery?" queried Smale with real or well-feigned surprise.

"She stoutly affirms that it is."

"Well, I'm damned! Either she's a consummate economist where truth is concerned or I have been neatly fooled," replied Smale, his brow deeply furrowed, his eyes staring fixedly at the pattern on the carpet at his feet.

"How did Lord Bygrave come by the receipt?" queried Vereker quietly.

"Although I never saw the correspondence, Bygrave told me she posted it to him on the receipt of the money."

"Were you aware of the transaction?"

"Certainly. She wrote to him saying that she was practically destitute, and he confided in me with regard to the whole situation. He told me that she was his wife and wanted to divulge that fact in a book of her reminiscences. This he was most eager to avoid, and to put her on her feet and evade any further trouble with her he said he had sent her the money."

"Then why should she deny that she gave this receipt for the money? She swears that she never received a penny from Lord Bygrave."

"I suppose because the transaction bordered very dangerously on blackmail. In any case a woman's pride is enough to urge her to such a denial."

"Did you handle the money at any time?" asked Vereker somewhat pointedly.

An angry flush lit Smale's eye for a moment, but swiftly vanished. "Rather a pertinent question, Vereker, prompted no doubt by my sudden departure subsequently from Bygrave Hall. I see the trend of your thoughts: the situation gave me an opportunity for a lively little swindle. To cover it I possibly had a hand in Bygrave's disappearance—it would be a distinctly opportune disappearance for me, eh? Well, I'm pleased to state that at no time did I handle the bonds. Bygrave simply gave me the receipt and asked me to conceal it in the secret drawer of his bureau. Think for a moment, Vereker; were I dishonourably implicated in this transaction of bonds, should I have been such a fool as to discover the receipt for you? I hardly think I'm a congenital idiot."

"Quite so, Smale; even as a piece of bluff it would have been unduly risky," replied Vereker pensively. "The whole affair begins to assume a bewildering complexion."

"As far as I can judge—though I don't know the lady—I should say she's an accomplished liar, much as I dislike saying that of any woman," added Smale as he turned up the collar of his dressing-gown.

"I wouldn't go as far as that," remarked Vereker. "I have met the lady and, if she has designedly deceived me, she must be a great artist. I can hardly believe it of her."

"She is a most prepossessing woman," said Smale, closing his eyes. "Beauty is a very dangerous weapon in the armoury of deceit. Believe me, I have been already wounded by the self-same weapon. You must be alertly on guard," he added warningly.

Vereker sat silent, buried in his own thoughts.

"She may be utterly innocent of the whole affair," he suggested at length.

"That is quite possible, Vereker," confirmed Smale, "anything is possible in this tangled business. I wonder what odds a psychological bookmaker would lay on the possibility of her not being innocent at all."

At this juncture Vereker rose from his chair. "I'm sorry to have troubled you about this affair, Smale, but I hope you understand the reasons which actuated me. I'm trying to get at the truth. You must also pardon the directness of my interrogation; it would have been a waste of time beating about the bush."

"Don't apologize, Vereker," replied Smale pleasantly. "I hope I've cleared the air somewhat, though at the moment it looks as if I had begotten a fog. If you want any further information, you had better write to me and address the letter to my home address. I shall not be there, but I shall eventually receive your correspondence. I must keep in touch with the guv'nor. I'm bound to the old home by the chain of pecuniary circumstance—at least until I can get on my feet abroad. Australia is the land of my choice. My only regret is that I can't offer dear old London a first-class ticket to accompany me."

He extended a friendly hand which Vereker, in spite of the many doubts in his mind, shook warmly.

"God speed," he said. "I hope you'll have good luck."

A few seconds afterwards he was in the street making his way slowly back to his flat. A look of weariness and dejection was on his lean, handsome face. His hands were clasped behind his back as he walked in his long-striding, leisurely manner.

"Drawn blank again," he muttered to himself, and added as an afterthought: "At least it appears so at the moment. I must go and see Mrs. Cathcart. She has something to disclose according to her last letter to me. Perhaps she can now shed a further ray of light on my darkness."

He arrived to find Ricardo washing up dishes and whistling an air from "Rigoletto" very much out of tune. At the sound of his footsteps Ricardo came at once into the studio, tea-towel and dripping plate in his hands.

"Well, Sherlock or Thorndike, or whatever you like to picture yourself, what of the interview? Did you singe the beard of the elusive Smale?"

"He was in, and I had a long chat with him," returned Vereker.

"Sounds quite mild. With satisfactory results, may I ask?"

"It has left me more bemused than ever, Ricky. Smale revealed himself to-day as cherubic; he was frankness and innocence personified; he was a thing of light. I ventured to his digs with the intention of extorting something amounting to a confession of guilt from him, armed, as I believed I was, with the deadly weapon of a forged receipt. I was nearly certain that he had forged that receipt. Under his self-possession and coolness and readiness to supply any information that I required, I saw the portentous mountains of my suspicions dissolve and slide away over the horizon and leave a smiling plain of trust and good faith. It was simply miraculous!"

"That chap would be worth his weight in gold as a company promoter, barrister or politician," remarked Ricky, hanging the tea-towel on a peg of Vereker's easel.

"I'm not sure yet whether he is innocent or not," said Vereker, thrusting his hands deep in his pockets and gazing blankly out of the window. If he is, it casts a very sinister light on Mrs. Cathcart—she is then a liar and a blackmailer."

"Which, of course, you don't believe for a moment?" said Ricardo, smiling.

"True, Ricky, perfectly true. Can you suggest anything?"

"Nothing more helpful than that you should rely, in the good old English fashion, on the spin of a coin."

Vereker disdained further conversation and still stood gazing out of the window, lost in thought.

"I wonder if I should go and see Mrs. Cathcart again," he soliloquized aloud.

"For God's sake do, Vereker. I know you're dying to," said Ricardo earnestly. "You remember my solution to the mystery of her last letter asking for an interview with you? You want to go and fall a victim to her charms. You can't deceive me, you know. Your absence will give me a chance of completing the next chapter of my dramatic story with some sort of verve. If you stay here I'll compose an ode to death or a lost soul, or—"

"I'm going to have a rest, Ricky," said Vereker, suddenly interrupting his friend. "My brain is tired and I'm depressed. Wake me about five o'clock, like a good chap, and have a cup of tea ready. I'll go down to Farnaby and see Mrs. Cathcart to-night."

"Very good, sir, and what suit of clothes will you wear this evening, sir? Brown shoes or black, white, brown or grey spats, sir? And the tie is most important."

Vereker's bedroom door closed quietly on Ricardo's flippant chatter, and he disappeared without further comment.

"By all the saints!" exclaimed Ricardo with a troubled look, "I'll write something on this and call it 'From painter to sleuth: the story of an unhappy metamorphosis.'" He strolled slowly back into the kitchen and gravely resumed his dish washing.

Chapter Seventeen

When Vereker arrived at Farnaby it was dark, and without wasting time he made his way to the narrow and deeply rutted lane that led to Bramblehurst. On leaving the main road he plunged into Cimmerian darkness, for there were no lamps, and progress became difficult and slow. Every now and then he sank ankle-deep in muddy pools, and heartily wished that he had brought a flash-lamp with him. At length he discerned the dark silhouette of a house against the lighter tone of the night sky, and knew he had reached his destination. Opening the gate and advancing a few paces up the gravelled approach, he was at once confronted with the disturbing fact that there were no lights in any of the windows of the dwelling.

All day long he had been in an unpleasant and depressed frame of mind, and the discovery that his journey had possibly been in vain did not tend to brighten his sombre outlook.

"Surely they cannot have turned in," he muttered to himself; "it's too early. They may, of course, be out, or perhaps they are using some room at the back of the house."

For some seconds he stood hesitant, deliberative, and then, striking a match, approached the front door and pressed the bell-push. He heard the bell ring shrilly in the profound stillness, but waited in vain for any answer to his summons.

"This fairly ices the cake," he ejaculated bitterly, and was about to depart when a sound of some movement within fell on his acute ears. He waited expectantly, hoping ardently that his hearing had not been at fault; but all again was as silent as the grave.

"A window rattling in a gust of wind," he soliloquized. This surmise, however, hardly convinced him, for he was aware that the night was profoundly still, and not a twig of tree or bush stirred to disturb the uncanny hush.

Not at all prone to imaginary fears, he felt himself invaded by an unusual sense of uneasiness and dread. Around him evergreen shrubs and yews reared a high wall of impenetrable gloom; an owl flung out a melancholy and eerie call from a tree near, and was answered afar off by another; some creature of the night rustled the leaves of the thick laurel hedge dividing the garden from the lane. Nature's marauders were astir and swift murder afoot. Shaking off with an effort his groundless nervousness, he walked boldly round the house with the intention of trying the back door, his heavy shoes noisily crunching the gravel. The very sound of his own footsteps seemed matter-of-fact and comforting in his present mood; but, strive how he might, Vereker was unable to rid himself of a feeling that something unusual and sinister ruled the moment. He experienced this all the more keenly because he was not at all given to presentiments or premonitions. He knocked loudly on the door, making the house reverberate with the tattoo, and stood with ears straining to catch the slightest sound from within. No reply was vouchsafed, and in his disappointment he swore vehemently, calling himself a feckless fool for not having wired that he was coming. Leaving the back door, he was about to make a detour of the house and set out for Farnaby village when, to his surprise, he discovered one of the kitchen windows wide open.

"Hello," he exclaimed, "this is odd! They have evidently forgotten to close it. It offers a golden opportunity for any passing tramp or loafer."

Then like a flash it crossed his mind that the sound of movement within which he was certain he had heard when he rung the front door bell might have its origin in some unlawful intruder. He considered for a moment what action he should take, and then, climbing swiftly and quietly in at the window, found himself in the kitchen. Thence he fumbled his way by the uncertain light of a match into the drawing-room, and discovered to his astonishment that all the choice pieces of furniture and *objets d'art* which he had furtively admired on his first visit had disappeared. The obvious conclusion was that Mrs. Cathcart and her adopted daughter had departed and taken their own belongings with them, leaving behind the furniture which belonged to the landlord. This was an electrifying discovery after her pressing invitation to him to come down and see her before her departure abroad. The match which Vereker had held aloft, and by which he had hastily surveyed the room, flickered fitfully to a stump and went out. The room was plunged in darkness. He was about to strike another when again he felt certain that he heard the sound of cautious movement somewhere.

"Anyone in?" he called loud enough to be heard upstairs, but his voice only echoed throughout the house and was soon engulfed in the profound silence.

"Enough to give anybody the creeps," he soliloquized, and determined to retrace his steps and firmly wedge the kitchen window on leaving.

His mind was in a turmoil. Why had Mrs. Cathcart so suddenly taken her departure? Where had she gone? It seemed to him that at every crucial moment of his investigation of the Bygrave case some one had vanished and left him baffled and disgruntled. Well, it was little use wasting precious time in futile conjecture in an uninhabited house surrounded by impenetrable darkness. He would have liked to explore the floor above, but the trains from Farnaby—yes, he must keep an eye on those trains. They ran at disconcertingly long and inconvenient intervals. He pulled out his watch and struck one of a fast dwindling reserve of matches. It was seven o'clock. There was a train at a quarter to eight; that would just give him time to make a cursory investigation of the room upstairs. Next moment the match in his hand had expired and he was standing bolt upright with every faculty on the alert. There was no mistaking the sound: it was that of a stealthy footfall, and it appeared to come from the staircase leading to the next floor.

"Who's there?" he challenged loudly, but received no reply. At that moment he cursed himself that he had not taken the precaution to bring his automatic pistol with him. He was about to strike another match and endeavour to discover who this lurker might be when, to his utter amazement, an electric torch opened a dazzling eye only a few feet from his face, temporarily blinding him with its powerful beam. Then, in the half-light behind the lamp, he caught sight of a face that left him completely aghast. It was the face of Lord Bygrave! But that face was lined and haggard and brutalized, and from its staring eyes there glared the light of a maniacal frenzy.

"Good God, Henry!" he exclaimed; but no sooner had he uttered the words than he received a smashing blow on the forehead with some heavy implement, and the whole word swiftly dissolved and slid into the dark abyss of unconsciousness,

He came to his senses it seemed an interminable time afterwards, coughing and spluttering from the effects of some burning liquid having been poured down his throat. It was brandy, and a warm glow seemed instantly to percolate through his veins. Some one had placed a supporting arm round his shoulders and was holding a flask to his face with his free hand. A candle lit up the room with a weak and fluctuating light, throwing grotesque shadows on walls and ceiling. His head was throbbing with an agonizing pain. Then a reddish mist seemed to envelop his immediate surroundings, and he slipped jerkily back into oblivion. When he regained consciousness once more an anxious voice was speaking to him:

"Come on, Vereker, pull yourself together like a man. "Get your teeth into life and hang on. You're all right. Bad flesh wound and concussion, that's all! Good job you have a thick skull! It was a wallop like the kick of a mule as far as I can gather. The brute must have used a life-preserver. Now then, there you are—have a little more brandy."

It was a voice familiar to Vereker and seemed to be chattering on partly to encourage its nervous owner, but in his dazed condition he could not place it. With an effort he looked up and found, to his astonishment, a pair of distorted, spectacled eyes gazing anxiously at him from the ludicrously childlike face of Sidney Smale.

"Better now, old horse?" asked the latter.

"Yes; but how the devil did you get here, Smale? This is Bramblehurst, Mrs. Cathcart's house?" queried Vereker weakly.

"You've spotted it first go," replied Smale. "It shows that your senses are beginning to regain their self-respect and coming out of their hiding-holes. Don't worry about anything for the present, and take another swig at this reviver: it will lace you up."

Vereker took an ample gulp from the flask, and soon felt decidedly better.

"Can you get on your feet?" asked Smale. "If you can manage it, we'll make an effort to get back at once to Farnaby. But first let me sponge the blood from your face and clothes. I have found a kettle and put it on to boil. It must be almost ready."

With these words he placed his arms around Vereker and, bringing him with a gentle heave to his feet, guided him to an arm-chair.

"Now sit there quietly; I won't be a minute," he said and disappeared into the kitchen.

He reappeared almost immediately with a basin of hot water and a clean handkerchief and, having gently but dexterously bathed Vereker's head and hands, bound the handkerchief firmly round his cut forehead.

By this time Vereker had regained sufficient strength to rise unaided to his feet, and with Smale's assisting arm and walking-stick protested that he was ready to proceed.

"That's better," remarked Smale encouragingly. "Now we'll quit this unhallowed spot or something worse may befall us."

"What on earth brought you down here?" again asked the bewildered Vereker, as they slowly and shakily walked along the path to the front gate of Bramblehurst.

"I had come to see Mrs. Cathcart about that receipt for bearer bonds. From your conversation this morning it seemed to me that I was under suspicion as a forger. Naturally I wasn't going to take that lying down—especially as I am about to make a hurried departure from England. I've no desire to return later and find that I've got that lie to lay. Lord knows I'm a fool, but I haven't yet stooped to crime. I knocked at the front door, though I noticed the house was in darkness, and received no reply. I was about to return when an amazing thing happened. I chanced to glance at the drawing-room window from the front door. Suddenly the darkness of the room beyond was lit up by the bright flash of an electric torch. A man's figure (yours it proved to be) was silhouetted clearly against the light. Then something shot out like a cobra striking from beyond the beam of the electric torch, there was a groan and you fell backward with a crash on the floor. Gripping my stick, I stole stealthily round to the back of the house, hoping that I might ambush the assailant. I had no desire to meet him face to face—I'm not a man of brawn—but there was just a chance that I could give him a shrewd blow when he wasn't looking. When I reached the back of the house the scoundrel had escaped. I heard his sprinting feet doing their damnedest across the paddock beyond, and at once came to your assistance. Who on earth could the man have been? A burglar, I suppose."

"It would be difficult for me to hazard a guess," replied Vereker cautiously. "I was blinded by the glare of the flash-lamp."

"It appears that Mrs. Cathcart has vamosed. I wonder where she has gone?" said Smale. "I should dearly like to clear up the matter of those bonds before quitting these inhospitable shores. I presume you journeyed down on the same errand?"

"I did," replied Vereker. "The result was as painful as it was unexpected, to say the least of it."

"It might have been worse," added Smale, "and you ought to sing with old Horace: 'Quam paene furvae regna Proserpinae et judicantem vidimus Aeacum.'"

"I ought to be thankful, I suppose," replied Vereker; "I've had a narrow squeak."

Chapter Eighteen

The journey back to London seemed to Vereker an endless affair. The blow which he had received had shaken him badly, and every jolt of the train was a sharp renewal of agony. In an unobtrusive way Smale was as solicitous about his comfort as anybody could have been, and Vereker in his heart was touched by the gentleness and care which his companion displayed. He was now beginning to feel a distinct remorse for all the hard things he had thought of him. Yet Smale had only himself to blame: his behaviour had, to put it mildly, been erratic enough in the circumstances to arouse the gravest suspicions.

As Vereker sat propped up in the corner of a first-class carriage, reviewing the almost incredible incidents of the night, he congratulated himself that some strange but beneficent chance had sent Smale down to Bramblehurst. He shuddered to think what might have happened had it not been for the secretary's opportune arrival. His mind then wandered off into a labyrinth of speculation on that unfathomable element in life which men call luck and, growing weary, he fell fast asleep.

On arrival at Charing Cross he took a taxi to his flat, where Smale, to his companion's surprise, firmly refused the proffered hospitality of a whisky and soda and decided to drive on to his own rooms.

"I'm done with drinks for the time being," Vereker," he said. "My temperament is one that cannot use such a blessing; it promptly starts to abuse it, and under alcoholic impulse I'm little short of a raving lunatic."

"Then you're better without, I suppose. Shall I see you before you go, Smale?" asked Vereker.

"Hardly, old man. I'm off early in the morning, and I have so much at present to think about that my time will be fully occupied."

"Ah, well, *bon voyage*!" said Vereker and, with a warm handshake, Smale leaped back into the conveyance, which glided away into the whirling maze of London's traffic.

On opening his door Vereker discovered that the ebullient Ricardo was still in possession. That youth was now writing furiously at his so-called *magnum opus* surrounded by the debris of a meal, and studiously finished his paragraph before looking round to greet his arrival.

"Crystallized ginger—high-frequency pep—that's what I call that love scene!" he soliloquized. "None of your amorous snail about it. It ought to calcinate every flapper in Britain and America. Then the screen rights, etc., etc. Lord, I hear the shekels rattling!"

Flinging down the manuscript, he at length turned round to welcome Vereker.

"Suffering humanity!" he exclaimed on seeing his friend's bandaged forehead. "What on earth has happened, Vereker?"

"Got a nasty knock, that's all. Don't worry, Ricky, I'm all right."

"If you'll give me the money, I know where I can get a bottle of brandy on the Q.T.—*I* myself prefer whisky. There's no elixir in this abandoned place."

"Yes, there is," replied Vereker. "Knowing your propensities, I hid it. But I'd rather have a strong cup of tea."

"Righty-o. I've got a kettle on the murmur. You'll have one in a few minutes. But who on earth fouled your intelligence department?"

"Pardon me, Ricky, if I'm not communicative to-night. I don't feel up to it. I'll tell you all another time. To put it baldly, I got an unexpected knock on the head when exploring Mrs. Cathcart's empty house down at Farnaby this evening."

"Well, I'm damned! You know you oughtn't to do these detective stunts single-handed. It's dangerous. Now, if I had been there the chances are that you wouldn't have been tackled except by a gang. I can use my dooks, as you know. But, talking of Farnaby reminds me, this very Mrs. Cathcart called here to-day at four o'clock. Isn't that strange?"

"Mrs. Cathcart?" queried Vereker, with undisguised surprise.

"The same. She seemed very disappointed when I told her you were away for the day and that I was uncertain when you would return. I gave her tea, or rather we made it together, and I was rather pleased you were away. It was delightfully jolly all on our own. Isn't she a stunner! If you haven't a prior claim, I think I'll fall in love with her without further delay. If you have, then name your seconds at once and choose your weapons."

"Did she leave an address?" asked Vereker.

"No, she didn't. She seemed rather overwrought; but she said she'd ring you up, because she particularly wants to see you before she goes abroad. There's something on her mind, I'm sure; women can't deceive the ripe and experienced Ricky. *Prenez garde*, Vereker!"

"Did she say where she was going?"

"The Riviera."

Vereker was silent and, throwing off his overcoat, sank into a comfortable arm-chair. Ricardo, taking the hint, brought him a cup of tea and prepared to retire.

"I'm going to turn in, Vereker. I can see you want to ruminate alone. I've to be up early tomorrow, I've just received a letter from my mother. She wants to see me. I hope it prognosticates cash. I'll have to give her a résumé of my life for the past few weeks. When she knows I've been staying with you, and working like a driven Egyptian, she'll be mollified to the tune of forty quid or so. I did the 'starving author in a garret' once, but it didn't mint a fiver out of my people. Unknown to me, they had seen me on the river with Freda the day before. We were busy at the moment with a bottle of Pol Roger which I had just fished out of the locker. But I mustn't hold you spellbound any longer, old wimple. Don't make too long a day of it. Good night."

"Good night, Ricky; wake me when you turn out, like a good chap," replied Vereker, and drank off his cup of tea at one draught. He now felt considerably refreshed and, as the pain from his wound had subsided, he poked up the fire and sat back at ease in his arm-chair. An evening paper lay on the table. He picked it up lazily and glanced cursorily at the headlines; further than that he seldom ventured. There was little news of importance, so he dropped the paper on the floor beside his chair and began to recapitulate to himself all the incidents of an eventful day. By far the most momentous fact that he had gathered about the Bygrave case was that Lord Bygrave was apparently alive but insane. Some damnable and evil thing had evidently occurred and sent awry that once keen and supple brain. Grief and horror commingled at his recollection of that drawn and frenzied face, those feverish eyes, that look of determined malevolence. What could have brought about such a dire change in so kindly, lovable and sane a man?

For a long while Vereker sat gazing into the cheerful, leaping flames of his fire, trying hard to find some solution to this mystery. Of course Bygrave must have been insane when he made the murderous attack on the man Twistleton at the Mill House at Eyford. This new knowledge shed a clear light on that episode and went a long way to corroborate Winslade's story, which at the time seemed to him utterly incredible. But why had Bygrave gone down to Bramblehurst? In his disordered brain there might have been born some thought of settling matters violently with his former wife—a sudden hatred, a cunning plan of murder. Thank God, Mrs. Cathcart had left in the nick of time! Vereker uttered a genuine sigh of relief. Had she received some warning? Her departure seemed to have been hurried. Where had she gone? Or was her disappearance simply due to an anxiety to avoid any further inconvenient investigation about the receipt for the bonds? It was hopelessly bewildering and, to add the last straw, Smale, for whom he had never cared much and whom he had always instinctively distrusted, had unexpectedly behaved like a trump.

Truly, human nature was utterly baffling! And human character remained steadfast it seemed only when running along the permanent way of habitual, daily life. Take away the familiar lines and fling that character into the medley of unexpected circumstance and anything might happen: your saint might turn devil, your devil saint. The guise in which a man journeyed through life was merely the flimsiest of garments that might be blown away by any chance wind of fortune or adversity. It was quite within the bounds of possibility that Smale had forged that receipt after all. At this moment the clock on the mantelpiece chimed ten, and immediately afterwards the telephone bell rang shrilly. Vereker rose and picked up the instrument.

"That you, Mr. Vereker?" came the question over the wire.

"Yes."

"May I come along and see you? Inspector Heather speaking."

"Do by all means, Heather; I shall be glad to see you. I want somebody to talk to."

"Then I'll come along at once."

A quarter of an hour later Vereker heard the rumble of a taxi and the detective's tread outside his door. On letting him in he noticed that Heather's face was unusually pale. The inspector, after glancing at Vereker's bandaged forehead without a word, doffed the soft felt hat that he was wearing and revealed his own head also swathed in linen.

"Good heavens, Heather, what has happened?" asked Vereker, consternation written on his face.

"I was just going to ask you the same question," retorted Heather, smiling.

"Take a pew," suggested Vereker, pulling another chair to the fire.

The inspector sank into it heavily and, looking mysteriously at Vereker, said:

"Come now, Mr. Vereker, tell me all about it."

Vereker leaned back and briefly related the adventures which he had encountered during the day. He noticed the light of surprise which glowed in Heather's eyes as he unfolded his tale, and then eagerly awaited Heather's narrative.

"A remarkable occurrence—almost incredible!" commented Heather. "Do you know that I also visited Bramblehurst to-night. It must have been about an hour after you had left. I was nosing round the place, after I had discovered that this Mrs. Cathcart— whom I particularly wanted to meet—had flown, and I was struck down in much the same way as you yourself, but from behind. Did you get a glimpse of your assailant, Mr. Vereker?"

"I did," replied Vereker laconically.

"Could you identify him?"

"Nothing so simple."

"Who on earth could he be?" asked Heather impatiently.

"It was Lord Bygrave," replied Vereker bluntly.

For some moments Heather gazed in dumb astonishment at Vereker. "You don't mean to say so!" he remarked, as if utterly bewildered, and then brought his hand down with a resounding slap on his knee.

That simple action worked like a flash of lightning on the dark sky of Vereker's confused surmises, but he remained silent, gazing stolidly into the fire as if nothing of importance had occurred to him, and in that brief space of time he learned that Inspector Heather was still running neck and neck with him in the slow-motion race of investigation.

"You went to see Mrs. Cathcart about those bearer bonds, I suppose?" asked Vereker with disturbing directness.

Heather's sharp, observant eyes glanced up quickly and an amused smile broke slowly over his features.

"That was one reason," he replied. "Don't you think she cleverly squeezed them out of Bygrave? I take it for granted you have discovered that they are still man and wife."

Vereker could not avoid a sudden start at this communication, and then burst into hearty laughter. "Heather, you are splendid!" he said sincerely. "How you get your information puzzles me; but, as for Mrs. Cathcart being a blackmailer, the very idea seems preposterous to me."

"And Smale, of course, you dismiss him too, without a stain on his character, after his behaviour of this evening?"

"I have just been looking at that problem from every angle to-night, Heather, and I am at loss to arrive at any conclusion at present. Perhaps you know more than I do about Smale. It seems an extraordinary coincidence that he should arrive at Bramblehurst at the moment he did—it was almost uncannily opportune."

"There is such a thing as pulling the wool over people's eyes," commented Heather quietly. "It only requires nerve and a convincing manner. I've seen so much of it in my experience that I may be unduly sceptical. The Good Samaritan is a very effective rôle when well played."

"If it was merely a rôle it was played with genius to-night," commented Vereker.

"All the more reason to be on the alert," warned Heather. "But, tell me, have you made any further progress in the elucidation of this mystery of Bygrave's disappearance? Have you formulated any further theory as to why he should vanish other than Mr. Winslade's incredible murder story?"

Vereker sat silent for a moment, thinking deeply, and then with impish but hidden glee replied:

"Having gone deeply into the matter since our last meeting, Heather, I have come to the conclusion that all my previous surmises were incorrect. One by one they tottered and fell, having no solid foundations. After much cogitation I have elicited the fact that the master brain in the whole baffling affair is Bygrave's. He is spoofing everybody. Winslade and Farnish know he's alive. I have seen him. He was the perpetrator of the outrage on you and me to-night. Of course the story of the murder of Mr. Twistleton was sheer moonshine, flung off to deceive Winslade as to whom he really met at the Mill House at Eyford."

"Whom did he meet?" asked the inspector bluntly.

"Smale, of course. Smale, his private secretary, knows every move of the game—a game of blackmail played desperately by Mrs. Cathcart, his former wife. You understand now why Smale appeared so opportunely to-night. He was undoubtedly there with his employer to checkmate the machinations of the lady. He's a clever and artistic liar and an excellent co-adjutor in Bygrave's plan. You will also remember, to revert for a moment to the Mill

House, that there was an open window upstairs when I made a thorough search of the place. Naturally, Smale had made his exit that way in case he should by any chance encounter Winslade on the road."

"H'm," grunted Inspector Heather, "and you think Smale impersonated Bygrave at the White Bear?"

"No; we'll have to drop that impersonation theory."

"I see. But why all this mystification on Lord Bygrave's part?"

"Can't you see that his wife has been blackmailing him? He doesn't want his early, secret marriage divulged now. He had definitely closed that chapter of his life and made his will as if he were a single man. He probably hates the sight of his wife. She, on the other hand, wishes to disclose the story of that marriage in her reminiscences—it would probably prove her brightest chapter—and he gives her £10,000 as settlement for her silence. Having received the money, she promptly, like most blackmailers, tries the extracting process again. Bygrave finally resolves to get her out of the country or, driven mad with rage, goes down to Farnaby to use physical violence as a persuasive. We were in the way of his prearranged plan, and he taps us forcibly on the head as a playful reminder that we should be at home and in bed long ago."

"And his further intentions?" asked Heather, looking dreamily into the fire.

"The rest is plain sailing," replied Vereker with a gesture of finality. "Having rid himself of his female incubus, he turns up suddenly at some tiny English village in a dazed and dishevelled state, like some bemused visitant from a distant and ferocious star. Another case of lost memory, thinks the constable leading him gingerly to the nearest police station. Next day the Press with gigantic headlines report the amazing discovery of Lord Bygrave, and there is a chorus of joy and sympathy from all sides. He is a great public figure; he has been overworking at the Ministry and broken down in health in his unflagging service of the State. A famous physician counsels a long rest and a sea-voyage as a restorative, and a grateful country is happy ever afterwards. You see the underlying cunning of the whole plan? Only one man—Smale—was to have been privy to all the facts, and he is promptly leaving England, doubtless with a nice little pension from his lordship. I must say this for Smale: he has been loyal through and through to Bygrave and was a labourer worthy of his hire."

"Why was Smale at the Mill House that night?" asked Heather pertinently.

"I'm rather hazy about that point," said Vereker, "but Bygrave, I imagine, was going to buy the house—you know he loves the district—and Smale was evidently down there having a look over it for him. Bygrave suddenly wished to give him some urgent instructions and was obliged to call there on his way down to the White Bear. It is a minor point in the mystery, I should say."

"Who was Mr. Twistleton?" asked the inspector, remorselessly interrogative.

"I think, if you make inquiries," replied Vereker, smiling, "you'll find that Mr. Twistleton had left the Mill House some days previous to his supposed murder."

"That's the first word of truth you've told, Mr. Vereker," replied the inspector quietly.

"Perhaps I've gone wildly astray in my deductions, Heather, but what else can you expect from an amateur? And your conclusions? Aren't you going to enlighten me and expose to me my crass ignorance?"

Inspector Heather smiled knowingly.

"I'm going to tell you some facts," he said, "frigid facts which you probably know as well as I do. We'll disregard for the moment the misleading squish you've just been spouting in a clumsy effort to put a joke across me. I won't say just how I have arrived at those facts, for of course I have a staff of agents who make matters comparatively easy for me. In the first place, Lord Bygrave—of this I'm almost certain—is dead. The story of Mrs. Cathcart's blackmailing him is sheer bunkum. Smale has no complicity in the business of Lord Bygrave's death whatever. Winslade and Farnish have as much acumen as my boots—probably less. Lord Bygrave's office staff—Grierson, Bliss and Murray—amiable nonentities, know as much about the affair as my hat knows about snipe-shooting."

"But hold on, Heather. Whom did I see at Bramblehurst to-night?"

"God knows. In your highly-strung state you must have imagined you saw Lord Bygrave. You have had him on your mind so long that such an hallucination is quite within the bounds of probability. The mind plays strange tricks at times."

"Quite so," agreed Vereker airily, "but I distrust that explanation. Then you have definitely concluded that Lord Bygrave has been murdered?"

"I said I was certain that he was dead," corrected the inspector. "I only surmise that he has been murdered."

"To put aside the squish I spouted to you to-night, Heather, and which lamentably failed to materialize into a joke at your expense, and to be thoroughly in earnest, I agree with you in all your conclusions but one. I will further add that I am as near certain as 'damn it' that Lord Bygrave has been murdered. I see clearly that we are both nearing the end of our labours. An even sovereign with you that I pass the post first."

"Taken," said Heather, extending his hand, "and, to adjust the weights fairly, I'll give you a line on the culprit."

"Ah, and he is?" queried Vereker.

"I'm not certain, of course, but what do you think about Lawless as an odds on favourite?"

"No, Heather, I don't like the tip. You are simply going on book-form, if I may continue the racing phraseology."

Inspector Heather rose. "I wish Mrs. Cathcart hadn't vanished so suddenly," he said; "it means we've got to track her down."

"Imperatively the next step," agreed Vereker. "You'll probably hear from me before long, Heather—or I may look you up for that sovereign."

"You'll be welcome, Mr. Vereker, and then we can go over the ground together just for the love of the thing. It ought to be an interesting post-mortem on the case. Good night."

Chapter Nineteen

Hardly had Inspector Heather taken his departure than Vereker's telephone bell rang, making him start with its sudden summons.

"I wonder," he soliloquized as he picked up the instrument.

"Is that you, Mr. Vereker?" came a well-known and nicely modulated voice.

"Yes; you are Mrs. Cathcart, I believe?"

"Fancy your recognizing my voice!" came the exclamation. "I called on you to-day about tea-time and was very hospitably received by your friend, Mr. Ricardo."

"So he told me. I had gone down to Farnaby to see you on rather an urgent matter, but found you had vacated the house."

"I'm so sorry you made the journey in vain, especially after my asking you to come down and see me, but I was obliged to hasten my departure, Mr. Vereker. I had very cogent reasons for doing so. I'm going to the Riviera, as you know, but please keep this strictly private and tell Mr. Ricardo to do the same. I wished to bid you good-bye before leaving and, perhaps more important to you, I have a little confession to make. There is something on my mind which indirectly concerns you, and I shall be glad to see you as soon as possible."

"When can we meet, Mrs. Cathcart?" asked Vereker.

"It has just struck eleven, and I am here in Graham Street, Number 56, quite close to you. Would you care to come round now, if it's not too late? I shall not retire till one to-night—I have so many things to arrange before my departure. I am staying with a friend, but every one has turned in except myself, so we shall be able to talk alone."

"I shall be with you in ten minutes."

"Thanks."

Vereker hung up the receiver and, seizing hat and coat, promptly set out for Graham Street. He chose to walk the distance, feeling that the exercise would steady him, for he had to admit to himself that his heart was beating with undue rapidity and that his nerves were distinctly shaky. He felt also that he was stealing a valuable start on Inspector Heather.

On his arrival at 56 Graham Street, Mrs. Cathcart opened the door of the flat herself and led him into a brightly lit and exquisitely furnished drawing-room, where a cheerful fire was flaming briskly. She motioned him to a comfortable armchair beside her own and, sitting down, turned and looked him frankly in the face. Vereker saw by her heightened colour and sparkling eyes that she was excited, and noted that in such a mood she was ineffably beautiful. He felt the colour rising to his own cheeks under the magic of her radiant gaze, and knew that she had intuitively divined his secret admiration of her.

"So you are going abroad, Mrs, Cathcart?" he said to open the conversation.

"Yes, and I'm sorry that I'm going," she replied, with a hint of sadness in her voice. "I came back to England to settle down and live quietly and happily in the country, but the Fates have decided, it seems, that such peace is not for me. The past thrusts itself ruthlessly into the present, and cruelly shatters all my dreams. Perhaps I deserve it—the mills of God grind slowly but grind exceeding small. To come to the point, however, I have been utterly miserable since I saw you last, and all on account of that receipt you showed me, purporting to be in my handwriting, and which was supposed to be an acknowledgment to Lord Bygrave for £10,000 worth of bearer bonds. You will remember that I stoutly denied having received those bonds and, in my rage, tore up the receipt."

"Yes," said Vereker, and something lumpish seemed to rise in his throat. "Is she going to go back on her first statement?" he asked himself, and felt his brow grow moist with sudden dread.

"I deny it as stoutly now, Mr. Vereker, as I did then," she said firmly, "and you will doubtless remember that you said you had a shrewd idea as to who had forged my signature."

"I thought so at the time, Mrs. Cathcart," he replied. "I had an idea that it might be Lord Bygrave's secretary, Mr. Smale. I have never been able to prove it. He protests that he never had anything to do with the handling of those bearer bonds, and I believe he has spoken the truth."

"Whom did he blame?" came the direct question from Mrs. Cathcart.

"I don't know that he blamed anybody," said Vereker hesitatingly.

"Didn't he suggest that I had done so?" asked Mrs. Cathcart,

"Possibly," replied Vereker weakly.

"And you believed it, Mr. Vereker?" she asked quietly.

Vereker at once looked up, and saw a face shot with pain gazing sadly at the fire. Tears had welled up in her eyes. Before he could reply she continued:

"Of course you don't know me well; I only wish you knew me better. I can quite see that such a receipt required a lot of explaining away. In the light of my marriage to Lord Bygrave (an incident in his life which he desired to be utterly forgotten, and which I at that moment was inclined to divulge in my reminiscences) it would appear to a stranger that the £10,000 was distastefully like hush-money. I cannot blame anyone not cognizant of the facts and ignorant of my character coming hastily to such a conclusion."

"I have felt ever since I saw you," said Vereker emphatically, "that you were incapable of such an act."

"I wish I could believe you," she replied, and next moment burst into bitter sobs.

"It's rather unfair of you to doubt my word, Mrs. Cathcart," said Vereker curtly. "You imply that I'm a—"

"No, no, no, Mr. Vereker," she hastened to correct, holding up a protesting hand to him. "I have expressed myself unfortunately.

Forgive me." She hurriedly wiped the tears from her eyes and, collecting herself, continued:

"You had every reason to draw such an inference, and yet it was an inference that I hoped against hope that you wouldn't draw. There are people one meets in life by whom one wishes to be well thought of. Immediately I saw you that wish was born in me. I cannot explain why: it's some obscure working of the subconscious mind, I suppose. When you came to me about that receipt and frankly put the matter to me, I lost my temper, but from that moment I had faith in you. I revealed to you the story of my marriage to Lord Bygrave, and I felt you trusted me and thought me an honourable woman."

"I did and do, Mrs. Cathcart," said Vereker quietly.

"But, Mr. Vereker, though I told you the truth with regard to that matter, there was a part of my life-story which I concealed. At the moment it seemed quite unnecessary to the investigation you were making. Since then, however, things have occurred which make it imperative that I should acquaint you with certain facts which I had hoped were for ever buried in the past. I must do so now to clear myself of any implication with the matter of those bonds and the disappearance of Lord Bygrave. After that I shall feel that my conscience is clear and that I am at last at peace with myself and the world—at least so far as my unhappy past will allow me."

Mrs. Cathcart paused as if to collect her thoughts, and at that moment Vereker raised a hand to the bandage about his forehead, which had loosened.

"May I ask, Mr. Vereker, how you came to hurt yourself?" she said solicitously. "I didn't like to be inquisitive when you didn't proffer any explanation. Are you in any pain?"

"No, Mrs. Cathcart, I am quite comfortable, thank you, but the bandage has worked loose."

"Let me fasten it for you," she said, rising quickly to her feet and bending over him. Deftly untying the knots at the back of his head, she readjusted the handkerchief, and in doing so her cool, soft fingers swept in an unconscious caress across Vereker's brow. Her proximity to him exercised again that magic thrill which he had experienced on a previous occasion. Her touch and an exquisitely delicate perfume emanating from her made the blood throb in his temples. A feeling almost akin to fear came over him. He had never before responded so swiftly and deeply to the personal magnetism of any woman; never before had he felt that the reins guiding his emotions, apparently so secure in his hands, might be so easily taken from his grasp by the overwhelming attraction of beauty.

"I think that's secure now," said Mrs. Cathcart, eyeing her handiwork critically. "Would you like something to drink? You are tired and want a stimulant."

"Not in your presence," he said, smiling, and it seemed to him as if the words had been uttered in spite of himself.

"It's very charming of you to say so," she replied, flushing slightly, "because I've got a long story to tell you. But you haven't let me know how you came by your hurt."

"It's entirely your fault," replied Vereker jocularly. "You see, I went down to Bramblehurst this evening, hoping to find you there. The house was in darkness, and I was just about to depart when I thought I'd go round and see if there were any lights at the back. There were none, but, to my surprise, I found the kitchen window wide open."

"Good gracious, I wonder how that happened!" exclaimed Mrs. Cathcart, her eyes wide with astonishment.

"I can't say. Thinking some one had effected an entrance with questionable motives, I climbed in and explored. I reached the drawing-room and discovered that all your personal belongings had gone and, coming to the conclusion that you had flown, I was about to retrace my steps when some one flashed an electric torch in my face. The next moment I was struck down by a violent blow on the forehead. On regaining my senses I beat a diplomatic retreat and returned to town."

"Did you see your assailant?" questioned Mrs. Cathcart anxiously.

"Yes, and in my excited frame of mind I thought it was Lord Bygrave. Since then I have come to the conclusion that it cannot possibly have been he."

At the conclusion of this narration Vereker noticed that Mrs. Cathcart had gone deathly pale and was trembling violently. She appeared about to faint.

"Can you give me a little brandy, Mr. Vereker?" she said weakly. "You will find a flask in the cabinet."

Vereker jumped up from his chair and, bringing the restorative, applied it to Mrs. Cathcart's lips. With an effort she managed to swallow the liquid, and in a few minutes the colour had returned to her blanched cheeks and she was once again able to sit erect in her chair.

"It must be he!" she exclaimed to herself distractedly. "It must be he! Am I never to escape from the beast?"

"Who do you think it was, Mrs. Cathcart?" asked Vereker solicitously. "Don't be afraid to tell me, and you needn't fear that you will come by any harm if you will just put yourself in my hands. I'll see Inspector Heather of Scotland Yard to-morrow, and he'll look after your personal safety."

"No, no," came the bitter cry, "don't inform the police—you must not—I beg you, Mr. Vereker!"

"Then may I—may I look after you?" asked Vereker haltingly.

"Will you, Mr. Vereker?" she pleaded, looking up to him with fear-haunted eyes and seizing his hands in hers.

"Certainly, Mrs. Cathcart, if you will trust me. But who is this man of whom you live in dread?"

Bowing her head as if in shame, she muttered:

"My present husband."

"Good God!" exclaimed Vereker in spite of himself. "But—but I thought—I thought—"

"I know what you are thinking," she interrupted almost fiercely; "and you are right. I have committed bigamy. There's no use my mincing matters. After what I have suffered a phrase cannot torture me any more. But I committed bigamy, as they call it, through the lying machinations of this Mr. Cathcart. His name is not Cathcart at all; it is George Darnell, and he is a full cousin of Henry Darnell, Lord Bygrave. I discovered this after my marriage to him in America. I met him in Boston during the height of my popularity as an operatic singer and, probably through his remarkable resemblance to my former husband, I fell in love with him. He proposed to me, and I had to reveal to him the fact that I was already married. Not many months afterwards he brought me a newspaper cutting announcing the death of Henry Darnell, Lord Bygrave, and, thinking that I was at last free, I accepted his renewed proposal. Our married life was unhappy from the very beginning. He is a cowardly man with an ungovernable temper and, after a few months, began to terrorize me into supplying him with money, which he squandered on other women. I left him and put myself in the hands of solicitors, who promptly saw to it that he should not molest me further.

"Then he actually stooped to forging my signature to a cheque for several thousand pounds. Not wishing to become the subject of gossip for a hemisphere, I let that pass, and he then informed me that Henry Darnell, Lord Bygrave, my husband, was alive and that the Henry Darnell who had died was Lord Bygrave's cousin. Under the threat that he would expose the fact that I had committed bigamy, he tried to extort further sums of money from me. I promptly flung up my career on the plea of failing health and secretly fled from America to escape from him. Since then I have learned that he underwent a long sentence of imprisonment for a very clever forgery previous to our marriage, and that that was the reason of his change of name to Cathcart. Ever since my arrival in

England I have lived in dread that he would pursue and persecute me anew, and now my worst fears have been realized."

"Did he resemble Lord Bygrave facially?" asked Vereker, his eyes alight with a new excitement.

"Very much so, but there is a sinister cast about his whole countenance, and when roused to anger he looks as if he were a maniac."

"He was without doubt my assailant at Bramblehurst to-night," said Vereker. "You have given me a living portrait of the man. Did Lord Bygrave know of his cousin's criminal career?"

"I cannot say, Mr. Vereker; but there is one thing certain, and that is on his arrival in England he would try to extort money from Lord Bygrave. When you brought me that receipt and also the envelope addressed to me in what you thought was Lord Bygrave's hand, I had a very strong suspicion that George Darnell was in England and was continuing here his nefarious career. That is the principal reason why I have suddenly decided to go abroad."

"Had you any other reason, Mrs. Cathcart?" asked Vereker tentatively.

"Yes," she said wearily, "I have. I will tell you some day—it has nothing to do with the Bygrave case."

Vereker rose preparatory to taking his departure.

"When do you leave for the Riviera?" he asked.

"To-morrow, without fail," she replied. "I cannot live a day longer in the same country as George Darnell."

"And if he follows you out there?" asked Vereker.

A look of terror sprang again into Mrs. Cathcart's eyes; she trembled and, drawing close to Vereker, laid a hand on the lapel of his coat.

"You said you would look after me," she murmured. "Will you keep that promise?"

"I will," replied Vereker. "If ever you feel in danger of violence from this beast, will you wire or cable me?"

"At once, Mr. Vereker," she replied. "You inspire confidence in me. I am not afraid when you are near me. Good night."

She extended to him a soft, faintly dimpled and beautifully shaped hand. He grasped it warmly in his own, and the next moment had pressed it swiftly to his lips.

"Good night, Mrs. Cathcart," he said. "May I see you off to-morrow?"

"Do come, Mr. Vereker," she said eagerly, "and I'll try not to cry as the train moves off."

Next moment Vereker was walking swiftly homewards. The stars seemed to him to be superbly bright, and his blood was racing madly through his veins. For the first time in his life he felt that he was in love.

Chapter Twenty

On arrival at his flat, Vereker slipped off his jacket and shoes, donned a warm woollen dressing-gown and slippers. Lighting a pipe, he sat down at his writing-desk. An hour later he was still sitting there scribbling as if possessed: he was drawing up an orderly account of his lengthy investigations in the Bygrave Mystery up to the moment of his discovery of the existence of Mr. George Darnell, alias Cathcart, as one of the principals in the case. The sudden intrusion of that unsavoury figure into the field of his observation was of paramount importance to Vereker. As iron filings fly and adhere to a magnet, so did all the loose facts which he had so patiently collected, and which had so far proved intractable, gather round this startling discovery and cohere as if by magic. He was too excited to sleep and, having completed a detailed summary of his work on the case, rose from his desk, poured himself out a stiff whisky and soda, and sat down in his arm-chair by the fire.

"One more piece to fit into the puzzle," he soliloquized, "and the picture is complete. The sequel to the discovery of Mr. George

Darnell is positively amazing, and Heather has an inkling of that sequel. That I know. I wonder if he has unearthed this all-important factor leading up to the sequel."

He thereupon swiftly drew up his plans for the morrow. He would go and see Mrs. Cathcart off on her journey southwards and immediately afterwards seek an interview with Heather. The inspector would at once set his trained pack on the hunt for Mr. George Darnell and run him to earth. Celerity was essential, for the quarry (now that he had scented danger, as was evident from his attack on Heather and himself at Bramblehurst) would take the first opportunity to quit the country.

Vereker finally turned in, but slept little. Excitement kept him awake and his brain, almost feverishly active, vacillated between reviewing the morbid episodes of the Bygrave Mystery and building very pleasant castles in Spain, castles in which there ever dwelt a very beautiful woman whom he knew.

The appointed hour saw him at Victoria Station patiently awaiting the arrival of Mrs. Cathcart. As the time drew nigh for the departure of her train he began to grow uneasy. He glanced anxiously at his watch as he kept a vigilant eye on passengers making their way through the barrier on to the platform. At length she appeared, and his heart leaped. She was heavily veiled and alone, but he recognized her at once by her bold, graceful carriage, that almost Spanish deportment which he so much admired.

"And where is Lossa, Mrs. Cathcart?" he asked. "I thought she was staying with you."

"She went back to school—a convent school in Belgium—about a week ago. This is her last term. She is looking forward to its conclusion because—well, it's a great secret—she's engaged to be married to a very wealthy young American. A very charming young man he is too: Lossa is one of the world's lucky ones."

"She is," echoed Vereker, "in having you as a foster-mother."

"Now, you flatterer!" said Mrs. Cathcart, and added tangentially. "You know, Mr. Vereker, I have often wondered what your Christian name is."

Vereker smiled broadly.

"My actual Christian name is Anthony," he said, "and my parents always called me Tony, but my name by use and wont—it was given me at college—is Algernon. It will follow me to the grave. It is my reward for having perennially played the buffoon."

"You don't mean to say you prefer Algernon to Anthony?" she asked, looking up at him seriously.

"I prefer Muriel to both," he replied, "and, if I may, I shall always call you by your Christian name."

"I wish you would, Tony," she replied, with a radiant smile. "And now we must hurry or I shall miss my train."

"If you catch it, I shall miss you, Muriel," he replied, and slipped his arm through hers.

As she leaned out of her compartment window she suddenly appeared depressed and very much subdued. Her bright loquacity had suddenly vanished and she was silent.

"You seem sad, Muriel," ventured Vereker, "and you ought to be as cheerful as a cricket, going off to sunshine and flowers and a heavenly sea."

"They are entrancing enough," she replied, "but to me—well, they often seemed to put, by contrast, a keener edge to grief. And now that I have met you and made one of the very few friends I have ever had a relentless Fate tears you away from me, and doesn't even, as consolation, disclose if I shall ever see you again."

"I am coming out to the Riviera as soon as I have finished with the Bygrave case," he replied; "and that won't be long. We've got to settle the fate of Mr. George Darnell and his confederate, and then for a holiday with my paint-box—"

At the mention of the Bygrave case Muriel Cathcart frowned and tossed her head as if to shake off the memory of an unpleasant and evil experience. Turning gravely to Vereker, she asked:

"Tony, do you really know what has happened to Lord Bygrave?"

"I'm afraid, Muriel, poor Henry Darnell is dead. He was murdered, and there is nothing more to do now than bring the crime home to the perpetrators. The chain of evidence is almost complete: their arrest is imminent."

As Vereker concluded his sentence the guard blew a shrill, warning blast on his whistle.

Vereker clasped Muriel Cathcart's hands in his own. She swiftly bent down close to him, and he kissed her.

"Au revoir, dear," she said, as the train broke into motion, "and don't be long."

"Au revoir, darling," he replied.

"You needn't bother to bring your paint-box," she counselled with a gay laugh, and next moment was out of ear-shot.

Half an hour later Vereker was back in his flat. On his arrival he found a letter lying on the floor of the hall, and picked it up. He glanced at the handwriting on the envelope and, flinging down his gloves and stick on a table, swiftly tore it open. It was a communication from Winslade:

Dear Vereker,

Just a line to let you know that Mary and I are now man and wife, and are just leaving England for our honeymoon. This news, I'm sure, won't surprise you, as you have known for some time that the event was in the offing.

Of more consequence to you will be the information that I have just received an urgent note from my uncle, from 8 Causeway Street, Kingsland Rd., E., asking me to send him a couple of hundred pounds, as he is destitute of money. It would be extremely difficult and inconvenient for me to send him this sum at the moment, as it amounts to all the spare cash I have in the world. I ask you as a great favour to try and help me out of my quandary. Would you see to it that he receives the money? As you are aware of all

the facts surrounding his unhappy case, there is nothing
that I can say further that can be helpful. Relying on you,
my dear Vereker—

Yours,

David Winslade

Without further ado Vereker seized stick and gloves and
hurried to the nearest post office. There he despatched a wire
to Winslade setting his mind at rest about the question of
immediately financing Lord Bygrave and wishing him *bon
voyage*. He then rang up Inspector Heather and asked him to join
him without fail at Jacques' for lunch, and hinted at a startling
discovery with regard to the Bygrave case.

"Good," replied Heather imperturbably. "I'm as hungry as a
hunter and will do the lunch justice, but you know, Mr. Vereker,
these foreign restaurants never keep a drop of decent beer."

"You shall have the run of the finest wine-cellar in London,
Heather," replied Vereker. "Beer's not good for you. You're much
too corpulent already."

"Wine's a fair substitute," muttered the inspector. "I'll be there,
one o'clock sharp. Good-bye."

Punctually at that hour Inspector Heather arrived and joined
Vereker at a table in a secluded corner of the famous restaurant,
where they could converse without fear of being overheard by
other patrons.

"Well, Mr. Vereker, what is the nature of your new and
staggering discovery?" asked the inspector without any preamble.

"I've found the missing link, Heather, the link that at once
makes all my deductions concatenate as they ought to and give a
background of purpose to all the incidents of this mysterious case,
which seemed utterly unintelligible before. It affords also a sense
of satisfaction to me, in as much as my reasoning ran in the right
direction and was based on correct deduction."

"And who is this missing link, Mr. Vereker?"

"No other than George Darnell, a cousin of Lord Bygrave's, who went to America when I was quite a kid in knickerbockers. He contracted a marriage out there with Mrs. Cathcart after persuading her by the production of a newspaper cutting that her former husband, Lord Bygrave, was dead. She was unaware that he was a Darnell, because he had assumed the name of Cathcart. This *alias* was to hide his identity, because he had some years previously served a sentence of imprisonment for a clever forgery in New York. He very closely resembles Bygrave in appearance, and it is this asset which has proved so useful to him in misleading us, his pursuers. You can at once see daylight through the fog which has all along enveloped our investigations."

"Where did you acquire this information?" asked Heather, pointedly interrupting Vereker's narrative.

"From Mrs. Cathcart, yesterday. She rang me up and told me all about her unhappy life with this criminal. But to revert to my story: it was George Darnell who induced Bygrave to visit the Mill House, probably to extort money from him. A quarrel must have ensued, or he may have deliberately planned to murder his cousin. I prefer the former theory, because Bygrave dead was not of much use to him from a financial point of view. It was he who impersonated Bygrave in that car ride with Winslade as far as the cow-pond, and also at the White Bear Inn. When Winslade told me his story of their visit to the Mill House I was (feeling that my impersonation theory was correct) particular to note the fact that before descending the stairs to join Winslade the supposed Lord Bygrave turned out the light on the landing above. Their conversation amounted altogether to a few sentences only, and excitement alters a man's voice to such an extent that Winslade failed to notice anything unusual in the timbre. I was very eager to know whether the lamp on the road, just at the Mill House gates, was alight when the two men entered the car. Winslade remembered that it was alight prior to his entering the approach, but was not sure whether it was so subsequently. If it had been alight Winslade could hardly have failed to discover the impersonation, because it shines full on the approach of the house. But I am certain (I will give my reason later) that it had been extinguished.

"You can understand now that Winslade really never actually saw George Darnell's face that night. His back was turned on Winslade while he extinguished the oil lamp on the landing above the hall; the journey to the car was completed in darkness; George Darnell was huddled in the back of the car until they had left road lamps far behind on the journey to Hartwood. Moreover, he has never been seen by Winslade since. His likeness to Lord Bygrave carried him through his visit to the White Bear Inn because he had not visited that hostelry for years. That egg-breakfast, tobacco, consumption of whisky, and key chain were all vital clues. The key chain bothered me at first, but when I examined the leather tab by which it is attached to the trouser button I found to my joy that the tab was torn, showing that it had been violently wrenched from Lord Bygrave's person. It evidently carried the button of his trousers until George Darnell reached the stile at the cow-pond. There it parted company with it, purposely to give me another vital clue. It is unnecessary for me to point out that it was George Darnell who stayed at Glendon Street, and further hoodwinked Winslade and Farnish by avoiding a meeting with them.

"At this stage of my story I must exonerate Mrs. Cathcart and Smale from all complicity in the acquisition of those bearer bonds. George Darnell, forging his wife's handwriting and knowing her status as Lord Bygrave's wife, extracted this money from him by a story of destitution. It may have even verged on blackmail for all I know, and have been the cause of the subsequent fatal affray at the Mill House, especially so if Bygrave had discovered that Mrs. Cathcart had never received the £10,000. Smale, who knew nothing of the existence of George Darnell, firmly believed that Mrs. Cathcart was the culprit, and had engineered a *coup* by threatening to disclose the story of their early marriage."

"How do you account for the complete disappearance of the body?" asked Heather quietly. "Who removed it during Winslade's comparatively short absence from the Mill House?"

"That is the vital point, Heather. It proves beyond all cavil that there must have been an accomplice in the crime, unless—and I can entertain no hope of such a contingency—Lord Bygrave is still alive and a prisoner somewhere."

"I have had the garden of the Mill House thoroughly dug up," continued Heather, pouring himself out another glass of Volnay, "and the mill dam and stream dragged without any success. I can only conclude that the body was removed in some kind of conveyance."

"Your conclusion I feel is unassailable, Heather, and when I mention the fact that there were car tracks right into the yard behind the house, and recent traces of lubricating oil on the ground when I explored the place, I think you will agree that the point is definitely established."

"Why did George Darnell trouble to stay at the White Bear and risk discovery?" asked Heather.

"He chose to pass the night under a roof in any case. He thereby also confirmed Winslade in his belief that it was his uncle and none other that he had driven from the Mill House to Hartwood. And—and—perhaps he was eager to secure something important in Lord Bygrave's gladstone bag—money, or even papers—that would have on discovery led to his speedy arrest. Another, but minor point: he left his signet-ring, which I was certain on account of its size was not Bygrave's, but was similar in every other detail. You know how often members of an old family wear plain signet-rings with the family crest engraved thereon. It was a tiny master stroke in its way."

"To revert to the question of that street lamp outside Mill House, Mr. Vereker," said Heather pensively, "what made you think it had been extinguished before George Darnell and Mr. Winslade emerged from the front door?"

Vereker was obliged to smile at this question.

"You're hot stuff, Heather," he replied. "I examined it and found that by climbing on to the front garden wall and breaking a pane of glass it could easily be put out. As a matter of fact, a pane had been broken and replaced just before I examined it, because the putty was still fresh. In my effort to prove my theory my wrist touched the heated metalwork of the lamp, and I burnt myself rather badly, as you know."

"You mean sprained your wrist," retorted Heather, with a loud laugh. "I knew you were fibbing, Mr. Vereker."

"Well, Heather, what's the next move?" asked Vereker, as if to change the subject, because the factor of his burned wrist had already given him a vital clue to the identity of George Darnell's still hidden accomplice.

"We must track down this Mr. George Darnell as speedily as possible. He may already have left the country, and that will entail endless trouble and delay in bringing the whole matter to a successful close. We must also find Lord Bygrave's body: that is absolutely essential. In the meantime we could, if we discover George Darnell's whereabouts, proceed against him in the matter of those bearer bonds and the forgery of Mrs. Cathcart's signature."

"I know where George Darnell is at the present moment," said Vereker quietly, and was delighted to see that his information had the effect of making a distinct impression on the phlegmatic and imperturbable inspector. Producing Winslade's letter, he tossed it carelessly across the table to Heather with the words, "As this discovery was not due to my brilliant work, inspector, I feel that I must share it with you and win my sovereign without taking any unfair advantages."

Inspector Heather scanned the letter swiftly and returned it. "That's splendid, Mr. Vereker," he said, rubbing his hands. "We'll place him under strict surveillance at once and keep him there until such time as we can put him under lock and key. But time is precious, and I must take leave of you. The lunch, I think, is mine; I owe it you. Au revoir."

Chapter Twenty-One

On Heather's departure Vereker sat quietly over a coffee and finished his cigar. His face was flushed and his eyes alight with excitement, for he had but one further move to make to conclude his investigations and bring his connexion with the Bygrave case to an end. As he pondered a look of anxiety settled on his features, for he was wondering whether the astute Heather had also got on the track of that culminating point in the mystery. He was rather inclined to think he had and was keeping the trump card quietly up his sleeve. He would soon see. As for George Darnell, he could safely leave that scoundrel in the capable hands of Scotland Yard, but he must lose no time in making his final coup by bringing to light his accomplice in the crime. With a pleasant nod to Jacques, who bade him good day with foreign effusiveness, he sallied into the street and hailed a taxi.

"I'm going to hire you for a goodish journey, driver," he explained. "I want to get down to Carrington, a house just a mile or so from Nutfield, in Surrey. You know Nutfield?"

"Oh, yes, sir; I come from Godstone, in Surrey, a couple of miles away."

"Good; well, drive there as quickly as you can. I want you to get there before the next train arrives at Redhill, the nearest station."

"Jump in, sir. I won't apply the brakes till I hear the front lamps buckle," said the driver, and the next moment they were on their way at top speed."

On arrival at Nutfield, Vereker bade his hire stop, and after inquiring of a villager the situation of Carrington House they speedily resumed the journey. Before reaching the entrance gate to Carrington House, Vereker got out and covered the short remaining distance on foot. As he walked briskly up the gravel drive he was constrained to admire how adroitly an old farm had been converted into a delightful country residence. Every point of the modern addition to the house and the carefully planned arrangement of surrounding garden and grounds revealed the consummate good taste of the occupant. The residence seemed an ideal retreat for a man of leisure with a love of the quiet of a rural existence.

"Just such a place as I should like to retire to when I'm past active service," thought Vereker. "Now, I hope that Mr. Grierson is in."

Mr. Grierson was in, and actually opened the door in answer to Vereker's ring. A look of joyous surprise lit up his face on recognizing his visitor.

"Well, this is a most unexpected pleasure, Mr. Vereker," he said cordially. "I'm delighted to see you. Come in, come in, or would you first like to have a look round my place? I seldom have the opportunity of showing it off to an appreciative eye."

"I should love to have a wander round, Mr. Grierson," replied Vereker, "but I must postpone that treat until I have the opportunity of coming down again. My time is very limited and my business urgent. I have to be back in town as soon as possible."

"Ah, well, come down in the spring, when the rock-garden is at its best. I pride myself that I possess one of the finest rock-gardens in Surrey. Let me lead the way into the drawing-room—or rather study and drawing-room combined."

On entering that room Vereker's swift eye was not slow to appreciate the beauty and fitness of the furnishing, and as his glance wandered round the walls he noted a magnificent collection of etchings. Here a Meryon, there a Whistler or a Seymour Haden. Only the choicest masters and specimens were represented.

"They must be priceless," thought Vereker, and wondered how old Grierson had been able to indulge in such an expensive luxury.

Mr. Grierson noticed that observant and roving glance of Vereker's. "My only treasures," he explained; "they represent the

savings of a life time. I have never regretted the renunciation of
other pleasures that was necessary to effect their purchase."

"They were worth it all," said Vereker, as he took a seat to
which Mr. Grierson waved him with an easy gesture.

"Well, Mr. Vereker," he said, "I suppose you have come down
to see me about the Bygrave case. I can think of no other reason
for the visit."

"I have, Mr. Grierson, and I think you can give me the
information I want."

"Did you call at the office?" asked the old man. "You know, I
have retired. I couldn't bear to think of further service under a
new Chief and, besides, my time was up."

"No, I hadn't heard of your retirement," replied Vereker. "No
doubt you have acted wisely. But, to come to the point, I have
made rather a momentous discovery with regard to the mystery of
Lord Bygrave's disappearance, and it concerns his cousin, George
Darnell. As an old friend of the Bygrave family, you possibly know
something of this George Darnell."

"Good gracious, has he returned from America?" came the
surprised question.

"Yes, unfortunately for himself, he has. You do know him, then?"

"Of course I do. I knew him intimately as a young man. Lord
Bygrave, George and I were all boys together."

"What sort of a man was he?"

"A very amiable and pleasant companion. Later on, owing to
his gambling propensities, he got into serious trouble and left for
America under a cloud. Lord Bygrave and he quarrelled bitterly
at the time, and they have never communicated with one another
since, as far as I know."

"You haven't seen him since his return from America
recently?" continued Vereker.

"Certainly not, and I only hope that he doesn't discover
my retreat. From information I received some time ago from a

friend in America, I hear he went to the dogs out there instead of rehabilitating himself and making good."

"Do you know a Mrs. Cathcart?" asked Vereker, and glanced up quickly to observe the effect of this question.

"Who is she?" queried Mr. Grierson with a puzzled look.

"She is supposed to be his wife. He contracted a marriage with her in America under the assumed name of Cathcart. On her part it was a bigamous marriage, because her actual husband, Lord Bygrave, was still living."

"Ah, then Lord Bygrave was secretly married," commented Mr. Grierson with mild surprise. "Years ago I heard a rumour about a clandestine marriage, but I never could ascertain whether there was any truth in the story."

"Well, with regard to George Darnell, there is a very grave suspicion and considerable evidence that he is responsible for Lord Bygrave's disappearance—perhaps even murder. Scotland Yard have now got him under strict surveillance and Inspector Heather, whom you have met, has gone to question him about the matter to-day."

"Heavens above!" exclaimed Mr. Grierson, raising his hands in horror, "What a dreadful business!"

"I have hopes that the inspector will wring a confession from him," continued Vereker, "but, as you know, the chief difficulty in bringing home a murder charge against him, or anyone else, is the fact that Lord Bygrave's body has not yet been discovered."

"Naturally. If the man is guilty, I can only hope that they will speedily remove that difficulty and bring the scoundrel to the gallows," said Mr. Grierson, and with a break in his voice added, "To think that my revered old Chief may have come by a violent end fills me with horror. I hope against hope that such may not be the case. The idea is monstrous."

"So, Mr. Grierson," said Vereker, glancing at his watch, "you can give me no further information about Mr. George Darnell?"

"I regret very much that I cannot. You see, it is thirty years ago since I met him. I wasn't even aware that he was alive."

"Thanks very much, Mr. Grierson; I'm sorry to have disturbed your peace by this intrusion about a very horrible affair, but you can understand that every fragment of information helps. The smallest fact may at any moment loom into proportions of unexpected importance. Now I must go."

"Shall I drive you down to Redhill Station?" asked Mr. Grierson. "You know, it's a tidy distance from here."

"You drive a car, Mr. Grierson?" asked Vereker with surprise.

"Oh, yes; there is not much traffic on these roads, and I'm still an active man as men of my age go."

"I won't accept your offer," continued Vereker; "I have a taxi waiting on the road for me. Thanks all the same. Au revoir."

"Don't forget, Mr. Vereker, in the spring. Ah, you'll see a sight to gladden your artist's eye when you see my rock-garden. Good-bye."

Chapter Twenty-Two

On reaching his taxi Vereker bade the driver proceed to Redhill and there garage his cab until he required it, which he intimated would be late that night. In the interval of waiting he decided to kill time in Redhill by having a meal and visiting a cinema for an hour or so. Later on, as soon as it was dark, he would walk back to Carrington House and, with the aid of an electric torch, explore the grounds of that house unknown to its owner.

"The polished old villain!" he muttered to himself as the taxi sped towards Redhill. "My story of George Darnell left him absolutely unshaken. What a nerve! And yet I cannot avoid the conclusion that he was Darnell's accomplice. He is the one man who is, or was, intimately acquainted with that scoundrel, a significant enough fact in itself, and if I hadn't observed on my first meeting him the lint bandage on his wrist, due probably to the very cause to which I owed my own injury, I might never have entertained any suspicion that he was implicated in the Bygrave Mystery. About his motive I am not thoroughly clear, but lack of money was doubtless the root of his participation in the crime. The manner and luxury of his life at present cannot possibly be accounted for by even the utmost thriftiness on his part in the past. His etchings alone are worth thousands of pounds, and the purchase and modernization of that old farm must have cost a small fortune. Where and how did he get the money? The possession of a car too! Apart from the cost of its maintenance that car fits in with the discovery that I made at the Mill House. Yes, Mr. Grierson, I am going to probe further into your affairs; I have a firm conviction that it will be fruitful."

On arrival at Redhill, Vereker dismissed his taxi and arranged with the driver to wait for him, at the last inn on the road to Bletchingley, until such time as he should make an appearance. After strolling about the town and feeling tired after his day's exertions, he sauntered into an inn for refreshment, and was about to give his order when an exclamation of surprise from behind made him turn swiftly round to ascertain the cause.

"Hello, Mr. Vereker. What are you going to drink?" asked Inspector Heather, with a laugh. "I hardly expected to meet you here."

"I cannot say the same of you, Heather," replied Vereker. "I guessed you'd be hot-foot on the trail as soon as possible, and I further knew that you wouldn't pass the nearest pub to the station without calling in for your pint of beer."

"Well thought out, Mr. Vereker! I suppose you have just paid a call on our old friend, Mr. Grierson, late of the Ministry of X—?"

"What makes you think that?" asked Vereker, affecting surprise.

"Oh, only a trifling matter of a burned wrist," replied the inspector, chuckling.

"It was a flimsy enough clue, Heather," agreed Vereker, "but it was a clue which I could not dismiss without involving Mr. Grierson."

"Flimsy enough, yes, but in conjunction with other clues a very helpful piece of evidence. Of course you were working on other information as well?"

"None whatever, inspector. My journey down to Carrington House was a bow drawn at a venture, and I felt the weakness of my position. I suppose you have turned up here for the purpose of seeing Mr. Grierson?"

"Yes, I must admit I have, and have taken the precaution of bringing two plain-clothes men with me. To-night, after a pleasant little chat with that gentleman, we are going to dig up his garden and unearth Lord Bygrave's body," replied Heather, with an air of supreme confidence.

"Of course you have information in support of the conjecture that it's there?" asked Vereker.

"Yes. To-day I had a lengthy interview with Mr. George Darnell, at the address you furnished me with, and under the cross-examination to which I subjected him he broke down completely and made a clean breast of it. As we surmised, he was blackmailing Lord Bygrave by threatening to make public his secret marriage, and he was also successful in extorting the £10,000 worth of bearer bonds from him by forging his wife's handwriting in a letter pleading that she was destitute. It was on this very business of blackmail that Lord Bygrave kept the fatal appointment at the Mill House with Darnell. But the man behind the scenes, the brains and engineer of all this roguery, was none other than Grierson. Now, in years gone by, this George Darnell and Mr. Grierson were as thick as thieves, and on his arrival in England Darnell promptly looked up his old friend. They very soon, it appears, began to exchange confidences, and quickly resumed their former intimate friendship. Neither of them had altered for the better since those days. Darnell had been imprisoned for forgery in America and Grierson had been secretly appropriating public money for years. Apart from Darnell's information, I had discovered this much some time ago, by instituting a thorough audit of his accounts at the Ministry of X—. Lord Bygrave discovered his defalcations by mere accident, so cleverly had they been executed and, to avoid a scandal, quietly cleared up matters out of his own pocket. He, however, insisted on Grierson giving him a written confession and tendering his resignation. This Grierson did, handing Bygrave the letter on the latter's departure for Hartwood, on a holiday. It was agreed that Grierson should leave immediately Bygrave returned from that vacation.

Naturally, when these two boon companions, George Darnell and Grierson, came to understand one another thoroughly once more they decided, as they were both short of money, to work together for their common benefit. There were distinct possibilities for making money at hand and they did not hesitate to exploit them to the utmost. As I have mentioned, the Mill House was agreed upon as the scene for a meeting between Bygrave and George Darnell, Grierson being at hand in another room in case of trouble. That interview ended in a violent quarrel in which George Darnell felled his cousin with a chair—in self-defence, he protests. Aghast at his action, he rushed into the bathroom for water, and on his return found Grierson standing over the prostrate man with a coal hammer in his hand. Grierson at once informed him that Lord Bygrave was dead and angrily upbraided him with having used quite unnecessary violence. Darnell is certain that Grierson, seizing his opportunity, finished the dastardly business during his (Darnell's) absence in the bathroom, by smashing Lord Bygrave's skull with the hammer.

Knowing that Winslade was waiting outside with his car for his uncle, Grierson at once worked out a most ingenious plan to avoid the discovery of their crime. It was the work of a master mind. Darnell was to wait in the room until Grierson, who was to jump from the window into the yard, had extinguished the lamp at the gate of Mill House, and then go down and meet Winslade as if he were Lord Bygrave. It was a bold and risky enterprise, requiring nerves of steel, but the situation was desperate. Darnell, however, succeeded beyond all expectation in his rôle, and managed to manoeuvre Winslade down to Hartwood out of the way while Grierson, who had been hiding in the garden after putting out the lamp, returned to the house to remove the body. This he did by dragging it down the stairs and placing it in the back of his car, and driving forthwith to Carrington House. It was also arranged that Darnell had to turn up at the White Bear,' still impersonate Bygrave, and ransack Bygrave's portmanteau for Grierson's incriminating confession. This all succeeded according to plan.

"And the body?" asked Vereker.

"Grierson subsequently informed Darnell that he had safely disposed of that by burying it in his garden beneath a rubbish heap close to the boundary wall."

"Admirable, Heather, admirable; and what are you going to do to-night?" asked Vereker eagerly.

"I'm going to have a brief interview with Grierson, tell him what we know, and then by lantern light exhume the body," replied Heather in a matter-of-fact tone: "You will, of course, accompany us?"

"An unpleasant business, but I should like to see the thing through," replied Vereker. "Of course you have arrested Darnell?"

"Darnell is dead," returned Heather. "He swallowed some poison or other after his confession and expired in the cab on the way to the police station."

An hour later Inspector Heather, with two assistants and Vereker, arrived at Carrington House. A light was burning brightly in one of the front windows on the ground floor, and on their receiving no reply to their summons Heather glanced in that illuminated window.

"Another tragedy, Mr. Vereker," he said.

Vereker quickly stepped over to where the inspector stood, and peered into the room. To his horror, he saw Mr. Grierson seated at a beautifully polished mahogany table; one arm hung limp at his side; the other; clutching a revolver, was thrust out in front of him, and his head, with its white, rigid face towards the window, rested on the table against that extended arm. A shining pool of blood had run from a ghastly hole in the forehead across the lustrous mahogany and dripped on to the light, fawn-coloured carpet below, creating a gruesome dark stain on that fabric. In front of the body was a writing pad on which lay some sheets of paper and a fountain-pen.

To effect an entrance to the house was the matter of only a few minutes, and soon Heather, Vereker and the two plain-clothes men were standing in the room of the tragedy, grouped about the body of the suicide. Heather was calmly examining the lifeless corpse, and jotting down notes in his diary.

"His last act seems to have been to set down a complete confession of his share in the crime," said Vereker, glancing at the sheets of written matter lying on the table. And he has addressed that confession to me," he added as he picked up the closely written leaves the more easily to read them.

"While you are going through that document," said Inspector Heather, "we'll proceed with digging operations outside. I'll let you know when we come upon the body, Mr. Vereker."

Vereker nodded his head and, leaving the room of the tragedy, entered the drawing-room next door where a bright fire was still burning. Switching on the electric light, he ensconced himself in a comfortable chair, and began to read.

Grierson's confession as to his share in the crime was a quiet, dispassionately written document. No trace of excitement or remorse or anxiety troubled the easy flowing sentences as they revealed the incidents of a most brutal and cold-blooded murder. That murder, it transpired from the document, Grierson had decided upon prior to George Darnell's appearance upon the scene, but his advent had at once been seized upon with alert opportunism by the old civil servant as dove-tailing admirably into his own plans. George Darnell he had used as a tool throughout the whole horrible business, and was quite prepared to send him to the gallows by throwing the onus of the crime upon him. He wrote:

> The extinction by hanging of a life so utterly worthless as his, George Darnell's, is no loss to the community, and my intention of so managing the death of Lord Bygrave that he should take my place at the end of the hangman's rope was forced on me by the fact that I required time to complete my monumental work on the World's Famous Etchers. Not that I consider my personal life any worthier than Darnell's, but just the possession of knowledge which I felt it imperative to bequeath to mankind decided me to make him suffer the penalty of an act which by the mere machinery of law and social order was undoubtedly my due. I therefore state as an act of justice to the man, now that my plans have failed to achieve success, that Darnell merely stunned Lord Bygrave when he felled him with a chair in the Mill House, Eyford. As Lord Bygrave's existence was inimical to my interests, for my retirement would have inflicted a further strain on my depleted exchequer, I gave him his quietus with a blow from a hammer. I think I am justified in believing that death was almost instantaneous and painless.
>
> The best laid schemes, however, oft come to grief, and I am now aware that Scotland Yard is slowly but inexorably drawing the net about me and that even you, Vereker, playing the amateur detective, have discovered something which remorselessly points to me as the culprit. I could not interpret your visit and your interrogation about George Darnell this evening in any other way, and am forced to the conclusion that he has been discovered by the police and made a statement incriminating me. This failure of my plan to evade the consequences of my act has come as a great disappointment to me and it is with infinite regret that I

now feel obliged to end my life before finishing my book. I therefore ask you, Vereker, to make a thorough study of my manuscript and attempt to bring it to a worthy conclusion. It is in the belief that you will not fail to undertake this task in the praiseworthy labour of human enlightenment, and for the furtherance of a wider study of Art, that I now meet the "Angel with the darker draught" with composure and a certain cheerfulness. In my safe you will find my will bequeathing my collection of etchings to the nation.

GREGORY FEATHERSTONEHAUGH GRIERSON.

Hardly had Vereker finished reading this amazing document, which filled him with horror by its frigid moral insensibility and insane egotism, than Heather entered the drawing-room. He was perspiring freely from recent physical exertion and his clothes and boots were thick with viscous mud.

"We have discovered the body, Mr. Vereker," he said, removing his hat and wiping his streaming brow, "would you care to come and see it?"

Vereker rose slowly from his chair. "No, thanks, Heather," he replied, "I have seen quite enough of horror to-day to last me a lifetime. On thinking the matter over, I have come to the conclusion that the moment has arrived when I can quietly and unobtrusively sever my connexion as a private detective with the Bygrave case. I heartily wish that I was not a trustee under my old friend's will, because, until I have finished my work in that capacity, the whole horrible business will be ever-present in my mind. After that, I hope to forget." "You're a sensitive type, Mr. Vereker. Recent occurrences have made a deep impression on you. But, bless my soul, you'll be as right as a trivet in a few weeks' time."

"I hope so, Heather, and now I'll bid you goodbye for some months. I am leaving England to-morrow for a long holiday on the Continent."

"Good-bye, sir, and God-speed!" replied the inspector, warmly shaking Vereker's proffered hand.

On reaching town, Vereker wired to Ricardo to pack and meet him on the boat train at Victoria the following morning. He also despatched a marconigram to Muriel Ellerton (she had reverted to her maiden name) advising her that he was starting on the morrow for Mentone, where she was staying, and that he was travelling unaccompanied by his beloved paint-box.

THE END

CPSIA information can be obtained
at www.ICGtesting.com
Printed in the USA
LVOW13s1528300518
578985LV00015B/167/P